Noire: A Dark Shifter Romance

Temple Maze Level One

Anna Fury

Editing - Kirsty McQuarrie of Let's Get Proofed

Proofreading - Mountains Wanted Editing

Cover - Books N Moods

Cover Model - Joey Berry (@joey_berry)

Cover Photo- Eric Wainwright (@wainwrightimages)

Map - Darren DeHaas (@theadventurousfuryk)

❀ Created with Vellum

To Mr Fury, who rates my books on a five-pant scale depending on how tight his get while reading them LOL. This is my sixth book, and the first one to get 5/5 pants from him.

Let's call that a win, shall we?

PS If that's hilarious to you, you can buy the sticker I made of his pants RIGHT HERE, and on my website at www.annafury.com/shop

A QUICK NOTE

Noire is a dark omegaverse romance, and omegaverse often deals with difficult topics like generalized violence, possessiveness, physical dominance, consent and more. This book has that in spades. It is intended for mature audiences due to the dark themes prevalent throughout my writing.

It's never my intention for a reader to feel triggered by something in these pages. If you're worried, please reach out to me at author@annafury.com, and I'll tell you as much as I can to make you comfy.

MONSTER GUIDE

While I made up some of the maze's monsters, some are loosely based on existing entities. For the sake of those not familiar with monster lore, I'll quickly lay out the monsters you'll see and hear about in this book.

Vampiri - humanoid with exceptional senses, incredible speed and occasional psychic ability. They are pale-skinned with black claws, lips and fangs. Vampiri are venomous and drink blood.

Rohrshach - humanoid with a featureless face, covered in an inkblot-style black blob that morphs and changes like the famous Rorschach mask. Not as strong as vampiri or shifters, so they hunt in packs.

Manangal - loosely based on the mythical filipino manananggal, a vampire-like winged creature that could separate it's lower half from it's upper to fly in search of prey.

Maulin Fox - I made these up, knowing I wanted something between a cat and a dog, but utterly wild and blood-loving. Tiny black foxes whose jaws split open to lock onto their pray and drink blood.

Minotaur - A 15-20-foot tall cross between a human and a bull with a humanoid body covered in fur but a bull head, complete with horns.

Naga - Half human and half cobra, naga have humanoid upper bodies with a flared hood behind a distinctly snake-like face. Their lower half is that of a snake.

Wendigo - Vaguely humanoid body with two arms and legs, but very tall and thin with saggy skin. A wendigo's face appears to be a deer skull complete with horns. They are cannibalistic and associated with cold, famine and starvation.

Kuraokami Dragon - Japanese ice dragon with a long snake-like body and short limbs. Of all the monsters in the maze, they would be the largest.

PRONUNCIATION GUIDE

Noire - Nwar (rhymes with car)
Diana - die-ANNA
Renze - renz (like friends)
Tenebris - TEN-uh-briss
Cashore - CASH-or
Ascelin - ASK-uh-lin
Liuvang - L'YOO-vang (like hang)
Vampiri - vahm-PEER-ee
Naga - NAH-guh
Wendigo - WHEN-d'go
Manangal - mahn-ANG-ahl
Lombornei - LAHM-bor-NAI
Tempang - TEM-payng
Siargao - See-ar-GAH-O
Rezha - RAY-zhuh
Vinituvari - vin-IT-u-VAHRI
Deshali - deh-SHAH-lee
Dest - rhymes with west
Sipam - SAI-pam (like dam)

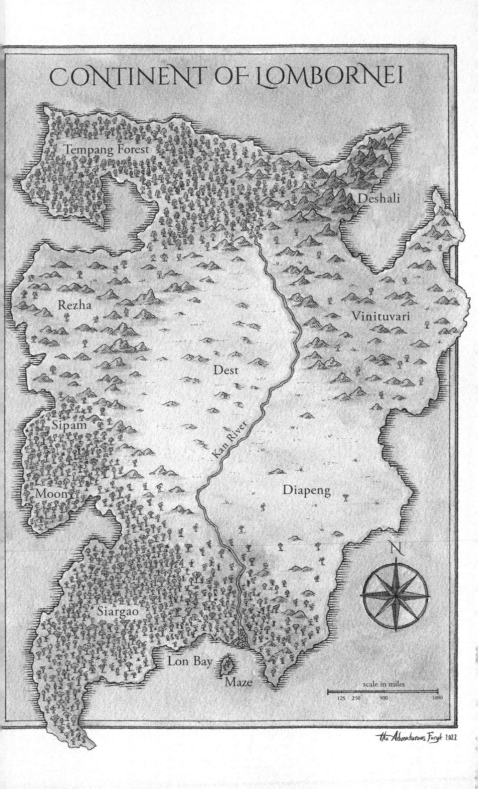

CONTINENT OF LOMBORNEI

Tempang Forest

Deshali

Rezha

Vinituvari

Dest

Kan River

Sipam

Moon

Diapeng

N

Siargao

Lon Bay

Maze

scale in miles

125 250   500   1000

the Adventurous Furyk 2022

A SHORT HISTORY LESSON

In the early days, the continent of Lombornei was ruled by humans, and it was lawless. Monsters kept to the shadows of the Tempang forest, living far from the human element and never mixing.

Eventually, a direwolf and a human woman fell in love. The wolf shifter sired a son, and the first alpha was born. Those hybrid genes spread quickly, and other monster crosses emerged as humans and monsters bred for the first time in history.

This new generation was less content to remain in the Tempang, and they desired freedom to roam and settle across all of Lombornei. Hybrids were bigger and stronger than humans, and within five hundred years, every province on the continent was a mixed region of monsters, hybrids, and humans together.

Most provinces lived in relative harmony, but not all monsters were thrilled at this new world order. Hybrids and humans built the province of Deshali on the edge of the Tempang forest, right

within claws-reach of every dark shadow that remained in the
forest.

The villain of our story was born and grew up in Deshali, her
soul twisted and torn by life among true monsters–eventually
turning her into the very worst one of all.

PROLOGUE - NOIRE
SEVEN YEARS AGO

S tanding in my personal car on the river train, I lean up against the window, watching the green jungle and glittering high-rises morph into the gritty Riverside District. The houses here are practically falling into the Kan River, some even propped up on stilts. The train jostles from side to side, but where most people would sit for this ride, I've always preferred to stand and look out the window at my kingdom.

A deep voice breaks through my peace. "Noire, Alpha Rand from Deshali is at the next station requesting an audience with you."

"Alpha Rand?" I glance up at my younger brother, Oskur, my enforcer. "What does he want?"

Oskur growls, "Says he has critical business with you, and in the name of Ayala pack, he is requesting an audience. Invoking the pack name to ensure a meeting is such a stupid fucking tradition."

Next to Oskur, my brother Jet rolls his eyes. "It's old-fashioned, but I think we should hear him out. He came across an entire continent to speak with you, and I thought he was killed when Deshali was decimated. I'd like to know how and why he's here, wouldn't you?"

I should listen to Jet when it comes to things like this. He's the strongest strategist in the family, always looking for approaches I wouldn't normally consider. Water flashes by the open windows as I inhale the beautiful waft of the Kan riverside—fried fish, dirt, common people. There's something strangely calming about the stench. I may live in a beautiful tower up in the verdant foothills, but riding the train down here along the river is where I get my best thinking done.

Sighing, I nod to Jet and Oskur. "Let's hear what he has to say."

Oskur nods and leaves the passenger car to make arrangements to stop as I look out the window, Jet coming to stand by my side. Like this, we're eye to eye.

"Last we heard from Rand, monsters were coming out of the Tempang to attack Deshali. I'm surprised he's still around," Jet says. "We haven't done a tour of other alpha packs in years, Noire. Maybe it's time to get a sense of what's happening in the other provinces again, as Father did."

"I don't give a fuck what's happening in the other provinces," I remind him. "Father cared far too much about the rest of the continent, forgetting Siargao has resources the rest of the continent needs. If you control Siargao, you control Lombornei by default. He focused too broadly, and it made him ineffective. We are better than he was, far better."

Jet nods, but I can see the wheels in his head spinning. The truth is I fucking hate traveling. I don't want to leave my part of the world because the rest of this continent and its people don't matter to me. My place and my rule are here. And it is firmly fucking cemented.

I growl when the train slows at the next station. Normally, when I'm on board, the train runs from up in the hills where I pick it up, all the way down to the mouth of Lon Bay. I'm intrigued why Rand has come all this way, though, even if it means my train has to make an atypical stop.

When it slows, Rand gets on. Standing by the window, I get the first whiff of an omega alongside his deeper alpha scent. Hers is heady, dark, enticing. It seems Rand has brought either a beauty to offer me, or something he thinks I lack. When Oskur enters the train car with Alpha Rand and a woman in tow, I narrow my eyes at them.

"Alpha Noire. It has been a long time," the older alpha murmurs, looking at me where I stand up against the open train car windows. I know what he sees: an alpha in his absolute prime. Rand, on the other hand, has not aged well. His skin is burnt by the sun, peeling off in many places, his hair nothing more than splotchy patches.

Rand is sick and dying. That much is clear.

If he were part of my pack, I'd have put him down by now. But he's not, so I take a step forward and glance at the omega behind him. Her eyes are downcast, as they should be, but she peeks up when I look at her. Long chocolate hair, stunning green eyes. She's gorgeous, although a little older, older than me by probably ten years, heading into her late forties. When I look closer, the hint of a faint scar slices from her hair down to her chin. It's barely there, but still noticeable.

Not that it would stop me fucking her.

I glance back at Rand. "You requested an audience, so let's hear it."

Rand's hands grip a cane he's using to hold himself upright, but he takes one hand off it to gesture to the omega standing behind him. "This is my daughter, Rama. I came to offer her hand in marriage to you, if you'll take it, Alpha Noire."

I bark out a laugh. "What leads you to believe I'd accept such a random, unbidden proposal?"

Rand nods. "It isn't traditional, to be sure. Deshali is devastated, overrun by monsters, and we have fought them for generations, Alpha Noire. You know this already."

He's referencing how he's called me for help twice in the past, and I did not grant it.

Rand continues, "I'm dying, as you can see. I need to cement a place for my daughter in this world, and Deshali has no marriage prospects for her."

I snarl as Jet comes to stand next to me. "So you thought you'd foist this omega on me simply to help you because you're dying?"

"No, alpha," Rand answers, lifting his head higher. "My daughter is brilliantly inventive, and the only reason we've hung on so long is because of her inventions to belay the monsters' advance out of the Tempang forest. But we can only do so much. However, we've recently discovered a gold mine in our kingdom, and we are reluctant to leave that, as you might imagine. If you marry Rama, you will get access to Deshali's natural resources. Plus, a beautiful omega who will birth you many pups to spread the Ayala name."

"Prove it," I snarl, not bothering to look at the hapless omega, even though she's staring at me now with open, curious eyes. "Prove a single fucking word of this bullshit, Rand. What this sounds like is yet another plea for help. I didn't grant it the first two times because you were foolish enough to build a city on the very fucking edge of the Tempang, the one place on our entire continent where the old uncivilized monsters still live. That's your problem."

Rand blanches but reaches into his thick coat and brings out a bag. Already, I hear coins rattling. He hands them to me, but I don't take them, waiting until he can't hold them upright any longer and the bag falls to the ground. The omega winces but looks up at me.

"Please, Alpha Noire," she whispers. "I would be a good

mate, and there is plenty more where this came from." She gestures to the bag of coins at my feet.

There's something about this omega I don't like. The way she spoke without being spoken to. The way she said "please." My alpha intuition pings as I take a step closer and grip her arm, tugging her out from behind Rand. He holds back a growl as I circle the woman, leaning in to scent her neck and the back of her shoulders, which she's left exposed. She shudders when I touch her, and not in a good way.

No. This omega wants nothing to do with marriage, and anything she says to the contrary is simply meant to fit her father's narrative.

She darts back behind her father when I finish my inspection and take a step back.

"No, Rand. Once again, no."

Rand's watery eyes meet mine as he brings both hands up. "Please, Alpha Noire. I am begging you to take her off my hands, to give her a place to be of use. Help her regain our homeland because there are riches there beyond your wildest imaginings."

The omega brings her head up, her expression carefully guarded. I don't like what I see and sense—a dark, deviant mind hidden behind her elegant features. There's a reason this omega is single. My guess is she's run off every potential suitor with the general air of distaste that wafts from her like a poisonous cloud.

I glance back at the father, narrowing my eyes. "You have nothing I want."

"Please," Rand continues. "She is exactly the type of mate a powerful alpha needs—beautiful, connected, and powerful in her own right. She can help you cement your foothold in the west."

I whip out a hand to grip his throat. "I already own every inch of Siargao, which means I own this whole continent. Every man, woman, and child does exactly what I wish them to do. This place was lawless before I took over from my father, but the city thrives under my rule. If I *ever* take a mate, I'll take one with her own assets." I glance at the omega, whose eyes narrow at me. "You and your daughter have nothing to offer me aside from a pretty face, and my pack is already full of those."

Behind Rand, the omega snarls, clenching her fists together. She's likely to be an absolute hellcat in the bedroom. Normally, I'd take her and enjoy her once or twice before they leave, but there's no way in seven hells I'm mating this beast.

"Your father would–" Rand barks. One glare from me halts him in his tracks as I loom closer. At his age, he's already sunken to half the size he was when I met him as a younger male.

"It doesn't matter what my father would or wouldn't do because I killed him and took his place. The only thing that matters is here and now, and I am fucking bored of this conversation. I won't make the deal because I have no incentive to."

"But," he blusters.

I step closer to him, pushing my chest to his, looking down at him, a reminder of how fucking powerful I am. I'm an alpha in my prime. My claw-tipped hands could rip his head from his shoulders in a second. There's no patience left in me for this topic.

Rand reaches down for the bag of gold, but I put my foot on it with a tsk. "That's staying with me for this colossal waste of my time."

"It's all I have left; I have to take it to the next place," he spits, suddenly full of vehemence. "And the next and the next until I secure a place for my daughter. I cannot mine more without he–"

"Not with this money," I snort. "And not with that daughter. Not a single thing about her screams that she wants a mate, so you've got more problems than a lack of assets. Go, *now*."

He stands and glares at me but reaches for his daughter's hand, leaning on her for support. One dark brow travels upward, his eyes sad as he takes me in. "I'm sorry, Alpha Noire."

Confusion curls in my chest at that. Sorry? He's...sorry? It makes no sense.

I glance over at my brother, Oskur. Of the four of us brothers, he's the biggest. Tenebris is still a pup, but I don't think anyone will ever outweigh my second-youngest brother. Oskur grips the omega by the back of the neck hard and guides her to the door. The father follows as Jet drops to a knee and opens the bag at my feet.

As he pulls the strings open, I'm happy to see it actually is full of gold coins, thick gold coins. Jet hands me one, and a quick sniff tells me they're real. I'm surprised this wealth existed in Deshali, but it's not worth fighting the monsters who remain in the Tempang.

Nobody trades in gold any longer, but these will still have value in some circles. I'm thinking of the alpha group I hunt with at the club on Fridays. A few of those males are collectors of ancient treasures such as this. I pick a coin up to examine it and realize it's printed on both sides with a pattern.

Jet rubs at the grime that coats the coin's surface as I frown. The pattern isn't a pattern at all; it's a labyrinth of sorts with an eye in the center. How...odd. I'm familiar with many of the old coins used in our history, but I don't recognize this.

That makes it more valuable. Already, my mind spins with ways I can use this to push and pull Siargao's seedier citizens around my personal chessboard.

Smiling, I go to put the coin in my pocket when I realize the pattern on the front is fading.

No, not fading. *Bubbling, melting.* I drop the coin back into the bag and peek in just as Oskur returns to the carriage.

"We were examining this coin, but it started bubbling—watch, Oskur," I bark.

Our brother strides over and picks up the coin as Jet takes a step away. "Toss them all out the window. That can't be a good sign."

As soon as the words are out of his mouth, the coin in Oskur's hand evaporates in a puff of smoke, filling his eyes as he coughs. Half a second later, Oskur drops to the ground as Jet roars.

I reach for the bag, kicking the fabric back over the top of the coins. But the second I do, the rest explode, filling the train car with curling black smoke. Jet and I roar, and then there's nothing as the train car's floor rushes up to meet my face.

My head is pounding, my heartbeat a steady thwomp in my chest. Even my fucking eyeballs are throbbing in my head. What in the fuck...

The black smoke. The omega. The godsdamned gold coins.

Glancing around, my eyes narrow. On the bed next to me sits a pile of gold coins, the same fucking coins with the labyrinth and eye pattern. These are all shiny, the eye winking at me maliciously.

Rand. Rand apologized on the train. Is this what he meant?

I jolt upright, only for stabbing pain to send me doubling over my lap, grunting in pain. I roll off the bed and sink down onto the floor, putting one hand out to steady myself. Glancing around, I don't recognize anything. Black stone floor. Black carpeting. Black stone walls.

Gripping the side of the bed frame, I manage to get myself upright as my alpha senses kick into overdrive. More grunting and cursing reach my ears. Oskur.

There's a door to my right, and I head there, expecting to find it locked. But it's not, so I stride through, peeking into a long hallway.

"Oskur," I call out quietly, knowing my brother will be able to hear me. Our alpha senses are incredibly strong.

"Here," he grunts. "Dying."

I stride up the hallway, the pain starting to fade from my head as I fling another door open. Another dark bedroom. Oskur lies on the floor, both hands on his head. "What the fuck was in those coins? Where are we?" His big chest heaves with exertion.

"Don't know," I bark. "Get up; you're not dying."

I turn and leave the room, listening for Jet. I find him the next room over, walking around the room with his hands balled into tight fists. "I don't recognize this place, Noire." Jet frowns, dark brows pulling into a tight vee over dark eyes. He looks so much like Father that I do a double-take for a second.

I leave his door and stride up the hallway, which ends in an open room. Living quarters with a kitchen on one side and a giant arched doorway on the other. Several more hallways lead off the main area. "Search," I bark to my brothers, tension building between my shoulder blades. I know every inch of Siargao, and I don't recognize anything here.

No doors, no windows save for the open doorway on one side of the room. It looks like another hallway. Jet and Oskur take a hallway each as I stalk toward the kitchen area, trying to get a sense of my surroundings. More dark stone, dark appliances, dark furnishings. Everything here is black. Behind the island, a small figure lies on the floor with a bag over his head.

Oh, fuuuuck. Dropping down, I whip the bag off and growl as I look into the face of my youngest brother, Tenebris. He's just a pup, barely eleven.

"Ten, what the fuck are you doing here?" I bark. "How did you get here, alpha? Answer me right the fuck now."

Ten's lower lip trembles as he looks up at me. "A woman led a bunch of guards to the house last night. She...she killed everyone, I think, Noire. I tried to escape, but she took me. The pack was running when she took me, and nobody could save me. Why did she take me, Noire? Where are we?"

I roar for Jet and Oskur, and make Ten repeat his story twice. Oskur questions the boy within an inch of his life as I jog for the arched stone entryway at the front of the quarters. Another hall-way. I jog down it. Another hallway, and another, and another. I don't want to get lost here, so I jog back and find my brothers, still questioning Ten as he sobs and curls in on himself.

"Enough," I snap, anger churning my stomach. Something is very, very wrong. "Ten, stop–"

"Good evening, Noire," a silky voice echoes through the cold room, stopping me in my tracks.

I whip around to find one section of the wall lit up like a tele-vision screen, a woman's sneering face the only thing on it.

The fucking omega from the train. Not Rand but the omega.

Balling my fists, I turn toward her but say nothing. This is her doing. I know it.

"No smart retorts, Noire? No scathing commentary about the state of my father's health or my utter inadequacy as a mate?" She doesn't wait for a response before she continues, "It doesn't matter because it was all a ruse anyhow. A ruse to keep you from looking skyward as my city approached yours. It was easier than I expected, to take it over from you. And now I own you, and anyone else who defies me."

There's so much there, I don't even know how to begin to unpack it, but boiling anger roars through my veins as my vision clouds, my fangs descending. I'm barely holding back the need to shift and rip something to shreds.

"Tsk tsk, Noire," the omega warns. "I'll make this very clear for you. You didn't help us when we needed it, and you could have. I'll never forgive you for letting Deshali fall when you had the resources to swoop in and push the monsters back. So now, you're in a maze of my own design. It's impossible to escape. And you will live there for the rest of your life. Not only will you live there, but you and the other monsters in the maze will do my bidding."

"I will never do your bidding," I snap.

The omega laughs. "Oh, you will. Take a look at your wrist; see the disk embedded there?"

I flip my arm over. A metal disk is now implanted along the underside, and it's flashing a red light at me. Godsdamnit all to the seven hells, I didn't fucking notice when I awoke. I scratch at the edges of the disk, sending a shooting pain up my arm.

The omega gives me a sinister grin. "That disk will tell you exactly what you're allowed to do and not do, every day for the rest of your godsdamned life. You work for me now, Noire. All of you do, even little Tenebris over there. But you're not alone in the maze. So be careful, or what remains of your life could be pitifully short."

"Let me the fuck out of here," I snarl. "Or you will rue the fucking day you came onto my train with those motherfucking coins."

"Oh, I don't think so." The omega laughs. And it's the laugh of someone who knows she's won. "Welcome to the Temple Maze, Noire."

CHAPTER 1
NOIRE
PRESENT DAY, SEVEN YEARS LATER

S triding across the open living area of our rooms, I scent the air for Jet and Tenebris. Sensing Ten, I head down the long hall toward my brother's quarters, growling at the way the security cameras pan to follow my every move. When I turn the corner, a screen inlaid at the end of Ten's hall shows a countdown timer. Only an hour and a half before tonight's hunt.

I'm certain the screen is not only a timer but a camera too. I spit at the tech and flip it the bird before knocking on Ten's door. His gruff bark is the only response he gives. Twisting the ornate metal handle, I push my way through and close the door behind me. Glancing up at the ceiling, I take note of the pinhole cameras in every corner of my youngest brother's room. Rama didn't install the swiveling globe-shaped monstrosities from the common areas in our quarters. The way she watches us is less noticeable here because the cameras don't follow.

Doesn't mean I'm any less aware of the truth. There is nowhere in this godsforsaken prison we can go that Rama's eyes don't see us.

Fuck Rama and this maze she's trapped us in. Seven years here haven't dulled my intense drive to get the fuck out.

I don't realize I'm snarling until my younger brother looks up from his chair. He's seated in front of the enormous black stone fireplace that lines one entire wall of his bedroom.

Sighing, Ten snaps his fingers in irritation, getting my attention. "I was hoping to finish this book before the hunt, but it's clear you need something, alpha. Spit it out."

"Watch your mouth. Why are you so tense?" I slide my hands into the pockets of my black jeans as Ten takes me in, pale eyes traveling down my body and back up. I take the opportunity to really examine my younger brother. He's grown up here in the maze, and these days, he's all alpha. Nearly as big as Oskur was. Bigger and brawnier than Jet. Mouthier than I'd like.

Ten sighs but bows his head, an apology of sorts. "Not tense. Alert. And invested in the ending of my book."

"Where are you tonight?" Anger prickles along the back of my neck when I think about Ten going into the maze for the hunt. It's not that an alpha is ever really in danger, but this fucking maze is full of all sorts of monsters. I might be the worst, but Ten is most definitely not. He's less of an asshole than Jet and me, even though he came of age in this hellish labyrinth.

"Maze too." Ten nods, chocolate hair falling across his light eyes. He's the only one of us brothers without the jet-black hair of our father and the dark eyes of our mother. "If we're down here, then Jet must be…" He breaks off as he gestures up at the ceiling.

"Yep. He'll be up in the Atrium tonight, balls deep in rich virtual-reality pussy so he can please the bored housewives of Siargao." I'm not bitter. I want nothing to do with that scene, but Rama rarely allows the three of us to be in the same place at the same time, with the exception of our quarters. Just another way to fuck with us.

Ten doesn't respond, but a lot goes unsaid between my brother and me in that moment. How he hates the way we're nothing more than assassins and prostitutes in here. How he'd give almost anything to escape this place.

"One day, brother," I whisper, low enough I'm sure the cameras won't pick it up. Alphas have extraordinary hearing. Ten doesn't bother to agree. He's not harboring hope we'll ever escape this prison. I don't harbor hope either. I harbor ill fucking will toward the woman who enslaved us here in the first place. If it's the last thing I ever do in this life, I'll get out of this place and destroy the woman who put me here.

Leaving Ten to his novel, I use my senses to locate my middle brother, Jet. He's at the opposite end of our quarters in the hallway we use for knife throwing practice. He likes to use it for other recreational activities because covert alcoves line the entire hall.

The sloppy sounds of fucking ring off the stones as my pupils dilate, nostrils widening. I round a corner to see Jet screwing a panting woman bent over a black velvet sofa. She could be anyone. A bored wife. Someone's daughter in need of a lesson. A junkie looking for the thrill of bedding an alpha male in his sexual prime. This sort of private, one-on-one show with Jet is one of the many ways Rama exerts her dominance over us. Jet has no more choice in this than any of us do, although he likes to pretend this is his preference.

We all have our skills, and Jet is exceptionally creative while fucking.

The woman is chained, arms stretched along both sides of the sofa's back as Jet rails into her viciously. The chains are meant to amp up his alpha libido, the same way the drugs they provide him get him ready to fuck rich women upstairs in the Atrium all night.

Jet turns his head only slightly to the side as I lean up against the dark stone wall and wait for him to finish. He pounds into the woman's dripping pussy over and over, cum pooling on the floor in a steady stream as she screams in ecstasy and he grunts his release.

I don't say a word as he slips out of the woman, wiping his still-hard dick off with a towel. Throwing the sticky fabric on top of her back, he presses a button set into the stone wall of this particular alcove. The woman's faint, satisfied moans ring in my ears as Jet rolls his eyes, walking past me. He doesn't turn to look when steel bars close down over the alcove and the back wall opens. Black-clothed and masked helpers come in, unchain the woman, and drag her away. We'll never see her again. Nobody ever risks coming back twice.

I tried to get out this way once. Killed three of Rama's beta workers and nearly got my leg hacked off by the descending bars before Ten dragged me back into the hallway. I'm a fucking lion pacing in a zoo cage. One day, I'll get out and raze everything to the ground to kill the bitch who threw me in here.

I follow Jet back into the main living room area of our quarters, frowning as I glance around. Our quarters are beautiful, or they would be if they were mine by choice. Knowing we're stuck here just makes me hate every black velvet sofa, every black stone on the wall, even the black fucking rugs. I suspect Rama made it beautiful because everything in the maze is for show. It's all one huge production for her rich clients. They want to see monsters being monsters in beautiful, seductive surroundings. They want to touch us and taste us from relative safety. They want to watch us do their dirty work.

Jet stalks to our fridge, still nude, and grabs water out of it, downing it with one great gulp. His broad chest still heaves from the exertion, his cock swinging around like a damn baseball bat. "Rama wants me in the first show for her VIPs, so it's ten solid hours of sex for me tonight."

"I didn't say anything, brother," I murmur, training my eyes on him. He glares back until, finally, his dark eyes flicker away. He still blames himself for touching those fucking coins. Reaching into the fridge again, he grabs a vial of purple liquid and downs that too, grimacing at the taste as it goes down.

I despise that he takes uppers to deal with his nights in the Atrium, but it is what it is. Jet needs it to handle the shit they put him through upstairs. I can't fault him for that. My pack is in survival mode the longer we're restrained here. Lesser alphas would have gone certifiable at this point.

Jet pulls a cigarette from a pack on the counter, fishing a lighter off the island at the same time. His shoulders shrug upward as he continues, his pupils blowing wide as the uppers hit his bloodstream. "I never thought I'd get bored of sex, but I can honestly say I am reaching my limit." Jet frowns and sighs again, sucking at the cigarette before releasing pale rings into the air.

It's not that Jet is bored, not really. It's that nothing will ever ignite or sate an alpha's intense sexual need but an omega, ideally our bondmate. I assume Rama knows enough about alphas to be aware of that. Maybe not, though, or she'd be dangling omegas in front of me constantly. A reminder of how her father offered her to me seven hellish years ago.

Jet's dark eyes find mine again. "I heard Rama put a fucking naga in the lower levels."

"Godsdamnit," I bark out. "She must be going deep into the Tempang. I've never heard of a naga settling in any of the provinces, unless the outside has changed…"

Jet shrugs again. "One of the rich bitches from upstairs told me someone tried to get out through the lower levels, so Rama found a fucking naga from somewhere and threw him in the basement to keep us away. Looks like your theory about the lower levels is probably right."

A dull ache spreads between my eyes as I pinch the brow of my nose. I've theorized the entire seven years we've been stuck in here that the lower levels hold the key to a way out. So far, I haven't found it, though. Sounds like I'm not the only monster with a bone-deep desire to leave.

A naga complicates things. I had planned to stalk the very lowest levels of the maze tonight during the hunt, but I won't risk a naga until I learn more. It's too dangerous, and nagas are too fucking big for me to take on without an army.

Once you become Rama's puppet, the only thing you're good for is fucking or killing the marks she sends in, or both. And Rama controls every moment of it through orchestrated bullshit and the disks buried in our arms. I have no army here, and never will.

"Where are you tonight?" Jet questions, handing me his cigarette after a deep puff.

"Maze with Ten."

Jet laughs cruelly. "Guess you're not off Rama's shit list after that stunt you pulled last month?"

"Hardly a stunt to kill her favorite handler when she dangled him the way she did. I've never *not* been on the shit list. She won't kill me; she has too much fun fucking with me."

"Still, you've been on maze duty ever since." He laughs. "Out there stalking and killing. Fucking is far easier, and you get to come."

"Who says I don't come when I stalk and kill?"

Jet ignores that, rolling his eyes. "Where's Ten right now? Shouldn't he be getting ready?"

"He's reading."

Jet's eyes soften for a moment. I know he'd never admit it out loud, but he worries for our youngest brother. Jet and I can handle this place, but eventually, it'll break Tenebris. He doesn't have the vicious, cruel, violent streak we do.

"We've got to get him out, you know." Jet's voice is thoughtful, quiet enough that I wonder if he's simply thinking aloud and not expecting a response.

I growl at my middle brother. "Finish getting ready, Jet; it's almost time."

Jet nods and takes another slow sip of the purple uppers, sucking in a hiss when the bitter taste coats his tongue. Snarling, I turn and head for my room.

Thirty minutes later, I'm armed to the teeth with weapons, zipping up a black leather coat, when Ten strides into my room without knocking. He takes a look at my leather. "Not planning to shift tonight?"

Shaking my head, I strap a serrated knife to my forearm, growling at the metal disk that flashes the fucking countdown back at me. It's embedded in my skin, tying me permanently to all the computerized systems and gadgets that make this gods-damned maze work. I despise not knowing precisely how much Rama knows about me because I'm unaware of what the disk does, other than count down to the hunt and give me permission to kill–or not. It's her own version of psychological warfare.

Glancing at Ten, I frown. "Don't feel like shifting tonight. Stalking in human form is just as fun."

Ten rolls his eyes but laughs. "I was going to run as my wolf, but I guess I'll stick around like this. Someone's got to keep you out of trouble. Not that you listen to me…"

"I'm never in trouble," I counter as Ten lowers his gaze, waggling his brows at me as he gestures around at the maze itself.

Growling, I snap my fangs at him. "Point taken."

The five-minute warning alarm sounds as he and I head toward the front of our living quarters. We can go anywhere in the maze at any time, but we tend to make a competition out of it amongst ourselves by standing in the doorway to our private quarters and waiting for the hunt alarm to go off.

Next to me, Ten snarls deep in his chest as he bends both knees and crouches, watching the screen that's set into the wall opposite the entry to our quarters. With two minutes to go, the screen comes on, and Rama herself smiles broadly at us, just like every other fucking night. A sheet of black hair hangs over one eye, the other done with wildly suggestive makeup designed to make her appear younger than she is.

"Your mark tonight is this man," Rama purrs. A photograph flashes up on the screen of an overweight white man's face. A tiny goatee lines his pudgy chins, expressive brown eyes looking at a camera he probably didn't realize was taking the last ever photo of him alive.

Rama continues in a raspy voice that grates at my sensitive ears, "Our client prefers the mark to meet his end via dismemberment or decapitation. Torture and play suggested but not required. Happy hunting, my children."

My eye twitches at her condescension. Deep in my mind, I picture her face and then my claws slicing her head from her shoulders. And I smile because, one day, I will make it happen.

There's never much more from Rama than a brief description of the evening's mark, but it doesn't matter. On my personal shit list, she is at the very top.

"Wonder what he did…" Ten muses as the screen flashes a sixty-second countdown.

"Don't know, don't care. I'm in the mood for violence." It's an easy retort.

I crouch down next to Ten, snarling when the countdown numbers move to the corner of the screen and the view changes to a room full of the wealthy elite–Rama's customers. Someone in that room paid a lot of money to get our mark thrown into the temple maze tonight. Someone wants that man dead. The reason could be anything–he had a secret, he fucked someone's wife or daughter, he had political aspirations, or saw something he shouldn't have.

I'll never know, and frankly, I don't care. But like every night, I memorize each face on the screen. Those are the people who get off watching monsters kill in the maze. Those are the people who profit off my suffering. Some faces I recognize from my time ruling Siargao, but most are new, the wealthy from other provinces farther inland. I will see them dead if it's the last thing I do. Rama's so confident the monsters will never get out that she lets us see the clients. It's a mistake. Because when I do get out, I will hunt down every fucking one of them.

The buzzer goes off, and Ten sprints up the hallway into the black depths of the maze with me right behind. When he and I hunt together, I always bring up the rear to have his back. It's how alpha packs work. The alpha brings up the rear, just like wolves.

We use our senses to sweep our way through the levels closest to our quarters, but there's no one here. Rama's minions must have dropped the mark somewhere in one of the lower levels or the other side of the maze where the vamps and rorshachs live.

We prowl up hall after hall, the mark's scent nowhere to be found until we get to the enormous maze's large stone chapel. The scent of fear is strong here, although the mark isn't here now. A quick breath tells me he *was* here, probably dropped here, but he's gone now.

The alpha urge to hunt overtakes the more logical side of my brain. My body focuses on finding the man we're meant to kill tonight.

Growling, Ten and I turn as one and jog through the chapel, along the pews, and out the back door into another dark hallway, following the man's scent. The floor is slick with piss, so he definitely came in here. A cackling laugh rings up the hallway as a human grunts and then screams.

The fucking rorshachs. Pushing in front of Ten, I sprint up the hall toward the smell and sounds of a fight. With my alpha eyesight, I make out the mark at the end of the hallway. He's surrounded by three of the monsters we call rorshachs. Their faces are eyeless, noseless masks of ever-changing textures and patterns, just like the famous inkblot masks from history. But they've got the ability to take on anyone's face for a minute or two. They were there the night Oskur was killed. They're the reason he's dead.

When I see them, murderous need overtakes all reason in my mind.

Bellowing up the hall, I sprint toward the group. The mark's eyes go wild when he sees us, and he scrambles to his feet and hauls ass as the rorschachs turn toward me. We're not supposed to kill other monsters in the maze; Rama makes sure we can't do that without retribution—starvation, pain, physical attacks. Not that monsters don't occasionally die here in one way or another.

I've never given a fuck about the repercussions. If I get a chance to kill something, I do it. Fuck her and fuck her maze. She wants to torture me far too much to kill me. I barrel through the group of smaller monsters, knocking two to the side but focusing on the largest of them. Ten backs me up immediately, blocking the smaller ones as they scramble upright and hiss.

I don't know their names; they don't speak unless they're speaking in the voice of the face they take, but this is the one who sacrificed one of his people to kill Oskur. He's still got a long scar down one mottled arm from my claws. I fuck with him every chance I get.

Slashing black-clawed hands across his chest, I roar with satisfaction as he screams in pain, a high-pitched sound that fuels my predatory instinct. The rorschach reels backward and takes off to get away from me, followed by the other two.

Ten stops beside me, chest heaving. "I suppose you're never planning to get off the shit list?"

"That was for Oskur."

Ten sighs.

I don't bother to say anything further as I jog up the dark hall after the fleeing monsters and our mark. Mere seconds later, we're in the opera house room. I'll admit, for a good show, this is a great place to end a life. Rama clearly thought of the cinematic aspect when she built the Temple Maze because there are all sorts of beautiful rooms to kill someone in. The opera house has great acoustics. The screams ring beautifully along the high, paneled ceiling.

The mark is in the middle of the stage, all lights pointed at him, his face a mask of terror as the rorschachs, and then Ten and I, push him toward the middle. Unfortunately for him, the vampiri stand in the shadows at the opposite side of the stage. This mark didn't put up much of a chase, but the sheer amount of aggression in the air now that we all surround him is enough to get my hackles rising, my competitive nature taking over as I stalk closer to the trembling human.

When I hear shouting, I look up the opera house's central aisle. The human contingent comes through the front door swinging baseball bats. The leader sees the collection of monsters on stage with the mark and frowns. He hates dealing with us, and we hate dealing with him. But the human element in the maze is the largest of the monster groups. Alphas are the smallest. Yet another way Rama continues to make fucking with me her personal mission.

I don't grace the humans with another look, but they turn to go as a group. If a monster finds the mark first, the humans have got no chance of being the ones to take him out. Rama's got it all planned out.

Onstage, one of the rorschachs morphs his face into a beautiful woman, although his body remains monstrous. The mark's eyes go wild as he shakes his head, stumbling backward as he screams, "No," over and over again. The rorschach stalks around the mark in a circle, berating him verbally before turning into its typical form again. The unfortunate man throws his arms over his face and screams into them, rocking on the floor like a child.

I should feel compassion, probably. If I were normal, I would. But I'm not. I'm an asshole and an alpha. I've seen thou-

sands of men cry just like this. At the end of the day, all of us
monsters have one job in this place: to do Rama's bidding or lose
our heads. Honestly, the hunt is the only part of the maze where I
get to still feel like myself. Stalking, hunting, chasing. The
blood.

Gods, I love the blood.

Next to me, Ten stands quietly, watching the show play out
as the rorschachs fuck with the man over and over until he's a
bumbling mess of snot and tears. They swipe at him with long
blue claws until he's bleeding all over the stage. Just surface
cuts, nothing severe. Nobody has permission to kill him yet. But
the man is falling apart. And the smell of blood only serves to
amp up the waiting tension in the room.

My mouth waters as I hover around the edges, watching the
lesser monsters fuck with the mark. The timer disk embedded in
my arm pings, and all the monsters look down at their own forearms at the same time. Apparently, the client is ready for the
grand finale. The disk counts down from thirty as we all crouch,
looking at the mark. He must sense the impending attack,
because dark, pleading eyes fly around at us, begging for his life.

We can't help you, little man, I muse. *We cannot even help
ourselves.*

My eyes wander across the stage to Cashore, the vampiri
king. He's a mean motherfucker, probably the closest thing to me
in this place. But we have an agreement–I don't go near his quarters, and his people don't come near mine. He tips his head at me
with an evil smile, waggling his forearm to show the fucking
disk that's approaching zero.

Go time.

An alarm sounds, and my disk flashes red, per usual. Not my
turn. Godsdamnit. Next to me, Ten visibly relaxes. I could swoop
in anyhow, but then I'd have a bigger fight on my hands.

Across from me, all the vampiri disks flash green as Cashore
roars in triumph. His people spring across the stage and descend

upon the mark, ripping into him with black claws and sharp teeth. His large body jerks once, twice as he screams, the sound of claws drawn across flesh ringing across the opera stage. There's a deep grunt from the mark and then the squishy noise of intestines hitting the wooden floors as the man groans.

Still seeing red, I watch a vampiri rip the mark's arm from its socket with a loud pop as the man screams, gurgling around a mouthful of blood. The monster brings the severed arm to Cashore with a bow as the vampiri takes it and looks across the stage at the rest of us.

Breaking the arm in half, Cashore sucks the marrow out of the bone, grinning at me before walking across the stage and tossing the arm at my feet. "A little consolation prize, Noire. It wasn't your night, but then again, it rarely seems to be. I wonder when Rama will ever find another client willing to pay the price for you to finish a mark…"

I snarl as I kick the arm toward the rorschachs, who descend upon it in a crazed fury.

In the middle of the stage, the mark's screams have slowed to the occasional grunt. He's not dead, but he's barely hanging on, drowning in pain. He won't last more than another minute or two, and when the vampiri are done, he'll be an eviscerated, dried husk. Mission accomplished for Rama's client.

There's a delightful ripping sound, and a slab of fat gets thrown out of the frenzy, landing with a squelch next to my shoe. I snarl at the vampiri as they rip into the man, balling my fists as I urge myself to hold back from taking over. Tonight is not my fight.

Next to me, Ten steps forward, growling, "Let's get outta here, Noire."

He's right; we should, but the dominant look on Cashore's face calls to the alpha side of my brain. He's challenging me the same way he always challenges me, every fucking night we hunt. I don't know if he's bored or just can't help himself.

Let's run the middle levels, Ten sends me through our mental bond. *Everyone is up here; it's a good time to examine some of those hallways again.*

I don't bother to nod, but Cashore cocks his head to the side as I back away from him, his expression triumphant.

The sounds of flesh tearing follow us as Ten and I head out of the opera house and through dark hallways toward the entrance to the middle levels. Already, the maulin foxes who clean up after the monsters flit in the shadows, waiting their turn to pick at the bones. Smiling, I wish them the best. They, at least, seem happy to be here.

We run for hours, examining doors and fake windows and looking for something, anything that might mean a way out. But like every night we do this, I can't find a single godsdamned thing that leads me to believe there's even a way out of this hellhole.

When we finally return to our rooms, I shower and lie in my bed, looking up at the dark stone ceiling. Every night I return here, temporarily defeated in my attempt to find a way out, that ceiling seems a little lower. I dread the day I wake up to find it right above my head, ready to crush me to dust.

Liuvang, I pray to the deity I scorned my whole life, *send me something, some sign. I have got to get out of here.*

CHAPTER 2
DIANA

I sort through the photos on my computer, searching for the perfect one. It's an in-the-moment shot of my subject, taken just days after he was thrown into Rama's maze.

Even the word "maze" sends a jolt of terror up my spine. It's shrouded in secrecy and rumors, but if you are put in, you never come out. It's Rama's dumping ground for anyone who defies or betrays her. Or anyone she simply dislikes. Now her wealthy clients have access to the maze too, paying her great sums of money to dispose of anyone they want.

I find the picture I'm looking for, sucking in a breath as I look at my subject. Dark hair is slicked back, revealing elegant, angular features and a square, masculine jaw. Everything about the way he's standing, looking across the hall toward the camera, indicates deadliness. He's intent, poised, the predatory look in his eyes seeping right from the file on my computer screen, sinking deep into the marrow of my bones.

This is a dangerous male. The most dangerous monster ever to rule Siargao. Before Rama took over, anyhow.

Alpha *Noire*.

Even his name means darkness, something I've always

wondered about. When he was born, did his parents take one look and know their son would be the most ruthless alpha to ever rule this province?

I met him once after he killed his alpha father and took over the Ayala pack. He came to meet my father to present himself as the new ruling alpha—a long-standing tradition amongst rulers. Our pack's province is on the far side of Lombornei, but Noire came anyhow. He nearly bowled me over with alpha dominance then. I was only seven at the time, but meeting him is a permanent imprint in my mind.

I drag the photo to the top left of the profiling document I'm working on for the client. She wants a full and complete picture of Noire. Who he is, every crime he's ever been implicated in, everything he's ever been convicted of, everything about his family and pack, and the details surrounding his abduction and entry into Rama's maze. I'll combine this with a full scene suggestion report, recommending to the clients how best to utilize Noire's talents to kill their chosen mark.

The work is gruesome, being the stage director of innocent peoples' final moments, but I have no choice in this–none at all. I'm certain Rama forces me to do it because it's a way to ensure death is always around me, and at her direction.

Staring down Noire's list of crimes, I shudder as icy prickles drag down my spine. Dismemberment, murder in all three degrees, assault with and without a deadly weapon, decapitation. He was once accused of sending a man's head to his wife in a box after the stupid male betrayed Noire. If a crime can be committed, Noire has been accused of it.

He's been in the maze for seven years, though, and Rama is in charge now. There's no more government, not that they had any power when Noire was in charge, or so I've heard. The client has asked for a complete profile of Noire, and I'm the very best at dredging up every nitty-gritty detail there is. In the few years I've had this shitty job, I've never been asked to profile him. He is almost never chosen to kill the marks, unless he was before I got the job. Nobody can afford what Rama charges for Noire. Until this client, apparently.

Satisfied my report is finished, I download the whole thing onto a thumb drive and ring a bell.

Precisely thirty seconds later, there's a rap at my door. When I open it, one of the street urchins who frequents this block shows up with his grimy palm held up. He knows the drill, the same as I do. We all work for Mistress Rama in one way or another, even Siargao's children. I hand him the thumb drive. "Straight to the docks with you."

He rolls his eyes as if it's obvious where he should go, and I suppose it is. Rama's goons litter the docks. They'll take this drive and deliver it to her so she can deliver it to the client. My job is done. It's on the tip of my tongue to remind the child to be careful, but I hold that comment back. I was a street urchin once, and I wasn't careful enough. That's why I'm stuck here now, working for the woman who rules this city under her bejeweled, elegant thumb.

Not that I've seen her in person in a very long time. But she appears nightly on every screen in the city for evening prayer. A prayer with her wellbeing and power front and center. A prayer that happens right after every screen in the city turns on to tele-vise the maze and the mark's demise. Another reminder of how very much she owns all of us.

The child snatches the drive and goes, and I watch my project disappear with him. Once he's gone, I turn back into my dismal apartment and walk to the window. Looking out, I smile when I see clouds rolling in over the hills. It's going to rain soon, and that's my favorite time in Siargao. Everyone else huddles inside, but I can put on my running shoes and sprint through the streets, along the shoreline as I watch the train crawl its way along the Kan River.

I run for miles when it rains. I run until I forget the memory of my dead pack and my dead twin brother. Everyone dead. I run until my emotions quiet into a simmer deep in my chest. Reaching into the secret compartment under my desk, I bring out the only photo I have of my twin, Dore. We're only seven or so in the photo, our arms slung around one another as I peck him on the cheek.

Our birthday. A happy time. Eventually, he and I were on the run from Rama's invading army, fighting for our lives, fighting for our freedom. She caught us, of course. With her superior technology and devious innovations, she caught *everyone* and subtly took over the Vinituvari province. And then she came here to Siargao and took it from Noire's Ayala pack overnight, dragging Dore and me along with her.

Lost in horrid memories, I reach down to my left arm and stroke my way along the intricately angular tattoo that goes up my entire arm and elbow. Father gave Dore and me matching tattoos when we turned eleven. I've often wondered about the timing; did Father know what was coming? Rama murdered him right after my fourteenth birthday.

I've always loved the tattoo's design, even though knowing Dore had the same one sends a knife straight through my broken heart.

Glancing out my window, I look at the floating city that glitters in the gray sky above Siargao's river valley. Rama's up there now, entertaining the wealthy. They live among beautiful, bright towers there and in Siargao's foothills, while the rest of us scrabble to stay alive down here by the riverside, praying for someone to relieve us of the woman who terrorizes us at every turn.

Growling, I head into my room, searching under my bed for my running shoes. They're threadbare at this point. I've nearly worn holes in the bottoms of them from my late-night runs.

A crack of lightning streaks across the sky, the clouds opening up to pour rain down on the valley. Smiling, I open the window to my back porch and raise the awning, providing a small, dry space. Moments later, a maulin fox slinks out of the growing shadows and hops up onto my railing, picking its way along until it's close to me.

The fox's lower jaw separates as he drops a tiny bone in my hand. He's been bringing me bones for years just like this, usually when it's rainy and he wants to come out of the cold. I scratch behind his ear and tickle under his chin as he rubs his cheek along the palm of my hand. When I'm satisfied he's happy with his spot perched on a dry section of my porch, I head back inside.

Moving my TV stand aside, I pull a panel off my wall and extract a large box. Taking the top off, I look at the hundreds of bones the fox has brought me over the last seven years. I toss the newest gift in with the rest and close the box, shoving it back in the wall and placing the TV stand back where it was.

I join the fox, lacing up my running shoes as he licks one paw slowly. Vibrant golden eyes meet mine as he cocks his head to the side.

Be safe, my friend, I think.

I imagine he understands me when he dips his head and focuses on me again, his gaze intent. We sit that way as the rain pours until finally the itch to run wins out. Stroking the tip of his chin one more time, I tell him goodbye and head to the front of my apartment just as the TV clicks on. There's no warning, but a man's screams ring out through my apartment. They ring through my open window too as every neighbor's television blares the death of tonight's mark.

Turning, I watch the beginning of the televised massacre. The clients nearly always agree with my scene suggestions, and I suggested the opera house for this man's final moments. The empty seats, the old-timey wooden stage, the velvet curtains–it's a beautiful place to die.

Plus, the vampiri in the maze always do the opera house

justice, and I selected them to be the harbingers of this man's death.

I don't stay to watch them kill him. I can't. "I'm sorry," I whisper under my breath to Rama's latest victim.

If I could help you, if I could change this, I would.

Holding back tears, I open my door and step out into the hallway. I jog down a set of stairs and out into the rain, pulling a hood up over my head as I look across the street. Two of Rama's goons stand there, watching me in the way they often do.

"Evening, gents," I snap, flipping them double birds as they growl. Everywhere I go, they're there. This whole town works for Rama in some way, and she loves keeping an eye on me because of who my father was. Just a reminder that she took everything away from me, and I have no choice but to live in her capital city and work for her. Controlling Siargao means she controls the whole continent, with the exception of the Tempang forest, of course. But the other provinces need the thick oil that's pumped out of the ground here.

The street is full of people scrambling to get inside, away from the deluge. I walk down the center as it empties, smiling as I lift my head for the rain to hit my face. It slides down my cheeks and neck, into my shirt. My smile deepens. This, at least, is something Rama can't take from me. The joy of a nighttime run in the rain.

Across from me, my neighbor, Trig, cooks bao in front of his restaurant. The rain is good for his business. When I turn his way, he looks up at me and blinks twice, slowly. Then he turns away, eyeing his patrons.

Still, I've received the message loud and clear. Two blinks for a need to meet.

I may be forced into servitude, crushed under Rama's boot, but I'll die before I give in and accept my current fate. Turns out I'm not the only one, and there's a growing movement of people who want to rebel against her somehow. Small, but growing.

I pick up a jog, heading toward the shoreline, and then I run along the Kan, people watching from dry porches as I pass. I push my muscles hard until I reach the mouth of the river where it empties into Lon Bay. Across the bay, an island stands, a solitary sentinel for the entire Siargao province.

The maze.

My father built the labyrinth, then Rama grew an island on top of it, and dragged the whole thing here, settling it at the mouth of the river once she took control. I can barely comprehend how she managed it.

"I miss you, Dore," I whisper to my brother's ghost as I look out at the maze island. It's as tropical as everything in this province, but seeing it makes me long for the rolling green hills and valleys of my homeland, Vinituvari. I miss the delicate, detailed architecture my father was famous for designing. I miss the hand pies. I miss riding my horse, Dove. I miss every fucking thing about where I came from. Shit, I even miss the cold.

"One day, Dore. One day, I will get retribution for what she did to you. I promise you that," I whisper again, more to myself than my brother. I don't know how I will, but something's got to give.

I watch the maze island silently for a while before turning and jogging up into the hills toward the graveyard near the end of the Riverside District. It marks the last bit of wildness before glittering towers take over as skyscrapers replace the trees, heading up the valley into the low, rolling mountains. The wealthy live safely in those buildings, using the big airport on top of one of the skyscrapers to travel to and from Rama's city in the sky.

Fuck all of them.

Slowing to a stop, I pick my way through the graveyard, to the spot where I collect rocks in memory of Dore. I didn't get to bury him; Rama made sure of that. But she can't tear his memory from my fucking memory banks, so this is how I make sure he's gone but never, ever forgotten.

I grab a small purple stone from my pocket and lay it gently on the pile, dropping to both knees. "I miss you, Dore. One day, Liuvang-willing, I will see you again, brother." I whisper that last prayer to the goddess under my breath. Praying to the fox goddess, Liuvang, is a sin, according to Rama, punishable by death. The only one anyone is allowed to pray to is Mistress Rama. She's a damn psychopath.

A sudden whirring noise whines behind me, the faint brush of wind brushing my blond waves aside, despite them being soaked. Whipping around, I'm shocked when an entire floating office, complete with a woman sitting at a desk, slides out of the dark clouds and descends until it's in the middle of the road. Inside the office, Rama sits at the desk, watching me, hands clasped together on the desktop. I haven't seen her in person in several years. Two at least, maybe three.

This is a bad sign, that she's here in person.

I stand, rain sluicing down my face as air pulses from underneath the floating office. Already, heady nerves bundle in my stomach, and I force myself not to clench my jaw as I pick around the gravestones and approach her. It's what she wants; I know that well enough from being forced to grow up under her thumb.

"Hello, Diana," she purrs, her voice throaty and seductive. I want to slice my claws across it and separate her fucking head from her shoulders.

"Hello, Mistress," I speak up, dipping my head. *Mistress bitch*, I add silently in my mind.

Rama stands in the office, and it maintains its floating position easily as she crosses the room. I see a faint distortion on the surface. It looks like I'm peering into an office with only three sides, but I'm sure there's some sort of force field across the front to protect her.

God, if only us regular people had access to tech like this. But she keeps most tech under lock and key, and nobody leaves Siargao.

"I'm sure you're wondering why I came down here personally, Diana," Rama begins, examining her nails before clasping both hands in front of her waist.

Not really, I want to bark, but I grit my jaw instead. "Was there an issue with my most recent profiling report? I sent it about an hour ago with one of the kids..." I trail off, unsure where to go from here.

"No," Rama laughs, "the client wants Noire's profile, and she's got Noire's profile, thanks to you. You've outlived your usefulness as a profiler, Diana. I have other plans for you now." Her face splits into an evil smile as I hear footsteps behind me.

When I whirl around, I see the goons, the same two who always follow me. "What's going on?" I bark as Rama hisses and points a dart gun at my face. She pulls the trigger, and before I can even register the anger, something pokes into my neck.

My knees give out, and I sink to the pavement, spinning as I fall to my back, the rain peppering my face like a hail of bullets. Distantly, I'm aware of Rama laughing as she directs the goons to do something. My hearing goes fuzzy, and the last thing I see before darkness takes me is a man's face.

One of the goons. He's got both middle fingers up and pointed straight at me. And he's smiling, his teeth black and crooked, his breath foul.

"Gotcha," he snarls. "It's finally your turn, little omega."

Voices surround me as I struggle to blink my eyes open. My mouth is one enormous cotton ball as I open it to say something and nothing comes out. The back of my head feels like a split log, pain radiating to the front of my face. My fangs descend, a protective move that happens involuntarily sometimes.

Snarling, I feel saliva drip down my fangs, coating my lower lip. Everything is fuzzy until I blink three or four times, and a black room comes into view. Black walls, black ceiling. I move to sit, but...I can't. I grunt as something pokes into me. Blinking hard, I glance down to see a corset.

A fucking corset. I'm wearing a cornflower blue corset and below that, a matching skirt.

"What do y'spose she did?" a harsh voice grates at my ears as I continue blinking, struggling to wrap my mind around the corset and matching skirt and a black room I don't recognize.

"Doesn't matter," a softer voice murmurs. "Not our place to guess. Finish prepping and keep your mouth shut."

"Where...where am I?" I grunt, finally finding my voice, even though it sounds like someone dragging me across gravel.

"The maze, of course," quips the first voice cheerfully. Then, a little more solemnly, "You go in tonight."

The maze. The fucking maze.

Struggling against whatever binds me, I bite at a hand as it comes close to my face. I still can't fully see past a foot or two, but there's a yip before someone backhands me, my head snapping back against something hard. Pain blooms at the back of my throat as a snarl rumbles out of my mouth.

"Try it again, bitch," the quieter of the two voices snaps. "It's our job to prep you, and you'll never make it out, so start praying to Mistress Rama that it's quick for you. Bite my hand again, and you'll go in missing a finger or two."

A mist of something that smells like pure sex hits me straight in the face as I try to leap back and can't, still strapped to some kind of platform, tilted upright so the two people can do whatever the hell they're doing.

The mist coats my face and hair until it drips from my eyelashes, and I start to get a sense of the two women in the room with me. The quieter one sprays a steady stream along my neck and shoulders as the second one watches her with a wary, guarded expression. "That seems like enough, Heti. Don't you think?"

"Mistress Rama said to coat her, so coat her we will. You don't want to answer to the Mistress if you forget a single part of the mark prep process, Del. I can promise you that. Finish her hair."

The chattier woman steps closer to me. "Please don't bite me, okay? I can't help you. I'm just doing my job."

I snap again, but she sighs and presses a button on a table beside her. Immediately, a strap goes across my neck, crushing my windpipe so hard, I can't even turn my head to the side. Another one flies across my face, slipping between my teeth as the woman grumbles, "I didn't want to do that to you. Why'd you have to fight?"

The quieter of the two huffs out a disbelieving breath and sets the mister bottle down. "No point talking to the marks, Del. They're dead, remember? Just do your best to keep your chin up and your head attached to your shoulders."

I struggle against the thick bands crisscrossing my body and neck, but I can't move as the worker fusses with my hair, piling it all on top of my head with metal pins that definitely couldn't double as any sort of weapon.

The fucking maze. I'm going into the fucking maze.

That bitch.

The wheels of my mind spin so fast that I can practically hear my brain heating as I struggle to think through this process.

The helpers finish messing with me, despite my struggle. Watching them clean up their tools sends my anxiety into over-drive, like their cleaning is a countdown timer to throwing me into the fucking maze to be killed.

And they continue cleaning, glancing at a clock on the wall that indicates the time. The room is painfully silent until the platform I'm chained to creaks and moves, sliding forward on a track toward an archway cut into one side of the room. The track seems to disappear off into the darkness like a horrible roller coaster ride from hell.

Despite knowing they won't help me, I can't resist the urge to beg them to let me out. "Please," I attempt to choke out around the strap. "Please, don't do this." Fear has my spine locked tight as the one called Heti smirks and Del's face falls a little. She clasps one hand over her heart as they follow my platform along the track, waving a sad goodbye to me as the platform heads through the archway and disappears, leaving the black room behind.

"No!" I try to scream. "Let me the fuck out of here!" My words are muffled around the thick leather between my lips. Gooseflesh crawls across my skin as freezing air slaps me in the face. The platform I'm strapped to rumbles noisily along the track, through a long dark hallway until it comes to a stop in front of a black stone wall. In front of me, a screen whirs to life, Rama appearing with a smirky smile on the brightly lit screen.

"Your mark tonight is this woman. The client wants her tortured and pulled apart in every possible way, drawing the death out as long as possible. Happy hunting, my children."

My face flashes across the screen for a few long seconds. I look…normal in the picture, as if they took it while I was walking down the street. Blond hair, blue eyes, freckles. There's a tension in the crinkles at the edges of my eyes, but I look…average.

The screen goes blank as I struggle against the bindings, although there's no point. This maze isn't designed for marks to get out. I've never heard of someone coming back from the Temple Maze. The platform creaks and begins moving again, floating through pitch darkness like a macabre circus ride. The blackness even eats up the light from the screen behind me until there's nothing, and I can't even see my body when I look down.

I suck in deep breaths, certain my heart is pounding loud enough for the entire maze to hear.

When the platform rounds a corner of the track and another stone door opens, there's a little bit of light. Then the stench hits, all unwashed bodies and filth. My mouth dries up as I struggle against the bindings, huddling in the middle of the platform. It continues creaking forward, until I'm able to see slats in the stone walls, claws and arms reaching through.

Oh God, the track here is only as wide as my platform, which isn't that wide. Every arm reaching through will be able to touch me. The monsters. Oh fuck.

Liuvang, please help me, I pray to the deity.

Most of the arms end in claws of all shades, and horrifyingly, there's a viewing window of sorts where I can see mouths, snouts, teeth, gnarled hands coated in sores. A few of the viewing holes have erect cocks poking through, deep grunts emitting from the monsters those swinging cocks are attached to.

I struggle not to scream-when a black-clawed hand grabs my hair and yanks it hard, snarls ringing through the small, cold hallway. Another hand reaches out and grips my breast through the bodice, squeezing hard enough to elicit a scream from me. That's what she wants, Rama. She wants the terror, the tease of how violent and ruthless the maze's monsters are. This is a prelude, something to terrify the maze's marks before the monsters play with them. Something to scare the shit out of me because, shortly, there will be no stone walls separating me from them.

I force myself to look forward, focusing on the end of the hallway as hands grip and tear at me, claws scratching at my skin until I'm bleeding from multiple stinging wounds. The monsters hurl insults and innuendoes like bricks, their filthy words sinking into my mind as I focus harder on the end of the hallway.

After what seems like hours, my platform reaches the end, and another stone door shuts behind me, enclosing me in darkness once more. It moves forward with a click and a hiss and then travels downward, the floor underneath me opening into a brightly lit room. My eyes struggle with the sudden explosion of light; everything here is golden and opulent. A gigantic circular bar enclosed inside a golden cage holds extravagantly dressed men and women, drinking.

Their heads swivel as the lights dim, and I see a stage. This has never been televised to the general public; I don't know what I'm looking at. But if I had to guess, this is a way Rama's wealthy patrons can enjoy the maze's monsters without being in real danger. The entire caged bar is full of wealthy-looking people, dressed to the nines and turning toward the stage. Small caged rooms line one side of the bar, and inside, it's easy to see men and women in various stages of getting fucked by monsters. But the monsters shimmer and shake like they're not real.

Virtual reality? Is that what I'm looking at? A safe way for the rich to experience the maze's beasts without worrying over their safety?

My stomach ties itself in knots as I resist the urge to be sick, my platform traveling down through the room and finally pulling to a stop. The people inside the bar's safety cage look up at me, pointing and laughing before the lights dim further, and a velvet curtain slides up on the stage. I can't pull my eyes from the scene as a huge alpha male stalks from the shadows, an erection clearly visible in his pants.

Noire's brother, Jet, the one he's closest to in age. I've profiled him a few times over the years, but seeing him in person is a shocking experience. He's fucking enormous, far bigger than I remember my own alpha father being, even in his prime. Jet slips his shirt off as the people in the cage take their seats and wait.

His pants slide off next, and then the crowd is presented with his naked form, his erect cock straining toward a woman chained to a table that pops up out of the floor. Jet shifts into his wolf and stalks across the stage, shoving his nose between the woman's thighs as she screams in terror.

My heart pounds in my chest as he paces around the table, scenting her before he shifts into human form again and unlocks one of her ankles from its chain. The woman brings her legs together quickly, but Jet yanks them back open wide and slaps her pussy with his thick cock.

Below me, the crowd goes wild, cheering him on. And then there's at least half an hour of him taking her in every possible way a woman can be taken. He's inventive and creative, and the crowd is crazed as the woman comes multiple times, despite her screams for him to stop.

Every now and again, the patrons glance up at me and point, snickering and laughing. I'm obviously just here to be presented to them. For them to know these are my last hours of life. I can't stop looking around the room, but my eyes return over and over to Jet and the way he fucks the woman in ways I could never have even imagined.

This room is debauchery in all its possible forms, and I'm so sick to my heart from watching it that I'm not even terrified for my life at the moment. I want to rage and scream and do something. But as the platform holding me shifts to move again, I can't resist another backward look at the performing alpha on the stage.

The woman is limp and catatonic at this point, but another platform comes up out of the stage, a muscular man tied to this one, his ass up in the air for everyone to see. Jet drops the woman and stalks across the stage to the man, but a door opens up in the wall above the stage, and my platform exits through it.

I hold on to that little bit of light from the ostentatious room, knowing it's the last light of any sort I'll ever see. With a click, the chains holding my arms and legs snap open, and the platform dumps sideways. I hit the ground hard enough to pull a grunt from my body, but then the floor opens up below me, and I *fall, fall, fall.*

When I hit the ground, the air whooshes from my lungs, my hair in a pile around me. And the very first thing I hear is a clicking hiss.

Oh gods, I'm in the fucking maze.

Not a single thing stands between the monsters and me.

CHAPTER 3
NOIRE

Another night, another hunt. Slipping a simple black tee over my bulky frame, I turn when I hear Tenebris coming down the hall. Striding across the room, I open my door and gesture for him to come in. The look on his face is carefully neutral as he inclines his head toward me, a respectful gesture from an alpha to *the* alpha.

"I went up to see the mark tonight." Ten's voice sounds easy, but there's a tense quality to it that lifts the hair on the back of my neck.

"Why? We never preview the marks."

Ten shrugs and walks across my room, leaning up against the black stone mantel with his arms crossed. "I've actually been up a few times this month. Just looking for something…different."

I lift a brow. "You went up alone? That's fucking foolish, Ten."

He shrugs again. "Everyone's too focused on the mark to bother one another. Anyhow, the mark's an omega. They doused her in enough pheromone to take down an ox, so they want her played with."

I bristle again. "An omega, are you sure?" We've never seen an omega in the maze. Nearly all omegas in Siargao were part of my pack or one other. I know every single one of them, and if Tenebris' early story is true, Rama killed everyone. "Do we know her?"

Ten shakes his head. "I couldn't place a scent through whatever they coated her with, but I didn't recognize her either."

My wheels spin as Ten stands, keeping quiet. Is it circumstance that Rama's putting an omega into the maze tonight? There's never been one the entire time we've been here, and I don't believe in circumstance.

Turning to my brother, I nod. "Where are you tonight?"

Ten smiles, but it doesn't reach his eyes. "Maze again with you. Which is a good thing. I'd like to see the omega a little more closely. Tall, delicate, blond, blue eyes. She's beautiful. Are they all like that? I can't remember anymore..."

"She's a dead woman walking," I remind him. I don't need to know anything else about her. And unless we get out of here, Ten will never take an omega. Maybe we can, at least, give him a good time tonight with this one.

Ten shrugs his shoulders. "I think this is the first time I've been excited for a hunt."

Whipping my head up, I cock it to the side and examine my youngest sibling. He leans casually against my fireplace, but there's a tension in the set of his shoulders and muscular frame. There's a predatory agitation about the sense I read from him right now. He wants to hunt this woman.

"What is it about her?" I snap, my alpha bark rolling over him as he bows his head to me.

"Nothing." It's a grumble, but it's a lie.

"Don't lie to me, Tenebris. What is this omega to you?"

He looks up, head bowed with respect. "She feels...different from the other women who get put here. Maybe it's just because she's an omega, and we haven't seen one this whole time."

The wheels in my head spin as I look at my brother and think about what he's saying. The more I think, the more certain I am that Rama sending an omega in here is no coincidence, just another way she can think up to try and fuck with us, me in particular.

For the first time, I regret not going to preview the mark. I'd like to get a sense of this woman before we hunt her tonight. In the end, it won't matter. She will die like so many others before her. It's just...curious.

The disk at my wrist flashes the five-minute warning. Ten shifts up off the fireplace and pads to the door.

Grabbing my favorite knife, I slide it in the holster across my chest and follow him. I spit at the screen outside my room that flashes the countdown timer like every other fucking night. Ahead of me, Ten chuckles low under his breath.

As we pass through the kitchen and living area, Jet holds a glass of purple liquid up to us in a mock cheer. "Just popped back down on a short break between performances. Happy hunting, my children!"

I frown, and Ten snorts while Jet downs the entire glass of uppers. It's so fucking much that his pupils blow wide almost immediately as he snarls at us both, tossing the glass into the sink.

I'll need to do something about this later. The increasing amount of drugs Jet's pumping into his system every night is getting out of control. He's going to become a problem if this keeps going.

"You and I need a chat later," I bark as Jet bows his head, mocking me as he bats his eyelashes. That's the drugs talking because no alpha would ever disrespect his pack alpha in this way.

I cross the room with swift intention, gripping Jet by the neck and throwing him up against the fridge. He dents the door and sinks to the floor, but hops back up with a raging howl, fists balled. The smell of uppers hits me hard when his mouth opens, but I don't back down. I never back down. I'm the fucking pack alpha, even of this sorry three-man pack in this fucking maze.

Siargao was my kingdom before getting put into this goddamn place, and it'll be mine again if it's the last thing I do. But for now, the maze is mine. And this high-as-fuck alpha is mine too.

"You forget your place, brother," I snap as I step into Jet's space, invading it as I whip a hand to his throat and squeeze hard enough to bruise his windpipe.

The alpha bark causes his eyes to lower, but he still struggles against the bond. That's the drugs talking again. Unless it's something more sinister, something deeper. Something like this place finally fucking with pack dynamics enough that my own brother thinks it's okay to challenge me.

I slice my dark claws across Jet's top two ribs and dig them under his skin, snarling in his face as he yowls at the pain. "This is a warning, brother. You know better."

Sweat slides down Jet's face as he squints his eyes against the pain. For him, it's hardly more than an irritation, but getting stabbed by our claws still hurts like a bitch. I slip my claws out, relishing the sound of bone on bone as Jet winces. Blood flows from the wound as he sucks in a deep breath.

The disk in my wrist flashes the sixty-second countdown as Jet's eyes go wide. "I've got to get upstairs. Can't be late. Can't be late. Can't be late."

When he repeats himself again, I narrow my eyes to observe him. There's an anxious tension scratching at our mental bond.

What happens if he's late? Something, clearly. I file it away for later investigation. For now, I drop his throat and indicate he can go.

He sprints for the door as Ten's eyes meet mine, full of sorrow. I don't return the look but head for the door to await Rama's nightly message.

Just before it comes on, Ten turns to me. "Did you have to do that? He's strung out."

"He disrespected me." That's all I need to say because, when I turn to look at Ten, he dips his head an appropriate, respectful amount and nods.

The screen inlaid across from our front entryway blinks several times, then we see Rama herself, looking smug as fuck as she begins her evening's directions.

"Your mark tonight is this woman." A picture flashes up on the screen, and I can see what Ten meant about her earlier. She's stunning. Clearly an omega, even from the little of her shown. Something in the focus of her eyes. If you know what to look for, pack omegas are just different enough from normal human women to be noticeable to an alpha.

"The client wants her tortured and pulled apart in every possible way, drawing the death out as long as possible. Happy hunting, my children."

Rama smirks on the screen, black hair swinging. I always imagine she's speaking directly to me when she comes on the screen. And that little smirk? Someday, I'm going to swipe it right off her face when I slice it from her body with my claws.

"As long as possible?" Ten turns to me as the timer flashes down from ten.

"Someone hates this woman," I grumble as he and I crouch in the front entryway.

Ten huffs. "Let's get to her first."

I turn to look at my brother as he crouches next to me, entirely focused on the dark hallway ahead of us. This maze is finally changing us, who we are, what we want. Ten's never been excited for a hunt before. I'm almost proud, although his interest amps up my competitive nature.

I want the omega first.

The buzzer sounds, and Ten takes off like a shot, me following up the rear, same as I always do. Tonight, Ten is focused. He doesn't bother sweeping the levels closest to us; they almost never drop marks at our doorstep. Instead, he heads right for vampiri territory. For whatever reason, marks often start there. Or in the middle levels where the humans can chase them for a while.

We round a corner, heading toward the chapel, and a scent hits me so hard I stagger and fall to my knees, sucking in deep, gasping breaths. Ten is frozen next to me, doing the same. Omega pheromones. I've never smelled them this strong before, although they usually prep female marks with some level of this. The scent sets off a livewire reaction in my body, every inch of me going rock hard in anticipation of whoever's giving off that smell.

This scent is blood in the water to a school of sharks, me being the biggest and baddest of them. This time, it isn't a general pheromone for monsters; it's specific to alphas. The mark smells like an omega in heat.

If I had any doubt Rama wanted to fuck with me, that doubt is gone. Someone wants this woman dead, and Rama's aware she's an omega, so she wants to torture me with this woman's presence for a while by rubbing it in my face—which means we aren't meant to kill this woman either. It'll be the vamps or rorschachs probably, maybe even the humans. Rama will want me to see this delicious-smelling mark ripped out of my hands for someone else to toy with.

I think not. Leaping back to my feet, I race through the hall, through the chapel where the scent gets stronger. But then other scents come to me. *Vampiri.* Competitive anger slices through the forefront of my brain as Ten growls next to me, panting with the intense need the pheromones produce in us both.

Far away, I hear footsteps and desperate breathing. The omega. She's running.

Sprinting in her direction, I calm my thoughts, ensuring my

footsteps are silent. She'll run right into us, focused as she is on whatever she's running from. An omega should be able to sense two alphas ahead of her, but an omega running for her life could miss the danger she's about to run into.

I hope she does.

The vampiri hoot and call happily when they hunt, and those noises ring up the long hallway toward us as they chase her slowly, playing with their food.

Peeking around a stone pillar, I can just begin to see her coming up the hallway. She's dressed in an old-fashioned blue dress. A tight bodice pushes up ample breasts so they spill out of the top. She's covered in blood already, blond hair falling out of the bun they put it up in. Tears stain her cheeks as she pumps her arms hard, flying up the passageway toward us.

A body barrels out of the shadows and knocks into the omega, slamming her up against the wall.

Rorshach. It screams in her face as its own begins to morph and turn. But before it can finish shifting, the omega bellows in anger and slices her arm upward, driving a knife up under the rorshach's chin. It screeches and hisses and stumbles backward as she yanks the knife out and gets to her feet.

She killed it; I'll be damned.

It's haunting to watch prey run right toward me, knowing when she gets to me, I will take her. In all the ways, I'll take her. Because I want to and I can. Watching her get murderous does things to my cock, stirring my natural need.

Across from me, Ten tenses. "More monsters are coming."

We're far enough away from the omega, and she's crazed with fear enough not to focus on us sprinting up the hallway quietly. She moves gracefully, long arms pumping as she steadies her breath, sucking air in quietly as blue eyes, the color of her dress, dart from side to side, scanning for danger.

I'm right here, female, I whisper to myself. *Keep coming.*

Ten and I hover in the dark shadows, watching as the omega skids out of the hallway and into an open room with dark stone pillars holding up the ceiling. Behind her, the vampiri hoot and call out to one another, and a rorschach snarls.

The omega pauses behind a pillar, taking a peek behind her as she grips the knife tighter in her bloody hand. She opens pink lips and sucks in a deep breath, scenting the air as her muscles tighten under the dress. I watch gooseflesh crawl its way along her skin as she glances around, starting to ascertain that Ten and I are here.

Next to me, he pants and tenses, centered entirely on the beauty now crouching down as she scents the air and prepares to run. Again.

Calm yourself, brother, I snap through our mental bond. *The chase is the best part of all this. Enjoy it.*

Ten nods imperceptibly and shifts forward onto the balls of his feet.

The omega glances around the dark room, looking up the nearest hallway, the one that leads almost directly to our quarters.

My dick leaks in my pants as I watch her look for the danger —me, the biggest threat to her in this whole fucking place. It's obvious she realizes she's not alone in this room, that the threats to her life are multiplied here.

Stay, I mentally bark at Ten as I step out of the shadows and into the room.

The omega's eyes widen as she sucks in another deep breath and grips her knife tighter, eyes traveling up my frame before she snaps her mouth shut.

I ball my fists as the noise of the other monsters' approach rings up the hallway. The omega's blue eyes dart to one side as she crouches, eyes flickering back toward me. Smirking, I cross the stone floor quietly, stalking toward her as my muscles bunch and harden in anticipation of taking her.

She'll run. I can sense it. And she should. *Not that it will help; I'll just enjoy it more.*

When I'm fifteen feet from her, I stop, cocking my head to the side as her chest heaves, accentuating the fullness of her breasts. She's so pale I can see the blue veins throbbing under her skin.

"I'm going to enjoy this," I growl as she blinks once, twice, her body already lighting up for mine. For a long moment, blue eyes lock onto my darker ones, and her gaze turns assessing, then wary. She's probably wondering if she can reason with me since we're the same species.

She can't.

"Run." My alpha bark washes over her as her mouth drops open, her body drawn to my alpha nature, despite knowing she needs to run from me.

She takes off like a shot, and I watch her go as Ten jogs toward me, panting heavily as he watches blue skirts disappear into the darkness. "Why'd you let her go? Godsdamn, Noire. She smells so fucking good; I'm losing my mind."

"Calm yourself," I snap. "And wait."

Behind us, the vampiri hoots come closer as need and lust amp up in my system. My cock strains against the front of my pants as my vision narrows to the hallway the omega disappeared inside of. Next to me, Ten whines and pants, shifting from side to side.

"What are we doing?" he groans. "Why are we waiting?"

"The chase is the best part of hunting an omega, brother," I growl as Ten groans again.

When the vampiri flood into the room behind us, I look at Ten.

Go, I whisper into our mental link.

He takes off like a shot, sprinting up the hallway after the omega. Like all omegas of our kind, she's fucking fast, and we gave her a head start.

I hear Cashore roar behind me as he watches us track the omega, running up the hallway.

Knowing other monsters are running just behind us sends my libido and natural dominance into overdrive. I follow Ten as he snarls and pushes toward the omega. We follow her up hallway after hallway until she makes a mistake, turning into a dead-end room.

She slides to a stop with an angry scream, spinning around with the knife out as Ten and I round the corner and pause. "Fuck you," she barks out, the force of her words slamming into me. She's strong, this woman. It's rare to find a mark with fight.

She's fucking godsdamned beautiful too.

Out of the darkness above her, a rorschach drops from the ceiling and throws the omega up against the wall. Her head hits the stone with a loud crack, the smell of blood permeating the air. The rorschach turns, creepy textured face morphing from face to face to face. It draws inspiration from the mark's mind, but when it turns into Rama and rounds on us, I'm shocked.

Instinct takes over then, and I dart across the small space, whipping out with my claws, separating the monster's head from its neck, reveling in the blood that sprays me.

"What the fuck are you doing?" hisses Ten, even as he reaches down and grabs the groaning omega, slinging her over one shoulder.

When we turn, Cashore is there, surrounded by dozens of vampiri. He leans into the room and sucks in a deep breath before glittering black eyes fall to the floor and take in the dead monster at my feet. "That was a foolish move, alpha. Rama will have your head for this."

"I don't think so," I snap back, stepping in front of Ten and squaring my shoulders.

Cashore's fake smile falls. "The mark is not for you. We all know it. The disk gave us the green tonight."

"And yet my brother has her, and we're taking her back to our rooms to play. So she *is* mine until the moment I say she's not. You heard the instructions; the client wants her played with. I'll take care of that part."

Cashore snarls, piercing black teeth flashing from underneath his equally black lips. "Hand her over, alpha."

I step closer to the vampiri king and snap my teeth in his face, reveling in the way one eye twitches as he shifts ever so slightly back. "Don't make me fight my way out of here, vampiri. You will not win, and I will get the girl anyway. Tenebris and I wish to play with her, per the client's instructions. You can collect the mark later when I am good and sated."

Cashore snarls and takes a step back. "You're outnumbered, alpha."

Gesturing to the dead monster on the floor, I smile, letting every shred of malevolence I feel into my wicked smile. "I don't give a fuck. As you can see. If I come out of this room swinging, some of your people will die. Do you want that?"

I see the moment he gives in and takes a step back. He doesn't want to lose anyone to my anger. He realizes just how few fucks I have left to give. I've broken the cardinal rule of the maze–don't kill the other monsters. I've broken that rule time and time again, and still, Rama doesn't come down on me as hard as she could.

Flicking my eyes to the side, I gesture for him to get out of my way, staying between the vamps and Tenebris as my brother sidles out of the room and heads up the hallway, the limp omega over his shoulder.

Raising my middle finger to Cashore, I give him my back and stalk up the hallway after my brother, eyes locked onto the blond hair dangling down his back. There's a red smattering of blood at the back of the omega's head. The rorschach flung her into the wall pretty hard. Hopefully not too hard because I want to play before it's time to end her. I'd rather her be awake enough to keep fighting.

Rama might be hoping to fuck with me by dangling this pretty thing in front of me like a toy. What Rama doesn't realize is precisely how much I'm going to enjoy this breakable doll before the disk embedded in my arm reminds me to give her up.

CHAPTER 4
DIANA

As I come to for the second time tonight, I shoot upright, then fly back down as pain blooms in my head hard enough to send black stars shooting across my vision. It blurs as I struggle to process voices. I'm not dead, thankfully. But I am laid out on top of a wooden table.

Turning my head to the side, I grunt in pain as my eyes blink open. An alpha–Noire–sits in a chair in front of me, one ankle crossed over his knee, fingertips steepled as he looks at me. I haven't seen an alpha male in years until I saw Jet earlier. I forgot just how big they are, how dominant they feel. Noire is enormous in real life, far larger than I could have realized from the profile I put together.

A second alpha comes into my view, but when I look up at him, Noire growls, a deep rumble that demands I return my gaze to him. When I do, a wicked smile marks his face, thin lips turning upward in a dominant smirk. When he speaks, his voice is so deep, I feel it all the way to my core and lower. "You came from outside the maze. Tell me about the city, omega. What of the Ayala pack?"

The Ayala pack, the famous alpha pack Rama decimated

when she took over Siargao. I've never met anyone claiming to be from the pack, although I've never left my area of the city either. "I don't know." My voice comes out small, barely a whisper as he leans forward.

"Don't lie to me. If you screwed someone over enough to get sent here, you know my people. Which means you know where they are if they're still around. Out with it."

His voice is a deep bark I can't resist and can't dance around. It's one of the bullshit things about being an omega, being physically subservient to the growly alpha males of my species.

"Ayala pack hasn't run Siargao since Rama took over. I don't know where they are these days, and that's the truth."

The alpha snarls and sits back as if he suspected this was the case but didn't want to believe it. He's been here for seven long years. Seven years is surely enough time to drive an already monstrous male to become something sub-alpha. If my research is accurate, there was no compassion in this male to begin with.

Dark eyes travel slowly back to mine. "Rama's never sent an omega into the maze. Why you and why now?"

It's another alpha bark that makes me want to roll over and show him my belly. He knows it because he leans forward in the chair and snarls again, and a whimper leaves my mouth at how that noise lights up my body. I'm tonight's mark. These males *will* kill me.

"She sent me here to fuck with you," I blurt out. It's probably the truth.

The alpha laughs, gesturing at my dress. "Why? Where have you been for seven years?"

"I worked for her," I admit. "Everyone does in one way or another. But apparently, I've outlived my usefulness." A bitter taste coats my mouth as I think about Rama's cruel words when she snatched me.

You've outlived your usefulness as a profiler, Diana…

"Wait," I moan, sensing the value of my life decrease as

Noire stands from his seat and steps into my space. I'm assaulted by his masculine scent, all warmth and heat, and something so intensely sexual, I have to squeeze my thighs together as slick coats them.

Noire reaches out, gripping my neck with one huge fist, black claws digging into my skin as the pain throbbing in the back of my head increases.

"Things are different outside the maze," I gasp out as he squeezes my throat. "Everyone works for Rama now. She is the Queen of Siargao. Nothing happens without her hand in it."

The alpha snarls as Tenebris comes into view, younger, although I can barely tell with the pain in my head hurting so damn bad.

"Let her down, alpha," Tenebris urges, dipping his head submissively even though he's nearly a head taller.

Noire's eyes scan my face, looking for what, I'm not sure. I'm looking at the former King of Siargao. He ruled everything with an iron fist, controlling the politicians, controlling the elite, controlling the seedy underbelly. This alpha ran every facet of Siargao society until Rama swooped in and yanked it out from under him, throwing him and his brothers into this maze.

Seven long-ass years ago.

Tenebris turns to me. "What did you do for Rama?" Even though he's younger and not in charge here, he's still an alpha. That fucking urge to roll over for him hits me hard, a whimper leaving my mouth as he snarls and steps closer, dragging his nose along my collarbone.

"Good, she smells so fucking good," he pants. "Do all omegas smell like this?" His voice is a deep whine. He's not much younger than me, and he came of age here in the maze. Plus, I know from profiling all the marks who've gone in that he hasn't seen an omega since he was young. In all my time in Siargao, I've never met another omega either, or an alpha, for that matter.

Noire leans in, one arm coming to either side of me as he gets right in my space. His nose goes to the base of my throat first before fisted fingers drag my head back, pulling a squeal from me as my head throbs. He doesn't care but sucks in breath after breath as he works his way up the column of my throat, under my ear, and back down along my collarbone.

"It's been a long time since I scented an omega." His voice is a deep growl as my thighs open of their own damn accord. "They're making her smell like a heat."

The young alpha whines again, wanting to step in and scent me, but he won't do it with Noire here.

Noire snarls and lets me go, rounding on his brother. "Tenebris, go upstairs; tell Jet to come down early if at all possible. I want to enjoy this omega before we have to turn her over to the vampiri."

Tenebris doesn't hesitate but stalks across the black living space and disappears out a side door.

Noire glances up at the cameras in the ceiling. "Rama wanted to dangle you in front of me. I'll ask you one more time. Why you and why now? I want details." He pulls his shirt over his head, revealing a thickly muscular body with a knife holster strapped to his chest.

My breath comes in huffy pants as his dark eyes lock onto mine. "I suspect she wants you to want me, and to watch the other monsters rip me away. Just another thing you can't have because of her."

Noire smirks and shakes his head. "I figured that part out on my own, omega. It won't be a hardship to enjoy you, but I will hardly care when your death happens."

"Maybe you should care," I snap back before I can rein the words in. "Because I can get you out of here."

His smile falls, turning into a furious scowl as he grips my neck and yanks me to the edge of the table. "What the fuck do you mean?"

CHAPTER 5
NOIRE

This fucking omega wants me to believe she can get me out? I've never believed in luck, and even if I did, this is too far-fetched. I'm done listening. I'm ready to take and take and take until I'm sated. Rama did one thing right; the pheromones she sprayed on this hapless omega are riling me up like no other mark ever has.

"My tattoo is a map of the maze," she blurts as I lean in. *Fuck*, she smells so godsdamn good, my mouth is watering, fangs fully descended. She must sense the direction my thoughts are headed because she keeps talking. "I can get you out, Noire. Please…"

"Open up." It's a simple alpha command that sends her body rolling up into mine, her hips pressing against me at the edge of the table. She's tall, even for an omega, probably close to six feet. But she's delicate and tense. She's prey, and every inch of my body knows it.

What she'll say next is anybody's guess, but this bullshit story about getting me out of here? I don't believe it for a second. She got put into the maze; she'll be dead tonight. And I want to have some fun first.

I reach for my knife and slice my way up her bodice as she gasps. It spills open immediately, pale breasts tumbling free. She moves to cover herself, an age-old instinct that doesn't mean shit in here. "Hands on the table. Keep them there."

She whines as she obeys my command, chest heaving as I lean in close to her. With both hands, I drag the bodice open, getting my first look at a semi-nude omega in years. I had no trouble warming my bed as the pack alpha, but it's been a long time, which is obvious based on how much pre-cum is pooling in my jeans already.

I need inside this woman, now. I need to fill her with my seed, to take her and possess her like the delicate toy she is. And then I need detail about this whole getting-me-out-of-the-maze plan. I don't believe her, but I want my brothers to hear what she has to say. After I fuck her.

Striking fast, I leap on top of her, slamming her upper body down on the tabletop. Before she can scream, I sink my teeth into her throat and flip us both, wrapping a leg around both of hers as I hold her tight to my chest. She's caught, the perfect, predictable prey that she is. Caught in my bite. I could crush her throat like this, and having her blood flow from the wounds to fill my mouth is almost more than I can take.

Like any good omega would, she fights the bite, despite the fact that it's a turn-on for us both that I could hold her here as long as I want. Her hips rock against mine even as she struggles against my teeth.

The godsdamned pheromones are making it nearly impossible to think straight though. This close, with her blood coating my tongue and sliding down my neck, her natural scent peeks through the shit they sprayed on her. She's all moonlight and grass and ferns. She's the scent of a midnight run, and it hits me so hard: if I don't bury myself inside that smell, I'll lose my mind.

Rolling off the table, I release the bite and grab an arm,

pulling her up off the ground and dragging her toward my room. She whimpers and yanks against me until I turn, snapping my teeth in her face. She flinches as I haul her roughly to my chest. "Your alpha father did a pitiful job teaching you to obey, omega."

"I wasn't raised by a fucking alpha, you assho–" Her words cut off as I yank her up by the hair and throw her over my shoulder, slapping her ass twice until she falls silent.

I stalk into my room, tossing her onto the bed as I take my pants off. She hits the sheets and flies to the headboard, chest heaving, which only accentuates pale pink nipples I ache to bite and mark.

Gods, what precisely did they spray her with? My libido is off the fucking rails looking at her in my bed. I've never been so anxious to fuck in my entire life. I watch her eyes spring wide at the crisscrossed bars that pierce the tip of my cock. The piercings were a coming-of-age gift for the future queen I'll never have, a way of paying homage to the pleasure I'd bring my omega when I eventually took a mate.

"Wait, please. Just look at my tattoo, and I can show you," she begs, and that plea is like a physical tug on my dick. I want her begging and pleading underneath me, screaming for my knot.

It's been far too long.

Hopping up onto the bed, I crawl my way across it, grabbing her ankles and yanking her down toward me. Rama's probably watching this right now, and even that turns me on. Let her watch me fuck this pretty little thing she dangled in front of me. Let her see I don't care when I dump this omega with the vampiri to take care of.

Snarling, I use my knife to cut away the front of her skirt, ripping it open. I'm unsurprised to find there's nothing underneath the dress. It was just for show anyway. Something to make her appear more feminine and delicate. It worked.

Between her thighs, a patch of blond curls is already damp

with slick. Leaning in, I drag my nose through her folds, her unique scent exploding across my senses like a bomb. The omega freezes then whimpers as I grip her thighs hard enough to bruise. I need a taste before I go mad.

Leaning in, I slide my tongue through her folds, circling the nub at the top that drives all omegas wild. Slick gushes from her, coating the bed as I growl, sucking air in deeply as her scent lights a fire in my core.

Focus eludes me as I lean in and lick my way down from her clit, down her entrance, lifting her hips with my hands to circle her back hole. I want to possess every inch of her. Snarling, I flip her and spread her ass cheeks, growling at the pucker that greets me. I want her here first.

Reaching between her thighs, I coat my fingers with slippery slick and run them along her back hole. This woman is just a plaything; I won't tease her the way I would a willing omega in my bed. But I want more than just shoving my dick inside her. I want to experience and savor in a way I haven't been able to. Touching her feels right, especially with the way her body betrays her. I want to soak in every scent, every vision of her. My mind, my eyes, my mouth–they're all fucking greedy and want a piece of her.

Glancing up, I laugh at the look she throws me over her shoulder. Abject terror, complete arousal. The warring sensations are too numerous for her to process. She's on the verge of coming and pleading for her life, all in one breath. "I can prove I know this place, Noire. Look right here." She points at a curve on her tattoo. "This is your–"

Without waiting for her to respond, I slide two fingertips inside her mouth. I don't believe this tale for a second. She chokes around my thick fingers as I revel in the soft heat of her mouth. "Silence," I growl as she sputters with my fingers pressing her tongue.

I laugh again as my need ramps up another level. Snarling, I gather more slick from between her thighs with my other hand and coat myself. Spreading her ass, I grunt as I slide the tip of my cock in and watch it disappear. She screams around my fingertips at the intrusion, locking up around me as pleasure shoots from the base of my spine all the way to the top of my head.

So tight, so fucking hot.

Removing my fingers from her mouth, I slide further in, pushing past the omega's resistance as she begs and pleads for me to stop, to listen. But I won't, not until this insatiable desire has blown my need away, not until the fire burning in my core is reduced to embers. She's asking me to stop even as her body takes over and calls to me in the way only an omega can. It's deep and primal, and her need rages through me like a hurricane.

Leaning over her, I slam my way home, heavy balls slapping against her as she grunts in pain. And that sound turns me on because I'm an asshole.

The omega grips the sheets as I slide out and back in, picking up a fast rhythm. Her ass is perfection. Hot, tight, gripping my cock harder than I remember this being.

Omegas are built for dominance, so even though this clearly hurts, based on the stiffness in her stance, her body produces more and more slick, coating the bed and her thighs as I take her. Reaching one arm around the front of her, I grip her hips and use that leverage to pound into her as she grits out a huffy series of curse words.

I teeter on the edge of orgasm, every inch of my body attuned to the pliable woman beneath me when I realize my brothers hover in the doorway. They know better than to come into the room of a pack alpha in the middle of fucking. But they're concerned; I read it in our bond.

I push those thoughts from my mind, focusing solely on the warm body beneath mine. The omega clenches around me as I fuck harder.

An orgasm slams into me with the force of gunshots, my body rocking as ropes of cum line the omega's asshole. The sounds of our sloppy fucking amplify as I fill her, her cries growing louder, my hips punching her into the bed. I can't stop looking at my thick length leaving her and entering her again, the way her skin molds around me like her ass was made to take my dick.

To my surprise, an orgasm builds again as I look at her, the need to bite her coming out of nowhere. Leaning over, I start up a fast rhythm again as I tug the corset from her body and toss it onto the floor. Her back is all creamy, smooth pale skin with the exception of my earlier bite mark. Until I sink my fangs into her shoulder, her entire body squeezing tight around me.

I release the bite and move to where her neck meets her collarbone, and sink my teeth in there again. And again. And again. I bite until her shoulder is nothing but blood and bruises, tears streaming down her cheeks as another orgasm blasts down my spine.

In my doorway, Jet risks entering as I slip out of the omega and flop onto the bed.

"What's going on, Noire?"

Behind Jet, Tenebris scowls. I know he craved her. But as alpha, I get everything first, including pussy. Snarling at Ten, I hop off the bed and ball my fists. "Why are you in my room?"

Jet holds his hands up. "You asked Ten to come get me, remember?"

Did I? The omega sits up in the bed, her face a mask of pain, and it takes everything in my body not to leap on top of her and fuck her again. My brain feels fuzzy and cloudy, and the only thing I can focus on is the naked piece of ass in my bed. I need inside her again.

But a threat is in my doorway, leering at her with greedy eyes.

"We aren't a threat to you, alpha. You look ready to pound us into the ground. Whatever Rama sprayed her with is throwing you into a rut. You can tell, can't you?" Jet's voice is reasonable as his words sink in.

A rut? I haven't had a rut since before the maze.

When he takes another step into my room, inching toward the omega, I launch forward, barreling into him as I take my brother to the ground.

"Don't touch her," I snap as Jet's fist connects with my chin.

CHAPTER 6
DIANA

In the room in front of me, Noire scuffles with his middle brother, Jet. I've profiled him as well, and I know that, of the three brothers, Noire is closest to Jet. Tenebris leaps through the doorway, tackling Noire as he and Jet fight.

My entire body is wound up tight, ready for release, slick and needy despite being taken in a way I was entirely unprepared for. I've never been taken back there, and now that first will forever belong to the alpha fighting tooth and nail just in front of the bed. Not that it matters. I'm likely to be dead in a few hours anyhow, based on how well my explanation of my ability to get the alphas out is going.

Jet bellows as Noire clamps fangs into his neck, ripping ferociously as blood sprays them both. The younger one leaps onto Noire's back as they fight. I press myself quietly into the headboard, not wanting to draw any attention to myself after what I just experienced. Slipping off the opposite side of the bed, I creep for the door.

Mid-punch, Noire's eyes flick to mine, and he snarls, throwing both alphas off him like they weigh nothing. He stalks across the room with big, purposeful strides, yanking me up into his arms and pressing us into the wall. All I can do is flail and plead as he drags my legs open and prepares to thrust inside me again. He's totally fucking unhinged as I scream and beat my fists against his chest.

"Omega," he snaps, bringing his lips to hover just above mine before a huge arm comes around his neck, dragging him away as I fall to the ground in a flurry of the remainder of my skirts.

"Stop, Noire, it's a rut. You've got to come out of it, alpha. We can't risk this now, not in the maze. She's the fucking mark, asshole."

The alpha drags Noire out the door with the help of the younger one, who gestures at me.

"Come."

It's one word, but damnit, my body complies because it's that fucking alpha command. I hover behind Tenebris as they drag Noire into the main living area. They manhandle him to the nearest wall, clamping huge thick cuffs on his arms before they let him go. He sprints to the end of the chains before being yanked viciously back by the immovable wall.

"Omega," he roars again, eyes intent on me where I hover behind the other two. Shit, fuck, I am in so much trouble. I never imagined he would be like this, that if we came face to face, he'd be so…alpha. I never imagined he wouldn't listen to me either, to what I had to say.

Turning to Jet, I put my hands up. "Please, I can get you out of the maze, all of you." My entire body is wired to run again, but I know they'll just enjoy the chase. And what they will do if they catch me won't be good. My heart gallops in my chest as I beg Jet with my eyes.

Please don't hurt me.

He laughs and grabs me by the throat, tossing me on top of the dining room table again. "You won't believe the amount of pure shit people start talking about when they get thrown in here.

The amount of times marks tell me they can help me, or pay me, or get me money, booze, women. You name it. They think we can or would help them. But we can't, and we won't. You're already dead if you're here."

Shaking my head, I point to the tattoo that takes up my entire left arm. "This? This is a map of the maze. The entire maze. I know this place like the back of my hand."

Two pairs of eyes laser focus on me as Noire bellows behind them. "Start talking," snaps Jet, glancing over his shoulder at Noire.

Licking my lips, I show them both the underside of my arm. "Years ago, my father was forced by Rama to build this place, long before she took over Siargao. He built it, but Father knew I'd be in danger, so he tattooed a map of the maze on my arm and taught me how to read it. Rama killed him and the rest of my pack and brought me to Siargao. I've been here ever since."

Jet looks skeptical. "I don't believe a word coming out of your mouth right now."

"I can prove it," I counter as Noire's raging grows louder and louder. Renewed concern for my physical safety slaps me as I shift backwards on the table. "What's happening to him?"

Jet grunts. "Whatever she dosed you with is throwing him into a rut for some reason. We need to get him out of the rut before we entertain any of what you're saying."

The younger alpha looks at him. "Jet, how the fuck do we pull Noire out of a rut? I've never seen this."

Jet frowns, looking over at where Noire bellows, pulling against his chains. I swear I hear a stone crack, but I must be wrong.

"Jet?" the younger alpha prompts him again.

Jet turns to me with a wicked grin. "Anger, Tenebris, that's the only thing that can pull him out long enough to gain control again. Right now, he's lost to lust, and if he goes all the way down that rabbit hole, it'll be a week before he comes back out."

Turning his attention to me, he smiles. "Good thing we've got Noire's plaything right here at the ready. Let's make him nice and mad by having our way with her for a while. If we take it far enough, he'll slip out of the desire long enough to want to beat our asses. There's a chance we can reason with him then."

I freeze as I take in his meaning, moving to slip off the other side of the table as both alphas turn their focus on me.

Tenebris, the younger one, licks his lips as he stalks slowly around one side of the table. Jet chuckles as he watches the younger alpha, winking at me. "Ten hasn't seen an omega since he came of age. He's going to thoroughly enjoy his first taste."

"Godsdamnit," I huff. "There are a few ways out, and Rama will try to stop us. Look at the fucking tatt–" The words cut off in my throat when Ten springs from his position and lands on top of me, crashing us both to the ground. I struggle under his incredible weight, but he's easily got two hundred pounds of muscle on me, despite my tall frame.

Ten pulls to a stand, one big arm around my waist and the other gripping my hair. My skull still feels like split kindling, but that's nothing compared to the terror of being at the mercy of two alphas.

Jet stalks closer to Noire, nodding in our direction. "Bring her over here, Ten. Let Noire get a good look at what we're gonna do to this soft little omega."

"No, no, please, we should hurry," I start as Ten snarls and drags me screaming across the carpet, throwing me down in front of Jet.

I back away instinctively as Jet tsks and shakes his head. "Don't get too close to Noire, little omega. If he gets his hands on you, I won't be able to get him off you a second time. Any logical thinking left in him is nearly overridden at this point."

Glancing behind me, I'm filled with terror at what I see. Noire strains against the chains, roaring as his eyes rake over me from top to bottom. His erection strains obviously, swinging and bobbing as precum drips steadily from him onto the floor. Despite my horror, my body recognizes a powerful sexual partner, and slick coats my thighs as I look at him.

Ten chuckles and sucks in a deep breath. "Ah, the body doesn't lie. Despite his violent taking of you, you want more, don't you? Fuck me, you're a pretty thing."

My gaze darts back up to his. "Please wait. Let's just leave, right now!"

"We can't, not without my alpha hearing this in the right frame of mind. Now, open those pretty thighs for me, or I'll open them for you."

At his compulsion, I spread my thighs open even as my stomach tumbles in knots.

Ten's eyes fall to my thighs, his pink tongue coming out to lick his lips as Jet continues talking, "Goddamn, there's nothing like omega pussy, nothing in this entire world." He falls to his knees in front of me, running both hands up my bare thighs as I shudder, falling back onto the floor. Already, my body wants him, his touch, his knot.

Jet turns to his pack alpha, gesturing between my thighs. "See this, Noire? See what I'm going to take? You think it's yours, but you're mistaken."

Noire bellows as Jet gestures for Ten to come closer. "Ten, stick your dick in her mouth."

I get ready to beg again, but the younger alpha straddles my head and takes his cock out of his pants. He's fucking huge too but unpierced.

Jet peers around Ten, dark eyes meeting mine. "Suck him off, omega."

There's no option as the younger alpha feeds his cock down my throat. He's surprisingly gentle, even when I hollow my cheeks and attempt to take as much of him as I can. A spurt of cum hits the back of my throat as he grunts and throws his head back. But when he starts moving, and I hear the rustle of Jet moving too, I make the mistake of looking up.

Noire screams in anger as Jet grabs my hips and shoves his thick cock inside me in one swift thrust. I groan around the dick in my mouth, unable to focus around the sensation of alpha cock in my pussy. I may have been terrified to come here tonight, but everything about their dominance and possessiveness was made to turn me on. I can only get past my biology so much.

Both alphas taking me at the same time is too much for my body; an orgasm racks my frame as I rock my hips to meet Jet, sucking Ten deep into my throat. Shockwaves ripple through my system as I scream out my pleasure, Noire raging as Jet laughs.

"I stole her first orgasm from you, asshole, and she feels so fucking good. I'll steal the next one and the next one until you come to take them from me."

Ten grunts as cum splashes against the back of my throat, his hips rocking slowly as I struggle around his thick cock.

"Get the fuck off her. She is *mine*," roars Noire as Jet slips out of me, hopping to a stand. Ten follows, grunting when his thick cock leaves my lips. He brushes the backs of his knuckles across my cheeks and holds out a hand to help me upright. It's surprisingly tender given what just happened. My mind is a mess of conflicting emotions.

One of the chains holding Noire back rips out of the wall then, and he uses his incredible strength to rip the other one free, stalking across the living space. He drags both chains behind him, chunks of stone still connected to them as he gets in Jet's face and lashes out, dragging his claws across the other alpha's chest, red ribbons of blood welling up immediately.

Jet flinches but bows his head. "Alpha, are you back with us? This is urgent."

Noire bellows, an angry roar that shakes the floor as I force my spine straight to watch the brothers' standoff. Ten steps in front of me protectively, shielding me from Noire's gaze, although I can't help peeking around his huge frame.

Jet keeps his head low, but his eyes glance up at Noire. "Alpha, this could be big. Are you here?"

Noire snarls again but presses his forehead to his brother's, his big chest heaving. "Barely. We need to talk."

Jet nods, not moving from the oddly gentle gesture. "Sit, alpha. I'll get you a drink. Ten, get those chains off him."

Noire nods and snarls at Ten, who steps to Noire with his head bowed, unlocking the chains. Noire comes to where I stand and leans in to drag his nose up my neck. "You need a bath. You smell like other alphas. But it'll have to wait."

I can't do anything but whimper. My entire body is bruised and worn from tonight's numerous assaults. Still, I let my forehead fall to Noire's chest as a rolling purr rumbles from between his thick pectoral muscles.

If the other alphas are surprised to hear their brother purr, they say nothing but watch in silence as Noire picks me up, sets me in a chair, and steps back, the sound stopping immediately. I'm ready to beg him to start it back up when he sinks into the chair opposite mine. Jet comes to his side with a glass of something amber, and Noire throws it back in one gulp.

"Talk." It's a one-word command I know better than to ignore.

"My tattoo is a map of the maze," I repeat, unsure how much he caught before.

"Your father built it; Rama killed him. What next?"

"I can get you out," I say simply. "And I want you to kill her for me."

Noire laughs, shaking his head. "In exchange for getting out of here, you mean."

I hold my breath, nodding.

He huffs out a breath as the other alphas sit next to him, one on either side. Seated like this, he looks like a king of the underworld, his loyal subjects flanking him, ready to do his bidding. Dark eyes land on mine, but there's no mirth, no joy in his gaze. "Why wouldn't I just force you to tell me how to read this map and then kill you and be done with this?"

He gestures at the elegant surroundings, his beautiful, dark prison.

"There's more than just this," I reply, keeping my voice low and even. "The maze is only part of Rama's temple. There's more to it."

"Why do you want her dead?" Noire's voice is ice-cold as he sits forward, placing one big hand on the table. His gaze never strays from mine.

"She killed my father." My voice comes out in a whisper as Noire frowns.

"So? Alphas aren't known for being kind and gentle fathers. Hard to believe you'd hold a grudge about him dying. Try again."

"That's it," I snap, harsher than I intended to as I run my fingertips along the tattoo, the same one my brother Dore has. *Had*.

"Try *again*, omega," Noire snaps. "I can taste the lie. You aren't here because of your father. Don't make me ask again."

Hurt and pain well to the surface of my heart as I ball my fists and think back to that horrible fucking night that set all of this into motion.

"I loved my father, you asshole." I don't mean to let the curse out, but it comes out anyway as Noire leaps to a stand, growling at me.

Noire grips my chin hard between his forefinger and thumb, eyes roving my face. Alphas have incredible intuition, but I let the truth of what I just admitted show through by not lowering my eyes from his.

"It's the truth," he whispers, more to himself than anyone, before turning on me with narrowed eyes. "Here's the thing.

Rama has a habit of concocting situations in the maze to fuck with me. So I'm trying to understand what's behind your appearance here, the first omega we've seen in seven years."

I can't help the frustration that infuses itself into my voice. "I don't know why she put me in here now. Does it matter? Let's get the fuck out and ki–"

Noire's teeth clamp down on my neck so fast I don't have time to hold back the scream that burbles out of my throat. When he lets go, I round on him, but he brings his lips to hover just above mine. "I'll allow that one time because an alpha didn't raise you. But never speak to me that way. Do you understand?"

"Yes, alpha," flies out of my mouth so fast I can barely stand it. When Noire's dark eyes meet mine, there's nothing but command and possession there. No compassion, no caring, no excitement for the reason I'm here. Nothing at all but a stone-cold monster.

CHAPTER 7
NOIRE

I n front of me, the omega winces when I snap my long fangs in front of her face. She smells like slick and cum and my brothers, and it's so wrong, I want to burn the entire maze down. I'm far too close to my rut, and I'm barely hanging on to my sanity. Every inch of her body is calling to me. From the way her head is cocked slightly to the side, baring her neck, to the flare of her nostrils and the way her chest rises and falls. She sways slightly, blood coating her lips from where she spit it out.

Leaning in, I lick her lower lip first, the bright scent of her blood slamming into my senses. I groan as I press harder into her, one hand going to her throat as the other grips her hair possessively. Bending her backward, I nip and suck at her lips. I want every ruby-red drop of her blood on my tongue.

"Open," I command, her lips parting. I suck her tongue between my lips, tugging at it with my teeth as she moans. If I'm on the edge of a rut, and she's the only omega in sight, the sheer amount of pheromones I'm giving off right now are probably enough to send her into heat.

I can't have that. But it takes a herculean level of effort to step back from her when Jet's eyes meet mine, worried.

"I don't buy a word of your story," I snap as Ten and Jet come to stand next to me, leering at the panting omega as she slumps against our dining room table.

Blue eyes are nearly black as hormones rock the omega, sending her body into overdrive. But she sucks in a deep breath and closes her eyes, breathing slowly before opening them for me again. When she does, I'm surprised at the renewed focus in her gaze. It reminds me of how I underestimated Rama and fucked up my life. I will never underestimate a woman again, and there's a thread of strength in this one that doesn't match her delicate, frightened appearance.

"I can prove it to you," she begins, lifting her tattooed arm and pointing to the alcove Jet fucked a woman in last night, just viewable down one of the hallways extending from this room. "These alcoves all link to a common area meant for the beta workers to come and go from. There are many layers of security, and it's not our best path out. But I'll show you that I know this place, or how it was designed, at least."

When I cock my head to the side and look at the omega, really look at her, she sits up straighter, covering her breasts with her arms, not moving her gaze from mine. Even when Jet speaks up next, she doesn't turn to look at him.

"There are cameras and microphones everywhere. How do you expect to get past Rama? She'll see us coming from a mile away. She's probably watching us right now."

The omega snarls, a wicked smile tilting the corners of her lips up into a vicious line. "What's she gonna do, send me in here twice? The cameras aren't as good as you think; there are blind spots. And in the event of a catastrophic revolt in the maze, it takes upward of twenty-four full hours for Rama to mount a response due to the way the security system is configured outside the maze. It's built that way to keep you from escaping, but it limits her ability to respond if you don't behave."

"Keep talking," Jet snaps as I take another step away from the omega. I'm barely hanging on to my sanity, and between her scent and the sass, I'm ready to drag her by the hair back to my bed.

She pushes off the table, but I keep my eyes on her face, resisting the urge to watch her full breasts jiggle. The front of the skirt is still ripped too, but she acts like it doesn't bother her as she looks at her tattoo, running her fingertips along a jagged curve and then striding to the alcove.

"My father built a few ways out of the maze, some easier than others. But what he did a really detailed job of was ensuring that, even if you accidentally stumbled on a way out, there'd be so many levels to the maze that you'd never get free before Rama could get you back in. Escaping here has to be an inside job; there's no other way."

Jet, Ten, and I stand just outside the alcove. My brothers are tense as fuck, ready to spring if this is all some bullshit to mess with us. The omega examines the stone wall inside the alcove and then presses lightly on the stones in a specific order.

To my horrific surprise, there's a telltale click, and the passage opens, just like it does when the beta maze workers remove the women Rama sends here for Jet.

Without a backward look, Diana steps into the darkness and disappears.

"Fuck," barks Ten. "We go in after her, right?"

Diana peeks her head back out of the darkness, winking at Ten. "You coming in here to verify I'm not lying or what?"

Ten huffs in shock at the omega's snark, but one growl from me, and the smile broadens as she winks.

My Gods, this female needs a healthy dose of punishment.

I go into the darkness first. I'm the fucking alpha, and I won't send my people somewhere I wouldn't go myself. It takes no time for my eyes to adjust to the pitch black as I follow the long corridor. Diana comes to my side and points at green paint on certain stones throughout the tunnel.

"See this? Where there's green paint, these stones can be removed but still appear to be there to you, allowing the workers to physically look in on any room in the maze. Nearly the entire maze works this way, except for the lowest levels."

"So despite the cameras, they can spy on us like this at any time?"

"Yeah," Diana confirms then seems to rethink her response. "Yes, alpha." Her voice is tight as she gulps hard, her throat bobbing.

I'm still raw from falling into the beginnings of a rut and getting yanked out of it with that bullshit Ten and Jet pulled. My need to fuck is amplified in the small, hot space of this hallway, and her response to me isn't helping. "Show me more."

Diana's eyes flutter as she sucks in a breath. "This isn't a good way out."

"And what about this?" I lift up the arm with the disk embedded in it as Diana nods.

"Rama made sure no one person ever knew everything about the maze; that's why she killed my father. He designed the maze and its security, and I'm sure she added on top of that. I don't know if she can kill you with that. I know she can hurt you, and I know her first plan of attack is always to turn the monsters on one another if someone needs to be controlled. That's what happened with you–" Her voice cuts off as blue eyes fly up to mine.

Hot fury rockets through my system as I take in her meaning. Grabbing her wrist, I squeeze hard as she yelps, dragging her behind me back out of the alcove and into the living area. "Speak," I bellow. "The whole thing, the entire fucking thing. What happened with Oskur? How do you know? Be precise."

Diana shudders and reaches for both halves of her corset, but

I yank the entire thing from her and shove her, reveling in the grunt that leaves her when she hits the nearest wall and slides partway down it.

"She gave the monsters you call rorschachs betas to play with for a full week for killing your brother. It was their reward for doing her bidding. She televised all of it, his death, the betas, everything to remind the common people how brutal the maze is, and how terrified we should all be of it."

Behind me, Jet roars in anguish, always having known there was so much more to Oskur's death.

Stone-cold fury lands in my stomach like a ball of dried cement. I can barely breathe around the anger, but when I look at the omega, I know one thing is for certain—I will get the fuck out of here, no matter what I have to do to her to make that happen.

Diana's quiet for a moment before looking up at me with wide blue eyes. "She'll do it again, knowing I'm trying to get you out. She'll offer the humans or vampiri something to come and finish off the mark and maybe kill you all too. Or kill one of your brothers but leave you. She will want retribution for you even attempting to escape. You're right about her watching us, she probably is."

"Maybe we should kill you and be done with it then," I snap, fisting my hands as I glare through narrowed eyes at the omega.

She surprises me when she stands taller, pale breasts pebbled in the cold of our private rooms. "I fully accept that this might not go well, that I might lose my life. I've already lost everything else important to me, so if that's the direction you want to take it, I'm ready. I can't promise I won't fight you, because even I've got a survival instinct…but I made my peace with this a long time ago."

"You're a crazy bitch," Jet snaps, coming to stand next to me with his back to the omega. "Can we talk about this? I snuck out of the Atrium…but if this is all a fucking ruse, I need to get back. Not that they don't know I'm here but still."

Not looking at Jet, I grab the omega once more and drag her back to my bedroom, throwing her inside. "Don't come out," I snap, pointing a finger at her.

She nods once, eyes narrowing at me as I close the door in her face.

When I stalk back into the kitchen, Jet and Ten are already seated at the dining room table. Jet's got a glass full of uppers in his hand, lifting it to his lips as he taps his foot rapid-fire under the table.

I grab the glass and hurl it across our rooms. "No more, not tonight. I need you here with me. Understand?"

Jet snarls but bows his head and nods before looking up at me again. "Do we believe her?"

"You saw the passageway." Ten sighs, gesturing toward the dark hallway with the alcoves. "But I don't believe the father story."

My brother's intuition is excellent; he'll make a good pack alpha one day in a pack of his own. *If I get him the fuck out of here.*

"One thing she's right about, Rama won't let us go easily. We're already in over our heads by not fulfilling the mark duty. Do we buy the tattoo piece?"

"I don't know," Jet says, hopping to a stand and pacing. "But she doesn't strike me as a liar. It's just a sense though. The story in and of itself isn't believable."

"I'd like to get more information," I admit. "If she's lying then maybe we're all fucked. If she's not, well, we'll never get another chance like this. I'm inclined to take it."

My brothers are quiet, torn, but they'll go along with what-ever I say. Standing, I turn from them. "I'm going to question her, but prepare yourselves to go. If I'm happy with her answers, we're going."

I hear Jet mutter out a long string of curse words as he and Ten head for the small weapons room that Rama keeps just stocked enough for us to fuck with the marks. "Don't fuck her again, Noire. We need your mind right." His warning echoes up the hall as my body stiffens in anticipation of opening my door and scenting the beautiful omega again.

I am in deep. Far too deep. Because fucking her is almost all I can think about doing.

CHAPTER 8
DIANA

F ootsteps along the hallway send me scurrying from the
door where I was listening back into the center of the
room. I fold my hands in front of my lap, trying to
appear nonconfrontational when the door opens quietly and
Noire stalks back in. My ass stings, my entire body tense and
sore. But when I look up at him, my body clenches with need,
slick dripping down one leg.

God, omega hormones are such assholes, and Noire is so
incredibly potent. Alpha dominance rolls off him and smacks
into me with a tidal wave of pleasure. Dark eyes meet mine and
don't move as he goes across the room and opens an armoire.
Inside, I see both doors are lined with knives. I know Rama
allows weapons in this place, and he's got quite a few of them.

"Tell me about where you came from, omega." It's not a
request, and I sense he's struggling to believe my story about
getting him out of here.

"My name is Diana," I whisper. "We don't have a lot of time,
Noire," I begin as he slips a knife out of his armoire and into the
chest holster he's still wearing. Another goes in right next to it as
he looks at me, demanding an answer with his intense stare.

"I'm listening, omega, and I won't ask again." Noire turns and grabs two more knives, strapping them along his belt. One in the front, one in the back.

"I wasn't lying about her killing my father and my pack; she did that years ago."

"I already know that," Noire grunts. "Where did you come from? What pack?"

"Winthrop." The last name I haven't used in nearly a decade slips off my tongue as I choke back a sob.

Noire's eyes go wide. "You're Edson Winthrop's daughter?"

Tears fill my eyes as I think back to my childhood. It wasn't perfect, but despite Noire's earlier proclamation about alpha fathers, mine was good and kind—until Rama slaughtered him and my whole pack. Dore and I escaped to the streets until she found us and took us in. First by force, but eventually we fell into line because we were children, and we had no other options.

"You had a twin," Noire says, but it's not a question.

A sob does leave my throat then as the first tears spill down my cheeks. "I did. Yes."

"Other siblings?"

I shake my head as my lip trembles, heat flushing across my neck and chest as Noire crosses the room to me, his face an unreadable neutral mask.

I refuse to beg for comfort from this alpha, but I want it. His heat, his warmth, his strong arms. They call to me as we stare at one another, neither of us looking away. What do I want from him? Retribution for my family? Comfort? Understanding? Because Rama took everything from both of us.

Noire steps in close, lifting my chin so I'm forced to look into pitch-black eyes that betray no emotion. "Get changed, Diana. We're going. Now. We are going to follow you, but if I sense at any point this will hurt my brothers, I will end you. Are we clear?"

Without saying another word, Noire hands me a black shirt.

Numb, I nod and take it, sliding it over my head, following in silence as we exit the room. As soon as we do, the screen just outside his door flicks on, and Rama's face comes on.

Noire turns and smiles at the maze's cruel mistress, his big body blocking me from viewing the full screen.

"You're not minding the rules, Noire," Rama purrs, her voice syrupy sweet. It claws at the memories buried in the back of my mind, slamming home how she tortured my brother, Dore, before slitting his throat.

Noire doesn't bother to respond as Rama sighs, her smile growing wider as she cocks her head to one side.

I peek around Noire, but when my eyes meet hers, a feral snarl leaves my throat. It's an animal growl that sends one of Noire's dark brows upward as he glances at me and then Rama.

"I want her dead, Noire," Rama says in a bored tone. "Blood play, dismemberment, those were the client's wishes. If you do not comply, I'll hurt your brothers. And then I'll kill you and this woman will die anyhow."

"Make me," purrs Noire, squaring his shoulders as Rama's eyes narrow.

"If you don't kill this woman, I'll send someone else, and there will be consequences." Rama speaks as if she's talking to a small, petulant child, and the effect it has on Noire is nearly instantaneous.

His entire body stiffens, but he doesn't bother to respond as he turns us both, placing his hand on the back of my neck as he steers me up the hallway.

When Rama huffs behind us, he turns on his hip, and I whip around in time to see him throw a knife up the hallway with incredible speed. It buries itself right in Rama's forehead before the screen sparks and clicks off.

At the same time, the disk implanted in his forearm lights up bright red, and his eyes find mine. "Let's go. I'm calling her bluff."

When we reach the open living area again, Jet and Tenebris are there, knives crisscrossing their bodies. Jet looks up at Noire, gritting his jaw. "It looks like we're going, then? We've got the weapons; what else do you want to bring?" He takes a beat, pointing at me with the tip of a knife in his hand, sending a shudder through my frame, although I stand taller to mask it. "Are we really doing this, Noire? You believe her? The disks are flashing red, we don't know what it means."

"We have to chance it," Noire snaps as he steps to the bag beside Jet on the table, opening it and looking in. Jars of a purple liquid shine from the interior of the bag. I don't miss the way Jet winces but straightens as Noire's eyes meet his. The big alpha says nothing but barks at Jet to get water from the fridge too.

When he turns to me, I meet his gaze and lift my chin. It's a bunch of bullshit the way alpha dominance makes omegas behave, and while these alphas are terrifying, I can't just roll over. I'm not built that way.

"Where to, omega?"

"We need to take the most direct route to the lower levels. Unfortunately, that means we'll probably cross some of the other monsters because the most direct route goes through other living areas."

Tenebris curses under his breath as Jet rolls his eyes. "Of fucking course." He turns to Noire again. "Noire, talk to me. Are we really following this fucking omega?"

Noire barks out a string of words in a language I don't understand, but Jet nods and turns for the door, taking the lead. Tenebris goes second, then me, and Noire follows behind me, silent as a ghost.

I take a quick look at my tattoo, tracing the intricate symbols that map out the maze. The map's legend exists only in my mind. Walking to the front of the alphas' living quarters, I find a stone inlaid in the ground with a small symbol on it. When I locate that symbol on my arm, Ten growls. "I knew these fucking symbols meant something."

"You're right," I agree quickly, nodding at him. "They do, but not without the map and the legend."

Tenebris grits his jaw but says nothing, hiking a bag up over his shoulder as he passes me. "Where to? Do you need anything before we go, omega?"

"Diana," I whisper. "My name is Diana. And, no, water is enough. We need to head to the left, through the chapel, and then there's a passageway there we need to take." Ten smiles gently at me as I whisper a thank you under my breath.

He nods and turns, Jet following him. I risk a glance at Noire, but his face is a mask of intense focus. His pupils are still wide from the rut, his body focused on me in a predatory way that calls mine to stand at attention. I freeze when he stalks the five feet or so between us, not stopping until he bumps into me, his warm skin heating mine through the thin cotton of the shirt he gave me.

My nipples harden into diamond nubs against his chest as he purrs and backs us into the nearest wall, lifting my tattooed arm to examine it. Black eyes flick back to mine. "You'd better be telling the truth about all of this." He looks up and gestures around the maze and toward his brothers' retreating backs. "If this is a ruse of some sort, and it hurts my brothers, your death will be nothing but slow pain. I'm saying it again because I want to make sure you are clear. Do you understand me?"

"I just want to get out, Noire," I whisper. "I want to get out and stop having to hide from Rama everywhere I go. I want to be truly free. I want *Siargao* to be free."

A shadow of understanding crosses Noire's face before he grunts, indicating I should follow the other alphas into the darkness. And follow I do, with the worst monster of all stalking at my back.

My body is a livewire as we walk purposefully through the

dark halls of the Temple Maze. All three alphas are on high alert, but given that Rama knows I'm trying to get out, I know she'll send other monsters after us.

By the time we get to the chapel, I know for certain she's fucking with us. It's far too quiet. We step through the chapel's doorways, the haunting scent of the black Alborada roses that grow throughout the maze blasting my nostrils. They're genetically modified to need no light, another feature of the maze my father put into place. He was a brilliant engineer and planner, but it makes the maze a real bitch to get out of.

As we enter the chapel, Tenebris snarls, "Where to, omega? I scent humans."

I sprint toward the altar, referencing my tattoo and the rim of the huge stone block itself until I find what I'm looking for.

"Hello, Blondie," I hear as a man emerges from one of the alcoves, brandishing a steel bat, a relic of human history so far in the past, I don't even know what the tool would have been used for. Now it only signifies incoming pain. I've seen televised sessions of humans killing marks. It's a frenzy of group violence I am not ready for.

Tenebris steps in front of me as Noire comes around the side of the altar, not paying the man any mind. "More humans are coming. We need to move fast. We can fight them in shift form, but if they all come, it'll be harder. Move, Diana."

Urgently, I scan my tattoo until I find the matching symbol on the underside of the stone altar.

"Now, Diana," snaps Noire as more humans begin to pour through the front door of the chapel, their catcalls ringing off the black stones.

Depressing the stone with the symbol on it, I glance at Noire as the altar slides on tracks toward the front of the dais. He's not looking at me but at the throng of human men who now pour in through the open doors.

Tenebris and Jet stand in front of us, snarling, when the first wave of humans attack. They're no match for the much bigger, faster alphas, and they go down fast in a flurry of black claws. But then more and more come as Noire starts roaring for his brothers to leave it. They're lost to the madness of the fight, slicing and roaring and ripping into the human men like they're nothing but meat.

When the first human gets a knife between Tenebris' ribs, Jet and Noire go wild and strip their clothes, shifting into the enormous black wolves that alpha males have access to. Noire barrels into the closest group of humans, knocking them to the side as Jet grips Ten by the back of the neck with his teeth, dragging him to the altar.

"In here," I scream at Jet as his wolf helps Ten to his feet, the younger alpha holding the knife as he grunts in pain.

Tenebris goes into the dark space below the altar without looking back, Jet gesturing for me to follow. I risk a glance at Noire, but he's still wolfed out, scattering pieces of the humans around the church as they attempt to overtake him.

Jet barks something out again in that language I don't know, and Noire roars loud enough to shatter some of the stained-glass windows on one side of the chapel, glass exploding everywhere as the humans take cover. The moment they do, he turns and sprints for us, shifting mid-run as we all pile into the dark space under the altar.

As soon as Noire is in, I feel for the symbol on the wall, and the altar trundles closed above us with a heavy click.

Flying over to Tenebris, I examine the knife in his side and slide it out as he hisses. Without looking up, I rip my shirt over my head and bite it, tearing it into long strips as Ten watches, his jaw gritted and eyes intense on me. Jet stands protectively to one side, looking up the hallway as Noire hovers behind me, an ominously naked presence.

I wrap the fabric around Tenebris' broad torso, tying it tight. "This'll sting, but as long as the bleeding stops, you'll heal fast."

He nods and grunts as Noire reaches out and hauls his brother to a stand.

Turning to me, his eyes travel down to my bare chest, the way my nipples harden in the cool air of the passageway.

I know Noire's libido is still running on high from the near-rut when he steps forward, leaning in to drag his fangs up my neck, nipping under my ear. My hips rock up against his as he snarls and runs both hands up my back, sucking in deep breaths along my throat, down into the hollow along my collarbone.

"Noire?" Tenebris' voice is tentative but urgent.

With a growl, Noire snaps his eyes toward his younger brother and stands taller, sighing. Reaching into his pack, he hands me another shirt before leaning in to nip at my ear and pulling out his own clothing.

I hold back a needy whine at his suggestive dominance and nod, pulling the shirt over my head. Noire puts his hand on my lower back and urges me forward to follow his brothers again.

The passageway is pitch black, but alphas and omegas have incredible senses, so we can see anyhow. I reference my tattoo from time to time, directing us from one dark hall to another.

"Wait, it's here," I say, quickly checking my tattoo. "When we go through this door, it'll drop us right into the middle of a living space, the one on the far opposite side of the maze from you."

Jet lets out a string of curse words as he rounds on me. "The fucking vampiri live there. Is there another way?"

"Yeah," I snap back, unable to keep the anger out of my voice as Noire comes up behind me, big body bumping into mine. "Yeah, we can take the long way around and do a tour of every single monster in this place, and hope we don't all get massacred after Rama offers them Gods-knows-what to kill us. Or we can go this way and directly to the lower levels, which is the best fucking way out."

Jet snarls and clamps a black-clawed hand around my throat.

I don't know where my sudden vitriol has come from, but Noire growls in my ear as Jet squeezes, "What have I said about speaking to alphas like that, Diana?"

I might have a death wish, but I also want us to keep moving. The longer we stay in the maze, the greater our chances of dying.

"You said not to speak to *you* like that again. You didn't mention your brothers."

To my surprise, Noire's booming laugh rings around us in the stone hallway, echoing off the black rock as Jet's grip on my throat tightens. Noire shoves his brother's arm away and turns me to face him. "Don't pretend you didn't know what I meant, omega. Another snarky remark and you'll deal with me."

It takes everything in me to resist snarking something at that precise moment, and Noire knows because he raises a brow and cocks his head to the side, challenging me to say something.

Stepping out of his grip, I look at Tenebris and Jet. "Let me go first. We need to go through the quarters here, so we'll have to speak with the vampiri if they live here."

Noire curses behind me. "Hate that. I'd rather go a longer way."

I shake my head and turn. "We don't have much time now that Rama is aware I know more than she thought. She has a stable full of monsters she can mobilize quickly. This is our best option, I promise."

Noire's brows furrow, but he steps aside and gestures for me to continue. When I depress the stone with the correct symbol, a floor panel creaks and opens. Gathering up my tattered, dirty skirts, I hop down into the darkness, followed by my three alphas.

Did I just call them my *alphas? Ugh.*

The moment I land and stand up, I sense monsters. It's the same way any prey knows they're being stalked. The hair on the back of my neck rises as Noire, Jet, and Tenebris snarl and surround me. My breath comes in short pants as I look around, even though I can't see anyone.

The panel above us closes as two vampiri step out of the shadows. There are more, I'm sure. Of all the monsters my father built the maze to hold, the vampiri scare me nearly as much as the alphas.

Stepping around Noire, I put my hands up as one of the monsters snarls, "Hello, little mark. Nice of you to bring yourself to our doorstep."

I've seen him televised before; he's the vampiri king's second, Firenze. Up close, he's even more terrifying than on-screen. Firenze is pale like all vampiri, blond hair pulled into a tightly woven braid that curls down the nape of his neck. This close, I see his teeth are black and translucent, dripping with... something. Venom, maybe? Oh Gods. There are so many ways this could go horribly wrong.

"I need to speak with your king," I respond, mustering up confidence from somewhere. Fake it 'til you make it, I suppose. "It's urgent. I have information for you."

"The only thing urgent in this place is our desire to feed," the vampiri barks back, taking a menacing step toward me as Noire snarls and comes to stand by my side.

The vampiri's eyes move to Noire as Noire takes another step fully in front of me. "Take us to Cashore. Now."

The vampiri's blank white eyes find mine again, and he shrugs. "We will tear her apart either way; you know the disk chose us this evening."

I shudder, knowing he's referencing the disk that picks which monsters get to kill the mark. It was them. Rama meant for this male, and the one next to him, and all the rest to rip me to shreds.

Noire barks back, "The mark is mine until I say she isn't. Cashore. *Now*. I won't ask again."

Both vampiri snarl but turn, and we follow them along two long halls to a large wooden door, intricately carved with interpretations of the Alborada roses that thrive in this part of the maze. Double-checking my tattoo, I nod at Noire when his eyes find mine, asking the silent question.

The vampiri turns the door handle and opens it, and I see into a room full of his kind, fake moonlight shining down on them. Ignoring Noire's warning growl, I follow the vampiri in with a nod, looking up at the ceiling in these particular living quarters. The stones here are inlaid in such a way that a faux night sky peeks through, a cruel reminder of just how close the monsters are to the outside world, yet somehow not close at all.

Tenebris and Jet pace around in front of me, Noire still behind in a protective triangle formation as my heart pounds in my chest. There's every chance this could go badly. My only hope is that I know a few things about this maze that could be useful to its monsters. My only item of value is my knowledge, and I have to pray the vampiri will listen to me long enough to hear what I know.

Monsters fill the room, coming in from deep alcoves I know stretch back into individual rooms, although vampiri typically sleep in mating pods together—a random fact I know from profiling them now and again. Snarls ring through the room, several of them crouching down as if readying themselves to chase prey. Every cell in my body screams at me to run, run, run.

Ten and Jet pause, both holding knives in each hand, crouched slightly. Behind me, Noire doesn't stop until his chest is touching my back, a deep growl rumbling from his warm body. "Where is Cashore?"

His alpha bark rolls over the vampiri, and even though they're a different species of monster entirely, it's easy to see the way his dominance affects them. Looking around, I'm surprised to see the majority of the vampiri step away from the deep roll of Noire's command.

The monsters part, and a taller vampiri with pitch-black waist-length hair and ice-white skin comes forward, hands folded behind his back. Calculating white eyes framed by pale lashes don't blink as he comes closer to us, cocking his head to the side as he assesses us. "The mark looks surprisingly unaffected by several hours in your quarters, alpha. I believe there were some client requests regarding entrails and blood play. Or have you forgotten our godsforsaken duty in this place?"

It's easy to hear the anger in his voice about being in the maze. I don't know where Rama found the vampiri, but there are probably close to thirty of them in this room. Far more than there are alphas.

Noire growls. "We need passage through your quarters."

The vampiri he called Cashore smiles, but there's nothing friendly about the way his lips pull wide, exposing black gums and black teeth. A clicking hiss leaves his throat, and another vampiri steps up next to him—a woman. She glares daggers at us as she steps to Cashore's side, holding a wicked-looking sword in a belt at her hip. Dark hair is braided along the sides of her head, falling free in the back, all the way to her waist. I'd call her beautiful if she wasn't so fucking deadly. I've seen them destroy marks when Rama televises it. The vampiri are horribly cruel.

Cashore steps forward. "That's hardly an explanation, alpha. It was foolish of you to come here. I allowed you to leave with the mark earlier because, as you said, my people may have suffered. But I cannot allow you to come into our quarters and demand…well, anything at all."

Another click leaves his mouth as the female stalks across the space, stopping just in front of Noire as Tenebris comes to my side, snarling. "Step away if you want to keep your pretty head," he growls at the female, brandishing a knife in each hand.

While all this is happening, Noire stands as if he owns this entire fucking maze, a king even here in this destroyed, devastated place.

Lurching forward, I raise my hands as though I'm surrendering, praying I can get them to just listen for a moment. "Stop, please. I know I'm the mark, but I have information that can help you, information about getting out of the maze."

Quick as a flash, the female vampiri shifts and moves, snatching me up by the hair before I have time to shout. Noire and Ten turn as one, but the vampiri moves again, and my head whips back. As soon as I can yank it upright, I realize we're across the fucking room already.

Oh shit, oh fuck. She was so godsdamned fast, I barely tracked the movement.

"Wait," I shout out as Noire stalks across the black stones with his fists balled. His eyes meet mine, full of alpha anger, ready to rip something apart to get to me.

Wait, I beg him silently. *Please, trust me, alpha.*

I know Noire can't hear me, but an understanding passes between us as he gets closer but pauses, looking directly at the female vampiri. "You touched what's mine, and I will shred your flesh from your bones if you hurt her."

The fist in my hair tightens, but the woman clicks at Cashore before kicking the back of my knees and forcing me down in front of the vampiri king.

Finding Cashore's eyes again, I put my hands back up. "Do you find your psychic ability dulled in the maze?"

Shock and awe cross his face before furious anger replaces it. The female yanks my head back so I'm forced to look up into Cashore's face. I can't help the squeak that comes out of my mouth. The back of my head is still tender from earlier.

In a second, Noire is on the female, slicing his claws toward her as she ducks away from him, roaring in anger but letting go of my hair. In front of me, Cashore looks bored as Noire rounds on the woman. "I warned you about hurting her. Back the fuck up before you lose your head."

The vampiri woman snarls but steps next to Cashore as Noire holds his hand out, pulling me upright. "Talk," Noire growls in my ear.

Cashore watches us, lips pursed. "What do you know of vampiri magic?"

Standing up taller, I meet his eyes and square my shoulders, feeling more confident with Noire's big body behind mine. I shift backwards, so his chest brushes against my back, and I swear I feel his strength threading through me. "I worked for Rama. This entire maze is built to handle certain species of monsters, including vampiri. There are numerous measures in place to control you. The Alborada roses that grow in this section are genetically modified to give off a pheromone that inhibits your psychic ability."

Cashore steps back and shakes his head, snarling.

"I can prove it," I press, stepping forward with one hand up. "Burn the roses in your quarters and outside the door. I suspect you'll notice a marked improvement with them gone. There are other measures in place to control you, but this is one. Help us, and I'll tell you the others."

Cashore narrows his eyes at me but nods at the woman with the sword. She immediately barks out a series of commands, and four vampiri dressed like her in black leather grab torches from the wall and walk around the room, lighting the roses aflame.

A hissing sound echoes through the stone chamber as the roses catch on fire and go up, hissing and popping as they burn to ash. Cashore drops to one knee as the smell of the roses slams into us. The female vampiri hisses and clicks at him, obviously worried as he falls forward, covering the back of his head with his hands.

She rounds on me with a hiss as Noire pulls me close. The vampiri hiss and click in concern around the room as Cashore roars in pain. Fuck. The fire must enhance the scent of the roses, and it's hurting him.

Jet and Ten are a tense wall behind Noire and me where they joined us as Cashore fell to his knees.

The vampiri female barks out a series of questions to

Cashore, not taking her eyes from us as he moans a response. Around the room, the roses are burning down to crisp, dead vines, smoke billowing into the room as Cashore rocks back onto his heels, closing his all-white eyes.

Deep in my mind, I feel a sudden intrusion. As if something is worming its way through the gray matter, eating me up as it goes. I squirm, gripping both sides of my head in my hands as I hiss around the pain.

Cashore blinks his eyes open. He looks too pained to smile, but his frown is equally terrifying. "Diana Winthrop, Edson Winthrop's daughter? My, my, my."

CHAPTER 9
NOIRE

E dson Winthrop? So Cashore knows the famous alpha
inventor? Winthrop was well-known in alpha circles,
but to my knowledge, Vinituvari did not have much of
a vampiri population. Jet and Ten bombard me with messages
through our bond all at the same time, but Cashore looks over
and chuckles. "You might as well be screaming your questions
aloud, gentlemen."

Godsdamnit, why did the omega tell him something that
gives him more power? I should have asked her what we'd have
to give up to get the fuck through here.

Cashore closes his eyes and sucks in a breath. When he
opens them again, he takes Diana's hand and pulls her closer.
She goes willingly, allowing him to look deeply into her eyes.

"How do you feel?" she questions, her voice soft but curious.

Cashore's black brows furrow as he looks at her, his face
inquisitive and concerned. "I have not had access to my ability in
years, Diana. What other tricks do you have up your proverbial
sleeve?"

Diana chuckles. "Can you not just read them in my mind?"

Cashore reaches out, drawing the back of his pale hand along her cheek as she stiffens.

Snarling, I step closer and pull Diana back to me. Her body relaxes when she hits my heat, and Cashore laughs.

"Oh, I see, alpha. This one is *yours*. All right. I'll allow it, for now." He turns back to Diana. "You did me a great favor, so I'll allow you through my quarters this once, but Ascelin, Renze, and I will be coming with you, wherever you're going."

Behind me, Jet and Tenebris growl immediately. The female, Ascelin, stalks around me, snapping her teeth. Tenebris turns to her when she passes him, taking an aggressive step in her direction as she pauses, eyeing him. There's a natural aggression between all the monsters in the maze, but I've seen Ascelin taunt Tenebris and Jet many times over the years.

Cashore clicks something at her, and she smirks, taking a step away from Ten, although she licks her lips as she does it. A tease of some sort.

"Let's go," I snap, urging Diana forward.

"Clear the room," Cashore roars as the vampiri scatter back along the hallways. Renze and Ascelin stay behind as Cashore turns to me. "I have questions, Noire."

"We don't have much time," Diana reminds him.

Cashore smirks. "No, *you* don't have much time, Diana Winthrop. Now, tell me more about your plans because I am highly interested in a way out of this maze as well."

Shit. She mentioned that, but he can read whatever she knows in her mind. Maybe even before she shares it all with me.

I snarl at the vampiri king, letting my fangs descend as he takes a step away from Diana.

She stiffens but nods, stroking her fingers along the intricately detailed tattoo. "If you knew my father, then you'll know he was a brilliant architect. When I was a child, he built this maze. Rama killed my entire pack once the maze was complete, and I've been living under her thumb in Siargao ever since." She lifts her arm. "This tattoo is a map of the maze. We're using it to get out. Right now."

Cashore blinks, bringing a palm to his forehead. "My gift is still murky, but I sense you tell the truth, Diana. As I said, I want a way out for my people. So if the way through is here, we'll be coming with you."

Diana looks at her arm and nods, pointing to the floor just beneath our feet. "Help me move this rug."

Gripping her arm, I give her a warning look. "We didn't discuss letting other monsters out, little omega."

Diana glances at Cashore and back at me. "We may not get out of here alone, alpha. It might be a good idea to work together."

We're between a fucking rock and a hard place. If I disagree with her, we'll have to fight our way out of the vampiri quarters, and they know what we're up to now. Shit, they might keep Diana and just read the way out from her fucking mind. I won't have it. Growling, I drop her arm and nod.

Cashore glances at Ascelin, and she and Renze go to the far corners of the rug, Ten and Jet at the other side. With a heave, they remove the rug, ripping it back to show the floor under-neath. Black stones lie in a circle around three eyes carved into the dark stone. Cashore swears under his breath as Diana crouches down, running her fingers along the mark and then referencing her tattoo.

The vampiri king's eyes meet mine, assessing as he frowns. He clicks something at Ascelin, and she leaves the room as Diana depresses a sequence of stones around the symbol.

Ten and Jet come and stand next to me as the symbol stone sinks and clicks over to the side on a track. More stones fall away and disappear as a set of stairs opens up in front of us.

Ascelin comes back into the room, handing Cashore a vicious curved blade that he straps to his back. "I do not like this, my king." She's using English to make it clear that she doesn't trust us. She gestures at Diana and my brothers, and sighs.

Cashore turns to her as Renze comes to stand on his other side. "Lissette is due soon, Asc. If we can help her, we must. At any cost."

The vampiri warrioress pales at his words as I try to absorb their meaning.

Due? The vampiri are procreating in the maze? I've never seen a child, though, and I've traveled every inch of this maze thousands of times.

Jet and Ten send a flurry of messages through our blood bond, but if Cashore hears them, he doesn't bother to respond.

"Due?" Diana questions Cashore. "With a child?"

Cashore nods, his face sad as he looks at Diana. "It is a long, sad story, Diana Winthrop. But if Ascelin, Renze, and I determine you are not lying, I will call my people so we may all leave this place."

Diana nods, not probing any further, and encourages us to move by taking the stairs first. I snarl when Cashore attempts to follow her.

He steps back with a huffy laugh. "Apologies, Noire. I did not mean to crowd your omega."

My omega. The words ring in my mind as something scratches at the edges of it. He doesn't know that all alphas train to deal with other monsters' abilities when we visit other provinces, so diving into my mind will be harder than he thinks. I dealt with a small contingent of vampiri in Siargao when I ruled. I am aware of their abilities.

Jet and Ten stiffen behind me, but I pace down the stairs after Diana as Cashore chuckles and follows. The dark engulfs us once more as Diana walks ahead of me.

For half an hour, we walk in near-complete silence as Diana mumbles to herself, checking her tattoo every other hallway or so.

NOIRE: A DARK SHIFTER ROMANCE   113

The quiet gives me a chance to observe her unencumbered by everyone else looking at me. I'm still at the very edge of a rut, ready to give in to that heat and take her for days. This is not the time or place, and my primary goal is to get out of this maze. But I can't deny that the way Diana's hips swing as she walks is a fucking distraction.

She looks over her shoulder, her elegant profile clearly visible to me. I let my mind wander to how she felt wrapped around my cock earlier, something I'd like to do again in the very near future.

If I get out of this maze tonight, there are three things I'll do, in order of importance:

Kill Rama.

Get my brothers to safety.

Fuck Diana until she's screaming my name and clenching around my knot in the throes of orgasm.

Behind me, Cashore chuckles in the quiet.

"Fuck off," I snap as he laughs again. He's not reading my mind, but I'm sure my focus on the beautiful omega in front of us speaks volumes.

Ahead of me, Diana pauses and finds a symbol on the wall. She turns to our group with a quick nod. "This should put us out into the lower levels. Do you know what's down there now? It's meant for larger monsters."

Ascelin comes forward, running pale hands over the symbol with a frown. "I have heard Rama put a naga in the maze, but I have avoided the lower levels for quite some time."

Cashore nods, giving me a knowing look. "The lower levels reek of wrongness to me. I cannot explain it, other than to say I hear voices there, which is a bad sign among our people."

"Fuck," snaps Jet. "I've been to the lower levels thousands of times. There's nothing there but more darkness. And maybe now a naga. So how do we deal with a naga?"

Turning to my youngest brother, I smile. "Tenebris, care to

enlighten the vampiri? How shall we deal with a naga?" Ten has always been the studious one, and he was fascinated by other monsters long before we came into the maze, always reading books about them. Even the maze library in his room is full of monster lore.

Ten smiles and glances at Ascelin before looking at Cashore. "Naga mate from birth, so if there is only one here, it will be wild with grief at being separated from its mate. Our only hope if we stumble upon one is to hold its attention long enough to get it to listen to us. We'll have to tell it we have a way out."

We all turn to look at Diana, but she stands up straighter. "The lower levels were designed to hold larger monsters—naga, minotaurs, wendigos. The only passages out of the lower levels are too small for those monsters to get through. They're dropped in from above. It's a way of locking them in, so to speak."

Ascelin frowns at Cashore. "That's why I hear the voices down there. Who knows what monsters exist there that we have yet to see? I tell you again, I do not like this, my king. If Diana is telling the truth, there are parts of the maze we have never seen."

Jet snaps his teeth with frustration. "There's never been anything down there until now. I was in the lower levels a week ago, and there sure as shit wasn't a naga there then."

Ascelin ignores him. "My king, please. Let us rethink this plan. Is this worth our lives?"

I look over, bored. "Come with us or not, vampiri, but rest assured, we are continuing on."

Diana gives Cashore a half-hearted smile, but beneath it, a thread of darkness lurks. This pretty little mark has already managed to surprise me this evening. What other secrets hide behind her elegant features?

I ache to find out.

"Let's go, omega," I command as cornflower eyes find mine and spark. Despite my taking of her earlier and my reassurance there will be repercussions for speaking to me with disrespect, she has to force herself to hold back. Deep inside Diana's mind, we are somehow on even footing, and I cannot have that.

Stepping up next to her, I watch her depress a stone, and the black stone wall slides open to reveal a passageway that drops straight down. Diana gathers the remainder of her skirts and hops in first. I follow her, hissing in a breath at the temperature drop of the lower level. The rest of our group drops down behind me, Ascelin and Renze snapping at the temperature change.

Ascelin opens her mouth to say something but stops when Cashore clicks at her in warning.

Turning, I frown. "What? What were you about to say?"

Cashore smiles, but it doesn't reach his eyes. "We dislike the cold, alpha. It's far cooler down here, one of many reasons vampiri avoid the lower levels."

Diana steps up next to me and smiles. "Vampiri slow down in the cooler weather. If it's too cold, they'll drop like stones. That's why they keep torches on in their chambers."

With that pronouncement, she turns and heads up the hallway as I glance back at Cashore. His face is white with rage, Ascelin snapping her teeth next to him as Renze draws his sword with an angry hiss.

Jet snickers at the vampiri group. "If it gets too cold and you pass out, I'm not carrying you."

I smile at Cashore, who still looks livid, before turning to follow the surprising omega through the maze.

CHAPTER 10
DIANA

Cashore stops rummaging around in my head as I pace up a dark hallway with Noire a wall of warmth behind me. Until we hear a bellow that shakes the hallway. It's inhuman, a roar and scream rolled into a growl that shakes my bones.

"The throne room," I bark. "There's a door there if we can hold it off long enough."

Noire grips my waist, our group falling immediately silent. In the darkness, he turns to me. "We need the nearest open space; something's coming fast." He says this as if he's not terrified of whatever just screeched up the hallway, but when I glance behind him, the vampiri all look horrified, Ascelin gripping her sword tight in one white fist.

Noire's fingers trail along my waist as he steps past me and heads up the hallway, his steps swift and sure. He knows the passages of this maze well, and that's clear when he takes two quick lefts and a right, dumping us out into a large hall with a throne at the end. Angular columns line the hallway, the stones here a slightly lighter color than the rest of the maze. There's not a great way out of this room if there is a naga, and it comes in.

"What's the plan?" hisses Renze from behind me.

Tenebris speaks up first. "We can't hide from a naga; they sense body heat, and they have incredible hearing."

"Our bodies are cold, alpha," snaps Ascelin, "let us use this to our advantage."

"Aim for the back of its hood," Tenebris continues. "Right between the eyes. It's the only place a weapon can penetrate naga scales."

"Split up," Noire commands our group. "Half of us on that side of the throne, half of us on this side. Something's coming; I can hear it, and it knows we're here. We must get it to listen to us."

Next to me, Noire turns to Jet. "If something happens to me, protect Diana at all costs. Get out of here. You know what to do from there."

Jet nods as I frown up at Noire, but his face is a carefully neutral mask as he tugs me behind him, standing just behind the obsidian throne.

You know what to do from there? The idea that Noire has a plan outside the maze that doesn't involve him eats me up. I hate the idea that he imagines not making it out of this place, but my heart warms in my chest knowing he told his brothers to protect me.

Long minutes pass where nobody says anything, and when I glance to the opposite side of the enormous throne, Ten, Ascelin, and Renze are poised there in obvious disquiet. When Renze looks up with a soft growl, my eyes fly toward the far end of the hall.

Shadows play in the dark doorway we first came in. *Something is coming.* Behind me, Noire slides his hand around my waist, up between my breasts to circle my throat. "Keep yourself safe, no matter what, Diana. Stick close to my brothers."

Nodding, I shift back into his heat as he stiffens and huffs out a breath along the shell of my ear. Goosebumps prickle down my neck and shoulders as Noire nips my neck. Someone hisses at us to be quiet—Cashore, I think—but I can't help the panting breaths that come out of my mouth as Noire grazes his teeth along my exposed neckline. "Even now, I'm half-tempted to take you, omega."

Throwing my head back into his shoulder, I expose my neck to him in the darkness of the maze, reaching to hold on to his forearms. I should be terrified of him. He's been nothing but rough and cruel to me. But somehow, unbelievably, I feel safe in Noire's arms, with his fangs at my throat. The worst monster is the one at my back, but I'm not afraid of him, not completely.

Noire pulls me tighter to him, growling low into my ear as his grip tightens. A terrible grating sound rings through the hall as my gaze shifts forward, heart leaping into my throat. It pounds so hard that I know whatever's coming can probably hear me, but Noire chuckles into my skin and plants a tender kiss at the base of my shoulder before straightening up behind me. His grip doesn't leave my throat, though.

I know he wants to keep me safe so he can get out, but it's easy to sink into his dominant possession.

Turning to the alphas, I nod toward the noise. "I need time to search the back wall, but the door is somewhere behind the throne. We need to keep him away from it. Deal?"

Ten and Jet nod, and Noire squeezes my hip.

A slithery grating sound rings louder up the hallway as our group prepares for whatever's coming.

Renze is the first to click in surprise when the head and shoulders of the monster come through the doorway. It's a naga—broad, red-scaled chest, a wide hood flaring behind slanted snake-like features. It's clearly a male by the set of his shoulders, his muscular stomach flowing into a thickly coiled body. He slithers into the room, and he's fucking enormous.

"It's a naga king," murmurs Ten under his breath, his eyes

narrowed. "See the pattern on his chest? It signifies he's royalty."

I've never seen a naga before because they mostly settle in the dusty and uncivilized western part of the continent, but he's nearly as tall as the columns themselves, his head almost touching the ceiling. He must be twenty feet tall without even rising up on his body.

The naga's tongue comes out to scent the air, and he snarls, gripping on to two columns with enormous hands as he leans into the room. His tongue tastes the air over and over as the remainder of his coils slips into the room and bunches up behind him. "Prey…" he whispers, the sound ringing off the dark stones of the room.

Noire moves from behind me before I can say a word, striding out from behind the throne like a king. He comes to stop next to it, the naga's eyes whipping toward him as it slithers forward another ten feet.

My first urge is to scream at Noire to run; we can't fight this thing. I've never seen a monster this big. But Noire wants out of this fucking place as much as I do.

He must have a plan.

"Prey," the naga whispers again, sliding up the aisle toward us as Jet and Tenebris slink off to either side of the columns, forming a box as the naga gets closer. His eyes dart from side to side as he looks at them but throws his head back and laughs.

It's a vicious, cruel sound, pitched low enough to rumble the stone floor.

Without warning, the naga leaps forward, crossing the space between him and Noire in the blink of an eye. He swipes out with one enormous arm, attempting to knock Noire into one of the columns. But Noire is faster than I could have believed possible, gripping the naga's arm and climbing up onto its back.

It's hard to even follow the movements as the naga writhes and coils, trying to dislodge Noire. They slam into a column, and the rocks crash around us as the rest of our group sprints into the clearing. Jet and Ten leap onto the Naga's front, attempting to drag it down as the vampiri all do the same.

With an explosion of fury, the naga shakes them all loose, and monsters fly around the room, hitting walls and sliding to the ground.

The moment the naga dislodges everyone, it rounds on me and shoots forward to where I stand next to the throne. There's no fucking way we can get past this monster.

"We can get you to your mate," I shout loudly to ensure the naga hears me.

The male slams to a halt, tongue flicking rapidly against his red lips, his eyes narrowed and angry.

Everyone is frozen, pulling to their feet as I face the naga king.

"Where is she?" he roars, flying forward and wrapping me in his scales, coiling up so I'm caught in his powerful body. The coils pull tight, crushing the air from my chest as his face comes close to mine.

My heart shrivels at what I see there: fury, distress, longing. His pain echoes in my soul. I feel...bad for him. Another monster who'd prefer to live out his life away from Rama, dragged here against his will to serve as her puppet.

"Your mate is in the maze too," I lie. I don't know if it's true or not, but I'll say anything I must to get us away from him. There's no way we can get past him. We'll just have to go another way, if we live long enough.

"I can...get you...to her." I gasp as the coils wind tighter, my ribs beginning to crack under the pressure of his tightly muscled body. Black spots dance in my vision as the breath steals from my lungs, my head falling back.

"Where is she?" he roars in my face, tongue flicking against my neck as he tastes me.

I'm vaguely aware of Noire leaping onto the creature's head, stabbing him over and over as the alphas and vampiri attempt to take the naga down. He unleashes his coils, flinging me across the room where I hit the black, glittering throne and fall to the ground.

The naga rolls and snatches Noire and Tenebris in his coils, twisting up tight as he roars for his mate and rounds on me again. "Where is she? Tell me now, and I'll make their death fast."

I gasp for air around the crushing pressure still squeezing my lungs. The naga slinks closer, crushing Noire and his brother in his coils when I see Renze and Ascelin fly through the air. The king senses them coming and whips his tail out, knocking Ascelin to the side, but Renze keeps coming, landing on the king's hood.

Almost faster than I can follow, Renze buries his sword in the center of the hood until it comes out through his mouth, the king roaring in pain as he releases the alphas and thrashes on the ground. Renze pushes off the king's head and leaps to the ground, rolling out of the way as he sprints behind one of the columns.

Noire and Tenebris jump gracefully over the thrashing king, careful to avoid a hooked barb at the end of his tail. Tenebris joins Renze behind one column, and Noire ducks behind with me, turning me carefully to face him. "Are you hurt?" Dark eyes scan mine and glance down to where I'm holding my ribs.

"I'll be okay," I whisper as he leans in and sniffs at my neck, growling into my skin.

The king flails in front of the room's throne, roaring as he scratches at the back of his hood, yanking the sword out and tossing it aside. He rounds on us, blood already streaming out of his mouth as he pants and surges forward. Noire, Tenebris, and I sprint for the other side of the room, crossing to where the rest of our group hides behind the other columns, but the king follows us in a macabre game of tag.

We round the throne just as he leaps up over the top of it,

throwing himself down in front of us as we scramble back, falling over one another to get away. But his movements slow, blood coating his entire neck and chest, dripping down. He lashes out, his tail whipping Jet across the chest as he flies against the wall, crushing his pack behind him.

I hear the crack of the uppers in his bag and watch the purple liquid seep out as Jet roars with anger.

"Get out of his way," I scream just as Jet falls forward and leaps upright, snarling at the swaying naga. "Draw him away from the throne, Jet! The door is somewhere in this part of the room!"

Jet sprints away from the king, but the naga's eyes barely follow him. He sways from side to side once, twice, then falls to the ground with a heavy thud, knocking us all to the stone floor, Jet flying sideways once more.

"Oh fuck!" I shout, throwing my hands up in my hair. "He's down in front of the wall. The door fucking swings open."

"You must be shitting me, Diana," Jet snaps as Renze comes to stand beside him, his chest heaving under the leather vest.

"Get away from the naga," I direct, scrambling backward just as Tenebris' eyes widen in understanding.

"Back up—as far as you can," he barks at our group. Without asking why, we all turn to do so, but the naga's body gives a horrifying squelch, and a cloud of mist rains down on us as Tenebris groans. "Godsdamnit, I hope he's the only one down here."

"Why?" barks Noire. "What the fuck is going on here?" He wipes at his face in disgust, frowning when it appears the mist has even gotten in his mouth.

I turn toward the group and sigh, closing my eyes and squinting them tightly shut. "Naga release a pheromone upon death, and if it coats you, it sends a signal to other naga when you meet them that you were in a naga's presence when they died. They're all reclusive, so they take this as a sign that you killed one of their kind. It's an immediate death sentence if there's another naga down here."

"Well, we'd have seen one already, wouldn't we?" Renze looks confused.

I point to the king's coils. "He's blocking the fucking door. There's no other way out in this section. We have to backtrack and go out the other side of the maze, which means going back down into the lower levels there. Those levels are all designed to hold the bigger monsters. It's entirely possible there's another naga, or something worse, something even bigger."

"I ran the lower levels last week," Jet reminds us. "There was nothing there..."

Grimacing, I turn to him. "The maze is designed to make it easy for Rama to insert monsters at various levels. She knows we're trying to get out. The likelihood of her putting something in the maze on the other side, knowing we're headed there, is very high."

"So, what next?" Noire's voice is cool and collected as Jet snarls and runs both hands through his hair.

"We follow the omega," Renze purrs coolly. "We protect her at all costs, and we get the fuck out of here. We knew it would not be easy, and Rama has not even begun to toy with us. We should expect that she will, as Diana just mentioned."

I look at the vampiri male with the disconcerting, too-white eyes. He smiles softly, but there's a sadness to it. He wants out, but he doesn't believe this will work.

Noire puts one hand on my back and ushers me forward. "Let's go, Diana."

Our entire group is pensive and quiet as we trek through the lower levels, backtracking toward the side of the maze that houses the vampiri living quarters. We can take another route from here, but it will be longer, and we'll spend more time on the other side of the lower levels. I'd love to avoid that, but unless we figure out a way to move the dead naga, we have very few other options.

Cashore pulls up next to me as we walk, despite a warning growl from Noire. I feel Cashore's gift rummaging around in my mind as I snap my teeth at him. "Get out."

The vampiri king's eyes narrow, but he does as I say, folding his hands behind his back. "I will be blunt, Diana. I need to get my people out, and I need to know that you have another way. A realistic way."

I turn to him, confused. "Why are you following me at all if you don't believe I'm telling the truth?"

Cashore nods slowly. "It is not that I do not believe you, but when we pass the vampiri quarters, I will ask the rest of my people to come. That group includes younglings, Diana, remember? Younglings we have protected from the maze for seven years. I will not further risk them, and I would not mention them again at all if I did not believe this was our one chance to leave this place."

Jet speaks up from in front of me, turning to walk backwards as he looks at Cashore. "Why would you have children in this place? Are you out of your mind?"

Renze speaks first. "Vampiri reproduce quickly, and our power is derived from sex. We have no way to prevent children from being born in this place. To my knowledge, we are the only group with females in the maze."

Jet nods. "I'd never considered that, but you're right. Of course, it's hard to tell the men from the women..."

Ascelin hisses next to Cashore, grabbing a knife from her chest-strap and brandishing it toward Jet. "Watch your mouth, alpha."

Jet winks at her before turning back around. I continue to follow but glance up at Cashore, who still looks at me with a blank expression. This close, I can see his eyes aren't truly white; there's an iris and pupil there but covered in a white film like a shark. "I truly know a few ways out, Cashore. And I will do my level best to help you get your younglings out of this place. I can't make you any promises, but I think you know that. I am not lying to you, though."

Cashore smiles, showing me dozens of razor-sharp teeth as his black lips part. "Good, Diana Winthrop. Because if you are lying, I will greatly relish fulfilling my duty for this evening." He holds his arm up, the disk still glowing a faint green, a reminder that the vampiri were supposed to take my life.

Ascelin laughs next to him, but it's evil and mean and devious. "If our remaining younglings suffer because of you, omega, I will suck the marrow from your bones while your heart still beats. You will feel every moment of pain until we end you."

Noire lashes out fast, swiping his claws at Ascelin's face as she chuckles and dances out of the way, batting her eyes playfully.

I hold back a shudder while Noire wraps a hand around my waist, tucking me into his other side, away from Cashore. "Don't touch the omega, vampiri. She's mine, and if you get in the way of my people getting out of here, you will deal with me." He snarls as Cashore laughs. And then we're at the vampiri quarters once more, the maze around us quiet and ominous.

"We stop here," Cashore barks, Noire stiffening beside me.

"No, we keep going."

Cashore rounds on Noire with a snarl, fangs descended as the white coating his eyes takes on a red hue. "Diana has already told us the lower levels will likely hold larger monsters. Do you really want to go down there without better weapons than you've got?" He gestures to Noire's knives, eliciting a growl as Noire pulls me tight against his chest.

"Are you saying you have better weapons?"

"I do," Cashore purrs. "I need a moment to gather my people, but if you can grant me a little time to do so, I will happily give your pack additional weapons so we may *all* leave this place."

I turn in Noire's arms, searching his face for any sign of understanding. It's clear from the angry clench of his jaw that he doesn't want to stop, not for a second. "Please, Noire," I murmur. "The more of us the better. There are worse monsters than naga in Rama's stable. We've only got one shot at this, and our chances diminish without good weaponry."

He looks over my head at Jet. "What do you think, brother?"

Before Jet can speak up, Tenebris does. "We need all the weapons we can get, Noire. Any one of them could mean the difference between us making it out or losing Diana and our only chance to leave."

Noire glances at Jet, who nods and, for once, has nothing saucy to say. Noire nods once to Cashore, and then we follow the vampiri trio back into their quarters.

The first thing we hear is a deep, wailing scream that sinks right into the depths of my bones.

CHAPTER 11
NOIRE

The vampiri scream sets my teeth on edge, grating at my sensitive hearing as Ascelin hands her long sword to Renze and darts off down a long hallway toward the noise. Renze turns to our group. "Vampiri birth is quite painful. We have had a youngling due for several days now. By the sounds of it, she is coming."

Diana looks at Renze in rapt fascination. "How do you protect them? How many younglings are in your group?"

Renze frowns over at Cashore, but the king nods at him. "Ten younglings left."

"Left?" Diana barks. "There were more?"

Cashore peers at Diana with a frown. "As I said, omega, we have protected the younglings from the maze when we could. But we have not saved them all. The maze has taken from us several times."

"Oh my gods," she whispers, tears lining her blue eyes. I shouldn't notice the way her cheeks flush or the way she takes a step closer to me as if my presence comforts her. "Do you have bones we need to take with us? How can we remember them? What do you need?"

Cashore frowns, looking meaningfully at the roses before glancing back at Diana. "The maze has already claimed the bodies of our dead younglings, Diana. There is nothing to take with us."

She chokes back a distressed noise and presses harder into my chest.

I shouldn't comfort her. If anything, she should step away because, out of the maze's dangerous hallways, my attention is focused once more on her intoxicating scent. Nothing can be done about the pheromones they doused her with, and my libido rises as she takes another step toward me, her skin hot against my arm through the tee she's wearing. Curiosity threads itself through the forefront of my mind, wondering why the scent isn't affecting Jet and Ten quite like it does me. The smell of Diana in heat was enough to send me into an immediate rut.

That is highly concerning because it indicates compatibility on a far deeper level than simple alpha-omega dynamics.

Cashore turns to me, changing the subject deftly. "Shall I take you to the weapons, alpha? You may have your pick of what you can carry."

Nodding, I grip Diana's hand and tug her along with me, maintaining vigilance as we follow Cashore down a dark hall and through a door. I'm leery of following him with Diana dangling like a prize between us. But Cashore sighs and turns to me in the darkness of the doorway. "We have a better chance of escaping if we work together, alpha. I will not attempt to harm you."

"Good," I purr back at him, not loosening my grip on the omega. "Because I think you know it would go poorly if you did…"

Cashore ignores the comment but flips the lights on in the room, not that any of the alphas need it. I sense his gift scratching at the edges of my mind as my brothers pace the room, eyeing wall after wall covered in knives, swords, and chains. The number of weapons in this room is staggering.

"Get out of my fucking brain," I snarl at the vampiri king. "I won't tell you again not to try that with me or my people."

Cashore has the bad sense to laugh. Renze grips his own sword tighter as he steps closer to his king.

Just then, a high trilling sound echoes through the hallway and open door, into the weapons room. Cashore whips his head around and stalks out, calling over his shoulder, "Help yourselves to the weapons. The youngling is here, and I must greet her."

Renze stays in the room with us, his gaze traveling from me to my brothers.

I run my fingertips up under Diana's shirt, stroking underneath one breast as I lean over her back, bringing my lips to her ear. "Find yourself some weapons, omega. I'll stand guard."

She turns and nods once at me, moving quietly across the room, silent on her feet like all omegas. I back up a step, leaning against the wall by the doorway as I watch my pack, keeping one eye on Renze. He relaxes when I do, sheathing his sword and crossing his arms over his chest, keeping watch the same way I am.

I don't miss how his eyes continue to fall on Jet, how he watches him far more than Tenebris. Alpha intuition tells me to keep an eye on him, that his focus on my brother is more than a general interest in a competing male.

Diana comes back to me then, tightening the straps of a chest holder filled with knives. I reach out, moving her fingers as I loosen it, moving one of the straps up over her head to the other side.

"You've got this on wrong, omega."

She looks up at me, and it's easy to see she's resisting the urge to snark something. When I tilt an eyebrow up in challenge, she bites her lip and keeps quiet. I tighten the strap, unable to stop focusing on how much the leather accentuates her full breasts.

Diana's nipples pebble underneath the shirt as my mouth starts to water. The sharp edges of my rut stab at the base of my spine as heat rushes to my cock. Gathering Diana into my arms, I pull her close and tug her head back, dragging my nose up her neck.

Gods, she smells so fucking good. Even beneath the fake pheromones, her natural scent shines through. It's warm and inviting, and the way she arches into me despite the tension between us only serves to stoke the flames building in my core. She remains wary of me, even with my body calling for hers, teasing hers. I want to push and pull her in every possible way until she's screaming release around my cock.

The trilling noise echoes louder, and Renze coughs. "The cord is cut, and the youngling is presented to the king. I must go meet her now as well. Feel free to come with us, or stay here with the weapons." He strides out of the room, careful not to touch the door. I eye him warily to make sure he doesn't attempt to close it.

Jet comes back and smirks at me. "Gonna fuck the omega right here, Noire?"

Diana's face schools into a careful neutral as she steps away from me, playing with the straps again. She turns to me, ignoring Jet's comment. "Let's just get out of here."

Nodding, I gesture for Jet to leave the room first, then Ten, then Diana. I follow up the rear as always, watching my people and keeping a wary eye for anything amiss. When we get to the common room, the vampiri step aside, and their circle opens to reveal a female vampiri in the center, holding a writhing infant in her arms. It's coated in blood, and the mother looks exhausted, but it sucks happily at her breast as Cashore looks up at me, face guarded and wary.

The vampiri around us trill again, a noise I've never heard

them make. It's joyous and happy, and for a moment, I'm taken back to my own pack, to the way we'd celebrate when pups were born. Despair crushes my chest in that moment as I close my eyes, remembering my people before Rama slaughtered them. Liuvang willing, some of them escaped.

I vow again to find them, if it's the last thing I do.

Hot anger builds in my system, rising until I channel it into focus—focus on getting out of here, on keeping Diana safe so I can use her knowledge. She watches the mother and child with rapt fascination, her pink mouth slightly open as she leans against the wall, cradling her ribs still. She turns slightly as if she can feel my gaze on her, body pivoting toward me as blue eyes find mine.

I don't know what to read in those eyes. Sorrow. Darkness. A twisted soul as black and complicated as mine?

Cashore comes up next to me with a meaningful look, his eyes flicking to Diana's back. "A word, alpha?"

Not taking my eyes from the omega, I nod, then turn to follow him. Through my bond with my brothers, I send them a clear message. *Do not let Diana out of your sight. I don't trust anyone.*

Cashore leads me down a hallway that's eerily similar to my own in the alpha quarters, opening a door and slipping in. I scent the room, looking for any signs of attack as he sighs. "It is just us, Noire."

Stepping in, I look around, but true to his word, there are only the two of us in the room. Not that I couldn't take Cashore in a fight, but this night is wearing my patience thin, and I'd prefer not to kill the vampiri king if I don't have to.

Cashore cocks his head to the side and smiles. "You think you could take me in a fight?"

"Stop reading my mind," I bark out.

He smiles again. "I'll have to thank Diana again for that tip regarding the roses. My full abilities are not back but are returning to me fast, despite your ability to ward against me."

I don't bother to congratulate him. An enemy who can read my thoughts sounds fucking inconvenient; although, for purposes of getting out of this place, it may come in handy.

Cashore nods, although the slimy feeling I get when he's reading me dissipates. "On the subject of Diana, it's clear she is multi-faceted in ways we did not foresee."

I bark out a laugh at that. Multi-faceted is one way to put it.

Cashore tuts at me with a smile. "Diana is…willful, but she's hiding something. Her mind is its own maze. Reading her is surprisingly difficult, even for me. That typically indicates years of psychological trauma."

Trauma. Somehow, when I think about someone damaging Diana in that way, rage fills my system. The mental image of Diana hurt and injured and afraid does not bring me joy. Earlier, when she was nothing but a mark to me, it was different. But tonight, she saved all our lives by distracting the naga. Still, a mark will often say and do anything to try to escape the maze. I still don't trust her, despite how wildly attracted to her I am on every possible level.

Cashore continues, "I won't risk my people, and I sense Diana has not been forthcoming with all the details around our exit from the maze. I believe it would be unwise for us to continue without a fuller picture of what she knows and why she's here."

"What do you have in mind? You've said she's hard to read…"

Cashore nods and smiles, a deeply wicked smile that reminds me how very predatory vampiri are. It grates my alpha senses as I stand up taller and snarl. Cashore snarls too, taking a step closer to me. "I need her distracted, overwhelmed. And while she is in that state, I will be able to read her more easily. I need to pick my way through Diana Winthrop's mind. You will be the distraction. Diana's memory is its own form of maze, Noire."

"Are you asking me to hurt her?" I growl out the words. Hurting her sounds far less appealing than it did a few hours ago.

"Hurt her, tease her–whatever you need to do to push her to a desperate edge. People in that state of mind are unable to hide their thoughts from me, despite training against it."

"Done," I snap. I won't risk losing another brother in this place, although I'll try teasing first.

"That would be a shame indeed," purrs Cashore, even though I didn't say that last part aloud. I whip a hand out and grab the vampiri king's chin as I press a knife to his chest. "What have I said about digging through my mind?"

"I am simply illustrating a point, alpha," Cashore smiles, his darkly translucent teeth peeking at me between black lips. Taking a step back, I nod in the direction of the common room. Trills still echo along the hallways. I'm ready to get the hell out of here.

When Cashore and I return to the main living area, Diana's eyes find mine, an odd mix of relief and anxiety showing through before she settles her face into a careful neutral.

The vampiri clears his throat, and as one, his people turn and bow their heads. "We leave tonight. Gather only what you must take with you. Go now to grab those items. We will continue this celebration when we are free of the maze." With that proclamation, the vampiri scatter along the hallways as my brothers turn to me.

When I find Jet, I reach into his bag for the purple liquid uppers, relieved to find one bottle still whole. I stalk across the room to Diana, handing her the bottle. "Drink it." It's a simple command, but I let the alpha roll through me and wash over her, smothering her with dominance.

Diana shudders but takes the glass. "Why?"

My gods, the sheer amount of disobedience from this woman.

Gripping her hair, I tug her head back and force her to look up at me. "Because there's plenty you're not telling us about who you are and what you're doing here, and I want to know every fucking detail. Right now. You're hiding something, Diana. I can feel it."

Cashore hisses from behind Diana, stalking soundlessly across the carpet as our eyes meet over her shoulder. Jet and Ten reach out through our mental bond, and I caution them to remain watchful.

Smiling, I nod at the vampiri, even though Diana can't turn and see. "You're gonna drink this, and then Cashore is going to read everything inside your mind, and we're going to see where that leaves us."

"Please, Noire, I'm not lying," she starts as I snarl and yank her head back harder. Cashore hisses again and comes to stand just behind her, leaning into her ear as I grip her jaw and pinch hard. Her mouth pops open as her eyes go wild. The vampiri takes the uppers and pours them down her throat as she sputters and coughs. Once she has a mouthful, I clamp her jaw shut and watch her swallow the purple liquid.

"Time to push her, alpha," Cashore purrs in a sing-song voice as Diana groans. I grip her jaw and force another few mouthfuls down her.

The effect is nearly instantaneous, just like with Jet. Diana's pupils expand until they overtake the blue of her iris, her chest heaving slightly as she balls her fists.

Jet and Ten come to stand just beside me; both are there if I need anything at all. They know better than to interrupt me when I'm in alpha enforcer mode.

I let a rumbling purr wash over Diana as I haul her close to my chest. It reverberates between us, her nipples pebbling for me, body tightening. She wants me. Despite how we got started.

Despite how roughly I took her in my bed earlier. A responding snarl leaves Diana's pretty lips as her fangs elongate, peeking out of the corners of her mouth. She's angry. Good.

Seeing those sharp teeth sends pleasure throbbing through my system. What would it feel like for her to bite me? I find myself pondering it as she pants in my arms.

"Tease her," purrs Cashore, nipping at Diana's ear as she shudders away from him.

Wrong, wrong, wrong. She doesn't want his touch.

Good. Because this isn't about her pleasure. This is about overwhelming her until she gives up all the secrets she's hiding in that steel-trap mind of hers.

"Tell me," I bark out. "Tell me everything about working for Rama. Tell me everything you know about leaving this place."

Diana fights the uppers and the compulsion I read from Cashore. His gift is like nails to a chalkboard in my mind; I can't imagine what it feels like to the omega on uppers. Diana snarls and shakes her head as I take one step closer to her, her breasts smashed up against my chest.

I purr again as she whimpers, the scent of slick slapping me across the face as her arousal amps up. "Tell me, pretty little omega. Tell me all your secrets." Reaching into her torn skirts, I slide my fingers between her thighs, chuckling when she parts them ever so slightly for me. I find her clit and pinch as she doubles over, Cashore yanking her back upright with his hand around her neck.

Anger flashes in Diana's eyes at the rough treatment, so I do it again, pinching her clit as more slick floods from her. This is the way an omega should respond to an alpha's need, rough as it is. Something about this woman brings out my darkest desires for pain and punishment.

Cashore leans into Diana's ear again. "Tell us about working with Rama. In what way did you work for her..."

Diana gasps, her eyes squinting tightly closed as I tickle my fingers along her clit, rubbing with even, soft strokes as she squirms between two monsters. "It doesn't matter," she grunts out, eyes flying open to meet mine.

I resist the urge to bellow and rage. I need details. "It matters to me, omega." My voice is husky even in my own ears as Cashore's eyes meet mine. *Push her.*

"I was…her profiler," she gasps out as Cashore's jaw clenches. He nods. She's telling the fucking truth.

"And that means what, exactly?" my bark whips around the space between Diana and me as she grunts against the onslaught of it and Cashore's gift.

Diana snarls and snaps her teeth at me as Cashore laughs. "More, Noire. Push her more."

Leaning in, I sink my teeth into her throat, just under her chin, blood filling my mouth and dripping down my fangs as Diana squirms against me, her feet losing purchase on the floor as I lift her off the ground. I release the bite and snarl into her lips, "Details, Diana."

"No," she pleads. "Don't make me!"

I bite her again, this time on her chest, just above heaving breasts I ache to suck and lick. She's clearly hedging, and the breath leaves her in a whoosh when I shove two fingers deep inside her and stroke. Diana's cunt clenches around me as she rocks her hips to meet me. "Tell me," I growl as I release the bite and look for another place.

"I profiled the mark and the monsters," she grunts. A deep moan leaves her as I stroke her inner walls, finding that spot that'll drive her wild.

"To what end?" I bark.

"To what end," Cashore repeats, his gift stabbing at Diana and me both as she grunts against the onslaught of my fingers. I shut him out as the vampiri groans at the slim expanse of creamy neck presented just below his mouth. The fiery poison he carries in his fangs begins to drip off his

NOIRE: A DARK SHIFTER ROMANCE   139

teeth, landing on Diana's skin as she yelps and squirms in my arms.

"What else, Diana?" I command as she sobs. I watch Cashore's poison eat away at her skin, burning it red and blistering it as I rub inside her with three fingers. Slick coats my hand, my dick lengthening in my pants as I growl and bring my teeth to drag up her neck, nipping under her ear.

Diana groans, sinking into me as her arms fly up to encircle my neck. She surprises me at every turn. All this hurt, all this pain, all this dominance, and still she doesn't run. What depths does this omega hide? I want to uncover every layer of her.

"I suggested scenes for the hunt based on the mark and monster profiles," she mumbles, her head lolling to the side as I bite my way down her neck, careful to steer clear of Cashore's venom. I don't want that shit in my mouth. "I've profiled every monster in here at some point. I've profiled every mark. I orchestrated...everything. Every detail of every death..."

I bite Diana's shoulder as she hisses and rolls her hips against mine. Cold fury sinks along a connection between us. *She created the scenes.*

"So, every time I killed, it was because you chose it?" Cashore's voice is a deep bark as Diana sobs and nods.

"I chose it; I chose all of it. Every moment of every death in this entire godsforsaken shithole." She's sobbing, shaking and angry as her words sink in.

"Every death?" I spit out. "*Every* death?"

Diana's blue eyes flash up to mine, and she shrugs, once. She knows what I'm asking. I need clear fucking confirmation. "Almost every one," she whispers.

"So, when Oskur died..."

A sob leaves Diana's lips as she nods again. "I profiled that too..." Her voice is a hint of a whisper as I roar with rage, shaking the ceiling as Ten and Jet pace around us. They don't know what to do with this information. This fucking omega worked for the woman who put us here. She planned Oskur's death. He is dead because of her. He died in the way *she chose.*

"There is more, Diana, I sense it," Cashore presses, looking at me. He takes the chance to speak into my mind. *Keep pushing, alpha; that is not all from her.*

"You're a greedy little thing," I purr. "You like this adventure, this trip into the maze to visit the monsters. I bet you came in here to get fucked by me. Did you profile this too? Did you profile our escape?"

There's a moment's pause where her eyes meet mine, and the truth shines so clearly through them as my breath halts in my chest.

"I did come here for you." It's a faint whisper, so soft I'm not sure she realizes she even said it aloud. Behind her, Cashore straightens and nods. *She's telling the truth.* He speaks this into my mind as I run circles around what she just said, trying to comprehend it.

"Rama killed everyone I ever cared about," Diana sobs as her body clenches around my fingers. She's overcome with emotion, tears streaming down her cheeks.

I'm so close to finding out all her truths. I can't let up now, even though watching her relive the horrors of her past doesn't excite me in the slightest.

"Why?" I demand, stroking her clit gently again as she sobs, her head falling back onto Cashore's chest as her eyes squeeze shut.

"Dore and I ran from her for so long, but we were just children. She caught us and brought us to Siargao. It was...awful, but we were together. We forced the bad memories away so we could stay alive, but as Dore got older and stronger, he questioned Rama constantly."

Diana shakes her head, her breath coming in great heaving sobs as her body ramps up the tension. She's miserable, high on uppers, and about to come all over my fingers, even though we're talking about her dead brother. This omega may be as twisted as I am.

"I knew she'd throw me into the maze one day when it suited her. And I knew I'd come for you when she did."

"Why?" I press further. Something about this story doesn't add up. Why me versus any other available monster, and why now?

Diana screams as her orgasm hits her, her body thrashing in my arms as my name falls off her lips like a prayer. I withdraw my fingers from her as her chest heaves.

Cashore groans as blood wells up along Diana's shoulders. Her body curls in on itself as I draw her orgasm out with another pinch to her clit, her teeth gnashing.

I'm halfway to coming in my pants watching her like this. But as her release fades, the shuddering of her frame turns into great heaving sobs as she points one angry finger at me. "She killed my brother, you fucking asshole. She slit his throat and threw him on a garbage heap the day we turned sixteen. You were kind to me once, when I was a child, when you came to see my father. And so, I thought, if anyone, if any-fucking-one could help me, it would be someone who was just as angry. I thought if anyone would take her down with me, it would be you!"

Diana throws her head backward, head-butting Cashore as he bellows in anger. Shoving her way out of his arms, she strides for the nearest door and sails through it without a backward glance.

Blood flows from Cashore's nose when I turn to look at him. "What do you make of that?"

The vampiri chuckles, his laugh wry around a mouthful of black blood. "I think she's your fucking mate, you hideous asshole."

The moment he says it, I know it's true.

CHAPTER 12
DIANA

D ore Dore Dore. *How could you leave me to deal with this shit?* I think to my dead brother as I stomp down a hall and into the backmost living quarters.

I knew the truth would come out; I just didn't think it would come out so violently. I don't know what I thought. I just knew I couldn't tell anyone when I first found the alphas that I worked for Rama so intimately. That I planned things that hurt them. But I had no choice…none at all.

But now? Now I need a godsdamned minute.

I know one thing's for certain: Rama will not want us to get out of this hellhole prison—no matter what. I obviously brought nothing with me into the maze, but my father didn't tell Rama everything about the maze's design either. Only I know every single one of its secrets.

A sudden pang at my shoulder causes me to double over in pain. The fucking vampiri venom. The only thing that can dissipate it is the sulfur baths in Cashore's primary living quarters, the room I came to. I suppose the good thing about knowing my way around every inch of this maze is that I can help myself more than a normal mark could.

I slip out of Noire's shirt and the battered, trashed blue dress Rama's minions outfitted me in, letting the ruined fabric fall to the floor. My entire body is tender. I'll heal fast because I'm an omega surrounded by alpha males–my body is built to take a beating and be ready for my alpha as quickly as possible. Even so, my ribs and shoulder are tenderized from the naga's coils and Noire's various assaults.

Tears slide down my cheeks nonstop as I look out across the enormous blackwater sulfur pool favored by the vampiri. My father designed the maze in some ways to placate the monsters, bringing in little bits of their home provinces as both a mockery and a comfort. Rama wanted them to remember what they lost, but to get complacent in the relative comforts of their quarters.

I step into the sulfur pool and stride across the black sand until I reach the very edge. The pool's edge drops off into a huge abyss that's miles deep and nearly half a mile across. At the very far edge, I can barely make out a black stone wall with various outcroppings. More monsters live there, more broken and battered heathens here to put on a show for Rama.

Fuck her.

Snarling, I whip around as the doors to Cashore's quarters open and shut with a small click.

Jet.

He meets my eyes but says nothing, ripping his clothes off as he hops into the pool with a big splash. I watch him dunk under, washing the blood from his body before swimming toward me and propping his back up against the ledge.

In that moment, he reminds me so much of my brother that my heart feels like it'll shatter in my chest all over again. If Jet senses what I'm thinking with his alpha intuition, he says nothing.

In the darkness around us, I hear chirping, and it brings a smile to my face. *Maulin foxes. My only friends.*

The tiny monster foxes who inhabit the maze are the scavengers. They're at the very bottom of the power totem pole, but they keep the maze clean, and they're wicked smart if you befriend them.

"We share a common ancestor, you know," Jet begins, nodding in the direction of the chirping. "Tenebris taught me that." His half-smile falls when he says his brother's name. He looks back up, and his eyes are bright with hope, hope that dimmed many years ago. Which I know because I've been watching him deal with this shit-ass maze for seven long horrible years, every time Rama televised the hunt.

Jet clenches his jaw before speaking. "Rama will not let us go easily. Whatever you do, get Ten out of here and away from this place, okay? Noire and I could handle being thrown back in here, but Ten is meant for something far better than his. He's brilliant, and that could be put to good use in the right pack."

"I can't promise to get any of you out. There's a very good chance this is a one-way ticket for me. But I'll do my best to get all of you out, especially Ten."

Jet nods and sinks lower into the water, dark eyes still tight at the corners when he looks over at me. "You planned all the hunt scenes? Really?"

"Is that so hard to believe?" I whisper, meeting his gaze. Jet's eyes narrow as he assesses me, almost like he's really seeing me for the first time.

"You put on a good show when you first arrived, acting like a scared little plaything who just happened to know a way out. Did you spill all your secrets just now?"

I sigh, placing my own head back against the rock ledge as my body knits my injuries back together.

Jet's next question surprises me. "Do you know why Rama always sends me to the Atrium? Why not Ten? I can guess why she doesn't send Noire..."

"She hates Noire with a bone-deep passion I've never fully understood. You're right, she didn't send him to the Atrium unless one of the clients specifically knew to request him because she didn't want him to experience pleasure."

Jet huffs out an angry growl. "So why me, then?"

Turning in the water, I muster up all the truth I can find and answer Jet honestly. "Your sexual creativity, especially on uppers, is unmatched, Jet. The clients love watching you, and doing that and interacting with you got them high in a way the maze wasn't initially designed to do. Rich people drunk on your pleasure often make bad decisions. You served as an incredible distraction for Rama to swoop in and get whatever she wanted. I profiled all of that too."

He nods as if he suspected it, but now that I've spent hours around him, I can read distress in his face. His voice is a bare whisper as he continues, "That night I was late when she had the guards shoot me over and over and then fuck that man, who asked for it? A client?"

The blood drains from my own face at his question. I'll never forget that night. "I don't know that level of detail. She televised it, of course, but that wasn't suggested by me. I can't really say...I just created the..."

"Profiles, right." Jet sighs and nods. "I'm guessing it had nothing to do with being late, and everything to do with psychologically attacking us at every opportunity."

"That's true," I whisper. "Even Oskur's death and the way it happened was meant to feel especially tragic," I say softly as Jet turns toward me.

"Tell me everything."

Sighing, I bring my legs up and wrap my arms around them. "Rama wanted you to fear the disks, to fear her power, to wonder exactly how much she was capable of. But I guess Oskur did something, and she asked me to profile you all for his death to have maximum impact. I lied, of course, to try to minimize it, but she does whatever she wants, regardless of my profile report. It doesn't always play out the way I suggest."

I'm an asshole for sharing what I did, but Jet's dark eyes close as he leans against the pool's edge. His jaw is tense, and it brings me back to watching them after the rorschachs killed Oskur. Remembering how Noire raged around the maze for weeks, destroying anything in his path. He destroyed their quarters too, but Rama put them back together as a slap in the face. She televised all of it so the citizens of Siargao could watch their former ruler reduced to insanity.

The chirping sound in the shadows intensifies, and I respond with my own series of clicks and kisses as a small group of the maulin fox dart across Cashore's carpet and leap up onto the edge of the pool. Two babies and their parents. I recognize them immediately.

Jet watches in disbelief as the foxes trot along the ledge and come up to me, nuzzling into my hand as I scratch their ears. "When Oskur died, I asked the foxes to bring his bones out of the maze. They can come and go, you know. They're so tiny. They brought bones to me for years. I've got them all collected on the outside, waiting to be taken to your family crypt if we get out."

"Where is the maze?" Jet questions. "If they've brought you bones for years."

Sighing, I turn to him. "It's underneath a man-made island in Lon Bay. The foxes swim the short distance to shore and bring me the bones, then they come back."

Jet grimaces. "We're underneath the fucking bay, so close to home?"

"Yeah," I affirm.

Jet opens his mouth to say something but thinks better of it and stalks over to me. The foxes break our touch and hiss at him, snapping and chirping as I soothe with little responding clicks of my own.

"Just be silent for a moment and hold your hand out," I

instruct him, pulling him closer as the foxes hide behind my head.

The powerful alpha male at my side crouches down in the water, bowing his head as he extends his hand. He smiles beautifully when the two baby foxes hop up into his palm and begin to roll around, nipping at his fingers. A laugh rings out across the pool as I tilt my head back, baring my neck to the grown fox.

Jet's eyes grow wild in disbelief as the mother fox's lower jaw splits open, many-forked tongue poking out to slide along the wounds on my neck and shoulder. She drinks up the blood before clamping her teeth onto my neck. Her partner comes and does the same, and I let them because this is how we connect. This blood-sharing produces a bond between me and all the maulin foxes in the maze, something I learned the first day one came to visit me. I can share sentiments and needs with them, and while we can't speak coherently in one another's minds, they can understand me. I have been befriending the foxes since the day Rama brought me to Siargao.

"What do you miss most about being outside?" I whisper.

Jet frowns and closes his eyes. "I miss music. I miss how close Noire and I were. Not that we're not close now, but it's different. This place has changed us all. He and I were so tight growing up, and this place has driven a wedge in that."

There is no suitable response to his sadness, so I rub the back of his hand and close my eyes, pushing my desire to help him out into the universe and hoping he can receive it.

"I've never said this to anyone," Jet growls. "But you surprise me."

I smile as I close my eyes, letting my connection to the foxes grow and blossom as they steal blood from me and heal my wounds, all at the same time.

Some days, I surprise myself.

CHAPTER 13
NOIRE

S tanding in the shadows outside Cashore's room, I listen to
Diana and Jet talk. I hear him ask about why Rama
always insisted on him being in the Atrium. I suck in a
breath as she talks about Oskur's bones, and I relive the rage
from when he died. Knowing Rama did it simply to fuck with
me cements my bone-deep desire to rip her head from her shoulders when I get out of here.

But something else stirs in my mind, now that Cashore
said it.

I think she's your fucking mate, you hideous asshole.

My body knew it before my mind did. The way she accepts
my particular overblown brand of violence as if she craves it.
The way her body pivots to mine the moment I walk into the
room. I've known her for mere hours, but when I look into those
blue eyes, I feel like I've known her for far longer. I knew she
was hiding secrets, and I knew how far to push her to pull those
secrets to the surface.

I never thought I'd find a bondmate. I figured I'd meet an
omega as devious as me who would serve the purpose as my
wife because the likelihood of me finding a bondmate in a pack

where I already knew everyone seemed unlikely. I had no desire to travel Lombornei to find a mate elsewhere.

I did not see Diana coming. Had I continued to travel to the other provinces, perhaps I would have met her when she was old enough. I remember meeting her as a child, but there is nothing left of the bouncy, happy pup she was when I met her in Edson's home many years ago.

The vampiri are gathering their things to leave, and while I'm anxious to be on our way, I need to have a conversation with Diana first. Things between us have changed because of Cashore's words. Already, I read a protective thread in Jet's mannerisms toward her. He's seated in the pool, but he's wary and watchful, keeping an eye on the entire room. I can feel it through our family bond.

He's protecting her because we all sense she's mine.

I open the door, my gaze finding Diana's as she tips her head up and looks at me. She's surrounded by the tiny maulin foxes that flit through the maze, scavenging off the mess the monsters leave behind.

When I stalk across the room and take my clothes off, hopping into the pool, the foxes suckling at Diana's neck snarl at me. They don't stop, though, which brings the sliver of a smile to her delicate features. I've never seen anyone befriend a maulin. They're wild and free, although my people tell tales of queens of the past who shapeshifted into maulins and ruled the world for a time before the first alpha was born.

Watching the fox and Diana connect is a near godly experience, my dick hard as a rock as she breathes softly in the pool across from me. Jet moves away from her and out of the water, nodding at me as he grabs his clothing and leaves. He shuts the door as I cross the pool slowly, watching to see the effect my proximity has on her.

Now that Cashore opened my eyes, I can't stop looking at her and thinking of her as something deeper and more connected than the convenient, stunning mark I thought she was. Sure enough, when I'm within a few feet of her, her back arches, nipples pebbling in the water as the foxes unlatch from her neck and skitter away into the shadows. I don't watch them go, but I can hear them licking Diana's blood off their jaws somewhere in the recesses of the room.

I reach under the water, parting Diana's thighs so I can step between them. She hisses in a little breath when my hard cock rubs up against her pussy. Knowing that I elicit this reaction from her is a heady feeling.

"You don't look ready to apologize..." she snaps as I lean over her, forcing her to tilt her head up to look at me.

A dark laugh pulls from my throat, an instinctual purr beginning to work its way up out of my chest, transferring goosebumps to her skin, her hips working against me already.

Natural. It's so fucking natural to do this with her. I need to know more. What will it be like to touch an omega, knowing the gods created this one to fit me? Reaching out, I stroke my fingertips along her collarbone and down between her breasts as she shudders, body rocking in the water as her hips find mine and punch.

The uppers Cashore and I forced down her throat are still running wild in her system, her inhibitions gone as she snaps her teeth. "If you came in here to tease me, get the fuck out, alpha."

Laughing, I wrap both hands around her throat and use that leverage to hoist her out of the water and onto the edge of the pool. Her upper body dangles above the void behind her, her chest heaving as she realizes how precariously placed she is. If I let her go, she could fall to her death.

I crave it, pushing her to the edge like this, knowing her life is in my hands, that she's at my mercy. Bringing one hand down, I grip her thigh and then release her neck, ensuring I have a good hold on her. I huff out a growl, hovering just above her clit as she whines and attempts to move her hips. She can't, and the pressure of my arms is the only thing keeping her from falling.

I want her to fall in other ways.

Leaning in, I lick between her thighs, dragging the flat side of my tongue from her ass all the way up and around her clit. I suck it between my lips then tug on it lightly with my teeth as Diana wails and pants, her hands finding my hair and threading through it.

"More," she cries out, struggling to move her hips to meet me.

"Your pleasure is mine, omega," I growl, nipping at her clit again as she gasps. "Mine to take and use. You'll come when I allow it. Do you understand?"

"Yes, alpha," she gasps as I suck at the sensitive skin between her thighs. Already her muscles tremble, and I find myself wondering how many times I can get her off before the vampiri are ready to go. I want to find out.

Teasing her entrance with my fingers, I slide two inside her and curl them as she gasps. Fireworks erupt between us as she screams my name into the void, over and over as alpha pride heats my core. *I* do this to her. I make her a slick-coated mess with the barest hint of my attention.

I need more, so much more. Now that I'm looking for a deeper connection between us, I feel it. That faint thread that ties us together in the most meaningful way possible. If I tend to that connection, if I stoke its flames, it'll become a fire that eats us both alive until we're bonded so permanently that even death can't separate us.

I've never wanted that, never thought it would be within my reach. I thought I'd take a wife for political reasons and pack connections. But then Diana came for me. She came into hell. My little liar came here *for me.*

Groaning, I hop onto the ledge, pulling Diana up onto her knees as I rub my cock head against her pretty pink lips. Her pupils dilate wider as she opens her mouth and sucks me down greedily, choking around my thick length. Watching her lips stretch and pull tight around me sends sparks down the back of my thighs as her tongue plays with my piercing.

"Diana…" I grunt out as she takes me deeper, the tip of my dick poking into the back of her throat as she chokes and coughs around me.

Fuck, I need more. I need to know how far I can push this little omega before she taps out. There's enough of a size difference between us that I curl myself over her back, essentially on all fours on top of her with my dick still in her mouth. This angle forces her ass up higher and her face down lower so she can keep sucking me off. But from here, I can slide my tongue between her thighs and eat everything that's already so wet for me.

Diana sputters around my dick as she rocks back onto my tongue, sucking in a breath before diving forward again and taking me deep into her throat. I pant into her ass, sucking at her pussy lips as she mewls around me, the vibration tightening my balls. I'm going to come so hard and so fast like this.

Reaching around her, I grip her throat with one hand, feeling her feed my cock down it. When she swallows around me, the pressure on my length is almost more than I can take. I squeeze her throat and hiss at the pleasure that rocks through my system. I feel how full she is of me, and gripping her throat is like squeezing my cock with my own hand all while it's trapped inside her heat.

It occurs to me as fire builds between my thighs that this omega may not have a limit. Because she's handcrafted for me, there may be nothing I can try with her that she won't fucking love.

That knowledge brings my orgasm shooting up through my system as I spill ropes of cum down Diana's throat. She coughs and sputters as I suck her clit into my mouth rhythmically, her slick drenching my face as she comes with me.

My hips pump up against her mouth, my cock buried deep in her throat as she chokes and gags, rocking backward to pull away from me. Growling, I grip her throat tighter. "Breathe through your nose, Diana. Easy, omega."

She groans but does what I tell her, my cock still spurting cum down her throat.

A needy pant leaves my lips as I sit back on my heels, giving her the space to move.

My dick leaves Diana's mouth with a noisy pop, sticky white release dripping from both sides. There are scratches down the length of my cock from her sharp teeth, but it only heightens the pleasure I feel.

Sliding off the precarious ledge into the water once more, I haul Diana into my arms and take her mouth. Kissing is dangerous. Kissing is a deeper connection than pure fucking. I don't kiss omegas. But Diana's pouty lips are swollen from taking me, and the need to suck at them drives me hard.

Diana is an enigma, devious and crafty and wrapped up in an irresistibly strong package. She could be my downfall, but right now? Right now, I don't care. Her lips part the moment mine touch hers, my tongue sliding alongside hers. The taste of my cum mixed with her unique flavor smacks into me as she groans, deepening the kiss with her arms threaded around my neck.

I need to fuck her now with my mouth on hers and her tight body pressed into mine. She fits me so fucking well. Our kiss turns needy, Diana devouring me just as hard as I do her. When she reaches down for my cock, lining it up with her entrance and spearing herself on me, I throw my head back at the ecstasy.

Diana takes that opportunity to bite her way up my neck, fangs sinking into my skin over and over as I buck up into her heat. Her pussy is omega perfection–perfectly hot and tight and responsive to every thrust of my hips. I could claim her right now; gods know my body wants it. But my mind spins with all the ways I underestimated a woman in the past, that move leading me to be stuck in this fucking hellhole.

My eyes find Diana's, but there's no blue left to them. She's still high as a kite on the uppers. I could probably ask her anything right now and get an honest answer.

"Did you recognize me?" she whispers as my thrusts take on a new force. "When you came to see my father all those years ago, we met. I was a child. But you were kind to me. You gave me a rose. Do you remember?" She grunts as I rock my hips harder. "Did you recognize me tonight?" Black eyes are bright on mine as her eyelashes flutter and her pussy clenches.

We're both about to come again. "No," I grunt. "You are a far cry from the bouncy, happy child I met all those years ago, Diana."

Shadows cross her eyes as she pouts, even while I fill her up.

"That doesn't mean I didn't recognize what you *are* to me," I grit out between clenched teeth. I'm on the edge of a sizzling orgasm that's going to obliterate conscious thought from my mind.

"Mine," she snaps as a grating noise thrums through the air.

Womp, womp, womp.

Anguish and irritation skate down our growing bond as Diana's eyes whips from mine to focus behind me. She leaps onto the edge of the pool, dripping water as she looks up into the dark area above us.

"Something is coming," she barks.

The warm air has changed, wind brushing lightly across my face as the thumping noise intensifies. It almost sounds like helicopter blades.

A dark shadow begins to come into view as I hop out of the pool and stand next to Diana. My body screams that something dangerous is coming, and I call to my brothers through our mental bond. *Get in here.*

"This is Rama's doing," Diana snaps. "She must be delivering something to fuck with us."

"What would it be?" I bark out. "Another monster?"

Diana nods as an actual helicopter appears from the dark depths of the abyss, flying down, down, down until it's level with us and I can see what's chained underneath it. A minotaur, a male, trussed up like a plaything but clearly fucking angry. It bellows when it sees us, and as the helicopter womps closer, I can see what's going to happen in slow motion. They're going to throw that fucking thing in here with us. It's enormous. My alpha nature bristles at the intrusion of another alpha male on my territory, in my space, interrupting my playtime.

Diana backs down into the pool, screaming for Cashore as the room's door flies open and monsters rush in: my brothers, Ascelin, Renze, Cashore, and a handful of others.

"What the fuck?" Jet roars. "Is that a godsdamned minotaur?"

Diana nods and turns to me. "It'll be on uppers and probably tortured prior to her setting it loose."

"Aim for the stomach and base of the spine," shouts Ten, drawing his weapons. He takes a step in front of Ascelin as the vampiri rolls her eyes and walks around him to stand by his side.

Gritting my teeth, I nod as the helicopter blades bring it close enough that we can see the pilot inside. He flips a switch, and the chains holding the minotaur begin to swing. When they let go, the monster lands with a splash in the pool, chains flying off him.

He's up far faster than I'd think he could be, bellowing his rage as he looks around the room. Someone leans out of the helicopter and aims an automatic rifle at the minotaur, unleashing a hail of bullets on his back as we all dive for cover to avoid them.

The minotaur roars in pain and leaps out of the pool, crossing the room impossibly fast as Diana leaps out of his way. He's easily twice my height with a man's body but a bull's head, complete with razor-sharp horns.

He came for her. He fucking came for *her* first. But she is mine. He's trying to hurt what's mine.

Red fury clouds my vision as I leap onto the minotaur's back, trying to get my arms around his neck, but he's huge. Probably fifteen feet of pure corded muscle. He reaches around and grabs me like a China doll, throwing me across the room as he rounds on Diana once more. There's a screen inlaid in these quarters just like the one outside mine, and Rama's face pops up onto it, a wicked smile curving her beautiful features.

"Tsk, Noire. Diana will never get you out of there. Best of luck to you, though; we are highly enjoying the show..." The camera pans to a room full of the glittering wealthy, eyes rapt on the screen as they watch the minotaur careen around the room behind me, tossing bodies in his wake, including my brothers'.

At this point I recognize every one of these faces.

I don't bother to tell Rama to fuck off as I turn to find both my brothers attacking the minotaur with their knives. Diana has one of the vampiri swords in her hand, stabbing at the minotaur's core as it roars and shakes the alphas off. It rounds on her again just as Renze and Ascelin leap onto its back, stabbing into its neck with their long swords.

Nothing fucking harms the monster, high as he is. With an angry scream that shakes the chandeliers hanging from the ceiling, the minotaur whips around and grabs Diana in both of his beefy hands, bringing her to his face as he opens his mouth wide.

He's going to fucking bite her. Moving as fast as I can, I barrel into him, knocking him down at the same time as Diana grunts in pain. I hear the cracking of bones that signifies a shift before I sense it in our threadbare bond.

She's fucking shifting. Very few omegas can do it; I've only ever met one—my mother. But right before my godsdamned eyes, Diana's body implodes on itself and a gigantic white direwolf stands in her place. Before the minotaur can right himself, she darts forward and clamps her jaws around his neck and shoulder, ripping into him with astounding ferocity.

He screams in pain as my brothers and I shift and attack at the same time. And then the vampiri get in on the action, stabbing until the minotaur leaps upright, shaking most of us off him.

Except for Diana. She springs off the minotaur's hairy back and bounds off the edge of the pool, using that leverage to catapult her back into his lower legs. He falls to the ground as she swipes her claws across the backs of his knees, ripping tendons as he bellows in pain.

I leap on top of his stomach, clawing over and over again as Diana leaps out of his way. The minotaur rolls fast, unseating me as he grabs her by the scruff and yanks her around to his front.

I hear a crack in her leg joints as her wolf howls in pain. The minotaur tosses her toward the ledge as I roar and fly across the room. I manage to intercept her trajectory as her body hits mine and slides to the ground, both of us narrowly missing the steep cliff's edge.

The vampiri rush the minotaur again, crowding on top of him like lions as he struggles against the torn tendons behind his knees. He goes down with a grunt as Jet and Ten join the fray, biting and clawing at his throat and stomach until he's a roaring mess of blood and torn flesh.

The sloppy sounds of sharp teeth ripping flesh from bone ring through the air as I cradle Diana in my arms. Her wolf whines as I shift back to alpha form and stroke her cheek. "Foolish girl, taking on that monster. Shift for me, Diana."

She obeys, screaming as her human voice returns. Her left arm dangles, clearly dislocated from its socket as Ten and Jet leave the fray and pace across the room, sitting to watch us in wolf form.

Looking up at Jet, I scowl. "Shift and help me with her arm."

A crack rends the air, and Jet's alpha form stands there once more. He crouches down by Diana as I start up a purr, tipping her chin to look at me. "Eyes on me, omega. Tell me what happened when I came to visit your father."

I remember what happened, of course, but I need to distract her while Jet resets her arm.

Diana grunts in pain when Jet grips her arm in one hand and places the other on her shoulder. Licking her lips, she looks up at me. "I was seven, and you had recently taken over. You came to my father for–" Her words cut off in a scream as Jet shoves her arm up swiftly back into its socket. The scream dies off into a sob as I haul her up into my arms, capturing her mouth.

I don't know how to be gentle, and frankly, I don't care to be that way. But in this moment, I devour her lips with a tenderness I didn't think existed in me. She sinks into my heat, tears streaming down her face as she pours pain and need into the strengthening bond between us. I take that pain and banish it with my kiss, and our connection turns into a tether, stronger and more insistent.

Comforting her is stoking the flames of what already exists between us. It's a dangerous game, but I find myself wanting to jump headfirst into that tie to bask in its glory. What could she and I be, if we unleashed one another?

"When did you first learn you could shift?" I murmur, stroking tears away from her cheeks as she smiles softly.

"You shifted and ran with your brothers when you visited our pack. I watched you and wondered if I could do it, and I could. But my father cautioned me that it's a rare ability and that alphas would want to control me. I've never shifted again until now."

"Still surprising us," Jet murmurs, alluding to his earlier comment in the sulfur pools beside us.

Diana's tears stop, so I stand with her still in my arms. Ten comes over with Diana's skirt and hands it to me. Without taking my eyes from hers, I lean in and wrap the skirt around her waist, clipping it in the back. She shakes her head and unclips it, letting it fall to the ground.

Tear-stained blue eyes flutter at the proximity of my lips to hers again.

I've got to get out of this shithole. I want space and time and safety to explore every reaction I can drag out of this woman. I want to know every fucking secret she keeps and holds close to her heart.

Diana moves quietly across the room, running her hands along the wall until she gets to a stone with two interlocked circles on it.

Jet snorts. "Don't tell me you've got an extra skirt inside the wall?"

She smiles at him as she depresses the stones around it in a sequence, and it swings out like a door. Diana reaches in and pulls out a small black disk, crossing the room to us as the vampiri crowd surrounds us to see what she's retrieved. "Ten, peel off the sticky side and put it in the middle of my back, please."

Ten glances at me for permission as I growl, but I give it because I'm curious to see what new toy she found that's been here in the maze the whole godsdamned time. She's so full of secrets that I'm not even surprised at this point.

Ten peels a sticky layer off the thick disk and places it gently in the middle of Diana's back, but she keeps her eyes on mine the whole time.

I take a step closer and tilt her chin up so she's forced to throw her head back and look at me. Diana's lips part as I lean in and nip at the lower one, but then I feel a rush of air and step back.

The disk at her back unfurls into long black ribbons that slide up and over her shoulders, crisscrossing over her breasts and down below her hips. Ten, Jet, and I watch in utter shock as the ribbons lock together with a zipping sound until they form what appears to be one complete piece of fabric.

A long-sleeved, skintight black shirt covers Diana's upper body, and the same fabric forms pants that extend all the way to her bare feet. The texture reminds me of shark skin but has the faintest of sheens to it. Reaching out in wonder, I touch the fabric and feel a slight electric zing.

Jet's the first to speak. "What the hell, Diana?"

"Nanite clothing." She winks at me. "My father never trusted Rama, and there are useful items here and there if one knows where to look."

I grunt my acknowledgment as Ten reaches out to touch the fabric in wonder. "I cannot wait to see what has happened in the outside world in the last seven years. This is…amazing. Is there more like this?"

Diana turns to him with a soft smile. "So many books, Ten. So much art. There's a whole world for you to explore, and I will get you out of here to explore it, if I can."

Ten's smile broadens as he nods at Diana. There's so much hope in his face, and the skeptical side of my personality wants to remind him there's a very good chance we won't make it out of here. I'm a realist, but I find myself unable to squash that dream for him. So what if this is the end for us, and he lives it hopeful and looking forward to the future?

Cashore comes up to us, blood trailing down his jaw as he licks blood off his lips. "Mmm, minotaur is the delicacy I didn't know I needed."

Jet fakes a gag as Cashore winks at him. "What have you been eating this entire time if not the meat that comes into the maze?"

"Sushi." Ten chuckles, glancing over at what remains of the minotaur. Most of the vampiri are on their hands and knees at this point, ripping the last shreds of meat from the minotaur's bones as the maulin hover around the edges. The moment the vampiri are sated, the maulin will crowd in and pick the bones and floor clean, dragging what remains of the minotaur somewhere. In the last seven years, I've learned they hoard bones, but to what purpose, I'm unsure.

Except for the bones of my brother. Those they saved for the stunning omega standing in front of me in a skintight superhero suit.

CHAPTER 14
DIANA

I'm surprised when Rama doesn't come back on the screen in Cashore's quarters to rail about the death of the minotaur. She's been saving him up for the right use for a while, torturing him with spiked chains and uppers. I couldn't do anything for him, just like I've been helpless to do anything for any of the monsters imprisoned here. I profile them; I recommend when to use them. I watch their psych evals come through and change and recommend them again.

Until now. I plotted and planned for years to get to the point where I could get the alphas out. It's my full intention to let the other monsters free if I can.

Turning my gaze back to Noire, I sense his mind is back on our mission: getting the fuck out of here. Despite renewed urgency, I can't stop my mind from returning to our time in the water. Noire is alpha perfection in the bedroom–dominant, strong, violent, playful. When he dangled me over the fucking ledge, I nearly came from the sheer terror of my life being in his hands. Rubbing my hand over my chest, I notice the connection between us is stronger now, clearer.

I wonder if it feels different to him? If it feels good...or if he's conflicted.

The minotaur was a distraction meant to slow us down. Rama is probably bricking up the few exits she knows about as we speak. Father made sure she never knew about them all, but I know she's smart enough to know she wasn't aware of every one of the maze's secrets.

She's a ruthless bitch, and she'll use every resource at her disposal to take me down, given what I'm trying to do. I'm simply evening the playing field by bringing the monsters to this war.

I turn to Cashore and gesture at his people. "We don't know what might be in the lower levels. Are you certain you want to bring everyone? Even the younglings?"

Cashore frowns, and I feel the scrape of his gift at the edges of my mind. "The families wish to stay until we are certain of what lies in the lower levels. It makes me...uneasy. But Renze, Ascelin, and I will go with you. If we determine it's not something else like the naga, we will come back for the younglings."

Ten winks at Ascelin. "Whaddya think, Asc? Ready to head into the fiery depths of the maze?"

"At least it's not fucking cold down there," Ascelin grumbles, Ten snorting at her comment.

"I'd hate to see you drop like a log and have to carry you out." His voice is a deep purr as Ascelin scowls at him.

"If you touch me, I'll chop your dick off and feed it to the maulin."

Jet laughs at their banter. "God, we need to get Ten in front of some omegas, stat. This is fucking painful to watch."

Chuckling, I take a knife from Noire's holster and slide it into a strap at my thigh as his brows rise.

"You have them all; I need one," I respond with a raise of my own brows. If Noire dislikes my sass, he isn't saying anything just now. Through the bond linking us, I feel something like wary interest. He isn't sure what to make of me after everything that's happened.

Good. I hope he never stops wondering if there are more layers of me to uncover. I want him to spend years unraveling every one of my intimate secrets. I've wanted that since I was seven and he was twenty. He handed me a rose when I met him in my father's garden. I knew he was mine then, and I've waited years for him. I should have been too young to think of him that way, but a bondmate is a rare and powerful thing.

I suspect the only reason he didn't know it then is because I was so young. He wouldn't have looked at me that way yet.

Turning back to Cashore, I gesture at Ascelin and Renze. "Your people aren't safe now that Rama knows we're working together to get out. Someone should stay to guard them, especially the younglings. The rest of us can go to the lower levels and open the gate to the next section that has an exit."

Cashore frowns and looks at Renze and Ascelin before glancing back at me. "What is Rama capable of that you think the vampiri here cannot defend themselves?"

I appreciate that he doesn't assume they're invincible. Nobody is. Not in this place. "There's every chance she's already inserting new monsters we haven't seen into the maze. She has a stable full that she's conditioned for years for situations like this, or if it's something the clients want. She has traveled nearly every inch of our world looking for monsters to kidnap and put here."

Behind me, Noire bumps my back with his chest and growls, bringing his teeth to my shoulder and nipping. "What is she likely to put in the maze next? Would you have any idea, profiler?"

I blanch at my former title but lean into Noire's heat, leveling my gaze on Cashore. "She's got manangal, fifty or sixty maybe? They were a client request, but he ended up being a mark before she needed them. I've profiled four or five types of monsters that clients haven't ended up picking, but I've always assumed Rama keeps them around just in case."

Cashore hisses in a disbelieving breath as he runs both black-clawed hands through his hair. Next to him, Renze and Ascelin snarl and glance around as if the very mention of the vampiric monsters gives them the heebie-jeebies.

"The fuck is a mangal?" snaps Jet, looking from me to Ten, who sighs as if he can't believe his brother isn't aware of every monster in the world.

Renze turns to Jet with a slow, deliberate frown. "*Manangal* are distant cousins of the vampiri. They can separate their upper body from their lower and fly. Throughout history, manangal and vampiri have fought, and vampiri were manangal slaves for thousands of years before a bloody war to free ourselves. There's a lot of history there. Manangal have never left the depths of the Tempang."

"They eat vampiri," snaps Ascelin. "One of the few monsters who would try that because of our venom. But manangal are strong, and our group is relatively small. We would likely not succeed in fighting fifty of them. Godsdamnit," she huffs, throwing her head back with a snarl.

Ten watches the frustrated warrior with a thoughtful expression on his face.

Renze reaches out and places his big hand on her lower back, the way a brother might, standing in silence as Cashore looks back at me. "Diana, are there ways for me to hide my people here in our quarters while we check the plausibility of the next exit? Secret passages or secret rooms? What are my options?"

I frown at the vampiri king. "There is a room above your quarters, but Rama is aware of it. There's no exit, so she couldn't put a monster in with your people, but they would not be able to escape either."

I don't think Cashore could pale any further, but he strides out of the room, I presume to speak with his people.

Ascelin and Renze follow him without a backward glance as Noire turns to face me. "Did you tell him the whole truth?"

Nodding, I meet Noire's eyes, willing the truth to show through. Through our blossoming connection, I push the knowledge I have, hoping he can read it.

A sliver of acceptance crosses his gaze, but his frown deepens. "Hear this, Diana. We may need the vampiri to get out of here, but if it comes to us or them, it's us. Do you understand? We cannot take on fifty of those monsters at once."

I nod again, tears filling my eyes when I think about children growing up in this maze. I grew up in a maze of a different sort, tortured and destroyed by Rama. I never want that for another child. I can't leave people behind if I have any choice at all, no matter what I'm saying out loud.

Noire cocks his head to the side as if he still doesn't understand me, but nods. As a group, we turn to leave the room. I click to the maulin who still linger in the shadows, waiting their turn with the minotaur's remains. When they hear me, they flow out of every dark shadow in the room and descend upon the battered body, ripping into what's left of the monster.

When I turn to my alphas, I see something like awe and interest from Jet and Ten. But Noire's face is a mask of controlled desire when he looks at me. It sends my thoughts to his rut, wondering if he's still suffering from being on the verge of it and getting pulled out.

Now isn't the time to test his limits, but I aim to–as soon as it's safe.

We leave the room to the sound of the maulin scraping flesh from bones behind us.

In the main part of the dark living quarters, Cashore speaks urgently with Ascelin, Renze, and three other vampiri. I've watched him consult them over the years. It's interesting to me that while Cashore is the equivalent of the king or alpha here, the vampiri rule themselves almost democratically. At least, if what's televised by Rama is any indication.

I'd laugh if I didn't find it admirable how devoted he is to his people, even after so many years in this place.

"Cashore, it's time," Noire barks out as the vampiri turns with a snarl, crossing the black carpet soundlessly as he snaps dark teeth at Noire.

"Go, I will catch up with you. I need to settle things with my people. It will take me a few minutes. If you cannot possibly wait a moment longer, just go. I know where you'll be."

Noire shrugs and turns, striding from the room without a backward glance.

Jet winks at Renze and then follows Noire out the door, although Ten stays with me, hovering protectively by my side. Odd how much things have changed since several hours ago.

Looking at the vampiri, I give them a sad smile. "I can't imagine the lower levels will be free of monsters. There's every chance this could go poorly, but I wouldn't leave your people here either. You're almost better to keep on the move. The faster we get out of here, the better. It takes Rama some hours to organize the manangal; they're difficult to control, as you know. But she's had hours at this point. She could put them in here at any moment. Or something else, something worse. She has many, many options."

Cashore grits his teeth and nods. "I sense your honesty, Diana, thank you. We will catch up shortly."

It's a dismissal, so I dip my head and turn with Ten, jogging until we catch up to Noire, who barks at me immediately, with Jet at his side. "Is there a quicker way down to the lower levels than through the chapel?"

I shake my head. "Not without going back down to the naga's room and through a long hallway. But the opening for the door is on the opposite side. There's no good way around this, and the next closest exit is in the depths of the trench outside the vampiri quarters. I want to avoid that level at all costs."

"Of fucking course," Noire growls. "Why the fuck did your father build this place this way?"

Anger flares in my gut then. Anger that my father worked for the monstrous woman who controls this place. Anger that he didn't see she planned to kill him. Anger at her for killing Dore and making me an orphan in every sense of the word. I'm suddenly angry at everything.

Rounding on the alpha, I snap my good hand out and jab a finger deep into his muscular chest. "It kept you in, didn't it? That was its only purpose."

Noire doesn't miss a beat, grabbing my hand and twisting it until I have to bend my entire upper body to follow my wrist. I yip as he uses the momentum to swing me up against the wall, my head cracking against the black stones.

Jet and Tenebris continue up the hallway, silent as church mice.

"Traitors!" I yell up into the darkness after them, tears springing to my eyes as Noire twists my wrist harder.

A snarl rumbles out of his throat, his fangs elongating as he brings his lips to hover over mine. "They've never seen me with an omega like this, but even they can tell when discipline is coming. They don't need to be here to see it."

Discipline?

"We don't have time for this, Noire," I snap as he sinks his teeth into my throat right under my chin. Blood wells up in my mouth, choking me as he squeezes tight enough that I can't breathe. One big claw slices a hole in the back of my gods-damned outfit, Noire sliding a hand in and down. He stuffs two fingers into my ass, dry, as he bites harder at my neck.

Black dots flash across my vision as I struggle to move, but I can't. His fingers probe, stretching and hurting as I struggle to find my breath around his bite. Noire growls, and the vibration of it rumbles my chest, my nipples pebbling despite the fact that he could kill me now.

Noire releases the bite as my head starts to fall to the side, my vision sliding to black. A slap rings out against my cheek as I suck in a deep, gasping breath, my head flying up. The moment my eyes find his, Noire smiles a wicked, evil smile that makes me want to back away from him. But I can't, because when I do, he slides another finger into my ass and moves, and the pinch fucking hurts.

"You feel that, Diana? That's a hint of what I'll do to your ass if you continue to defy me. You think you have some power here because you know the way out, but it's simply not true. I will always be the alpha when it comes to us."

I squirm against the invasion of Noire's fingers as he leans in and nips at my lower lip, tugging it so hard that I pant out a huffy breath as he chuckles. "You came down here for me; you came into this maze to find me and get fucked by me. Never forget which of us has the real power in this situation." He steps back, sliding his fingers out of my ass, which he slaps hard enough for the noise to ring up the hallway.

Gesturing in the direction Jet and Ten left, he snaps his teeth at me suggestively. "Go. Now, Diana."

Rubbing my ass, I hold in the grumble I wish I was brave enough to emit right now and trot up the hallway until I catch up with the rest of our pack.

CHAPTER 15
NOIRE

I'm certain Diana isn't done testing me, not by a long shot. Even now with a sore ass and blood still trailing down her chest, lustful need rolls off her in pheromone-laced waves that have my dick hard as a rock in my pants.

I've been in this maze a long time, and it turns out even I'm not immune to the power of a beautiful fucking omega. Knowing my bondmate walks in front of me and I haven't claimed her as my own is driving me wild. My people told bedtime stories of fated bondmates, how claiming one another can unleash incredible powers, how it can make them both stronger and faster. How it changes the shift in ways that are different for every couple. I've only ever known two bonded pairs.

Diana moves quietly in front of me, glancing over her shoulder every so often as I stalk behind her, keeping my eyes on the maze. It's quiet. Too fucking quiet.

Diana leads us through the chapel, only pausing when we hear a scraping, scratching noise. Jet and Ten stop at the same moment as Diana.

"What is that?" Her voice is barely a whisper.

Around us, the chapel is eerily quiet. Even the maulin who

have a nest here are making no sound at all. Light shines in through what remains of the stained-glass windows, illuminating the church in a dramatic glow. The maze is built that way to really put on a show for clients who want to see a mark finished here on the altar. Alborada roses crowd the entire dais, growing up the walls and framing the windows. It's a hauntingly beautiful, eerie place.

The floor is still littered with glass from the panes I broke earlier. One of the remaining stained-glass windows breaks with a deafening crash as Ten flings himself on top of Diana, knocking her to the ground. Winged bodies flood through the broken glass, filling the front of the chapel. Dozens of monsters leap in through the windows and turn as one toward us.

Rama's face pops up on a screen behind the altar, and she laughs. That's it; that's all.

They must be the manangals. Long, leathery splotched limbs hang from thin, emaciated bodies. Their faces have two small eyes and a huge mouth full of translucent dark teeth.

The creatures go wild at the sound of Rama's voice and begin to shed their lower halves, just as Cashore explained. We all watch in horrified disgust as the animals separate the lower halves of their bodies from the upper, legs and intestines hitting the ground with a squelch. Then the legs shudder and shift and stand on their fucking own, charging toward us as the top halves' wings beat the air. The monsters shriek and hiss, and the legs seem to respond, veering into formation as they attempt to herd us into a group.

"Shit, we need to hide," screams Diana. But where? The whole point of this place is there is nowhere to hide, except for the tunnel underneath the altar where we went down before.

Diana reads my thoughts at the same time, but the monsters hover around the altar, still splitting in two.

Monstrous lower limbs stretch and snap loose as one of the manangal rockets through the air toward us with a shriek. Its arms are too long, too thin, with pale skin stretched over impossible-shaped bones. It's the least human thing I've ever seen. The legs scuttle quickly toward us on the floor.

The monster heads directly for me, most likely sensing I'm the biggest threat. But Diana surprises it when she leaps on its back and slams a blade through its skull. More manangal separate and shriek toward us, but the majority fly straight past us for the hallway.

"They just want us out of the way, why?" snaps Ten as he stabs a creature and watches it fall to the ground, others barreling past us as the sound of their wings hitting the walls rings through the chapel. Even the detached legs brush past us with spider-like hitched movements, following the upper halves out the front door.

The last wave floods through as Diana's face pales. "Cashore. They're going after them. We have to go back!"

"No!" I snap. "Better for them to be distracted. Let's go."

"No!" she barks. "We can't leave them. Younglings, Noire. I said I'd help them get out. I said I'd help, Noire! There are children in there!"

"And I told you that when push came to shove, it was us or them. What do you imagine we'll do, Diana? Beat fifty or sixty of those monsters? Some or all of us will die in that process. I told you not ten minutes ago that we would leave them if we had to. Get moving. Right the fuck now."

Diana glares daggers at me, but I learned long ago that it's every monster for himself in the Temple Maze. I'm an asshole, but I need to give my pack the best chance of getting free. A huge pack of vampiri is not what we need slowing us down, giving Rama more time to get creative.

"I won't repeat myself," I bark at Diana, letting an alpha command roll off my tongue to slap her.

She blanches under that particular power but the vehemence in her eyes doesn't dissipate. If anything, she stands taller, but Jet and Ten are already trotting out of the chapel's side door as Diana faces off with me.

I let loose an angry laugh. "If you think I'm going to forget about this, you're wrong."

"I could say the same," she snaps, the earlier wound at her throat starting to bleed again as if even her body wants to remind her what crossing me means.

When I take a step toward her, she blanches and turns, jogging after my brothers.

"Having fun, Noire?" Rama's voice rings through the empty chapel.

Turning to face my greatest enemy, I smile at her, watching her own smile turn sharp and bitter. "I'll be having all the fun in the world when I rip that smile off your fucking face. See you soon, omega."

Rama's smile falls as she spits into the camera, her voice threaded with violence. "I'm toying with you, Noire. It's been fun to watch you scramble, watch you think you have a hope of getting out. But even Diana doesn't know everything about this maze. Just keep that in mind if you decide she's trustworthy. She betrayed me by trying to get you out; how hard would it be for her to betray you?"

I beam at Rama, throwing up a middle finger as I turn and stride through the chapel's side doors after the devious omega who could very well be my downfall.

Catching up to my pack fast, I urge us on. "Rama is losing her patience," I grumble as Jet nods, his jaw clenched hard. In silence, we move through the maze, down level after level until we're on the edge of the huge doors that mark the end of this part of the maze. After this, the levels are larger, more open. Big enough for a naga to slip through. Or something else.

Diana pauses outside the door, looking at me. "We need to be wary of whatever's down here. We should just assume the lower levels are no longer empty."

I nod my agreement, gesturing for her to continue.

"There's a big room down here with the hot springs pool area. There's a hidden stone gate there we can open with a lever across the pool. When we do that, it'll open into a new section of the maze you've not been into. From there, we've got a few options."

Jet growls next to me as we hear faint voices. The humans. They don't normally come to this side of the maze, but no doubt Rama's offered them something to come after us. I wouldn't usually worry about the humans, but in a large enough group, they're dangerous, even for us.

Diana hears the low voices at the same time we do and swings the door open to the lowest levels. If the humans follow us in here, and there are new monsters, they'll be in for a fucking surprise. I almost hope they do.

We follow Diana through the door, pacing quietly through the lower levels on high alert. I can't scent any other monsters. When we get to the huge grotto that forms the bottommost room, I finally sense something. It's the hair-prickling feeling I get at the back of my spine when there's another predator in the room.

"Something's here," I hiss as Diana pauses behind a column, looking around the room.

"There," she whispers, pointing to a steaming pool of water down below us, even as she winces from the shoulder injury. The entire underground lake is filled with rocks that spout steam into the air. When I look where Diana suggested, I see the very end of a coiled tail tucked around one of the rocks.

"Another naga," hisses Jet. "You've got to be fucking kidding me. And we're coated in that pheromone, right? So we can just assume it's gonna go wild when it's close enough to smell us?"

Diana bites her lip and nods as Ten runs his hands through his wavy hair, growling under his breath.

Suddenly, the hooting calls of the humans ring through the hallways. They did fucking follow us. This is an opportunity.

When I look back, the coiled tail is gone, but across the lake, a naga rises out of the water. Jet gulps next to me. "Didn't realize they could be bigger. This one's the size of a fucking house, Noire. We barely stopped the other one long enough to talk to him."

"Hush," Diana chides, pointing toward the far side of the pool. "See that side pool there? The door handle to open the gate between the two sections is there. That's where we need to go."

"Yeah, let me just stroll down there and see if it'll let me take a fucking swim, Diana. How do you propose we do this?" Jet glares at Diana, but she glances at him with a wry smile.

"Bait, Jet. We need bait."

"Well, the humans are coming," I offer, pointing behind me. Even now, their catcalls are getting louder as they follow us. I'm surprised Rama didn't let them in on what they're heading into, but I suspect at this point, she's throwing everything she can at us.

Diana looks behind me. "This is not ideal. Once we open that gate, it's just one long hallway to another large area. We don't know what's there, so if we get stuck between two huge monsters, we're fucked."

"I'm open to suggestions, omega," I bark back. "How did you imagine this going?"

She doesn't answer but looks up at Ten and Jet. "One of you lead the humans here, and I need the other to distract the naga. Noire and I will go across the pool and open the gate."

"I'll distract her," Ten offers.

"Her? How can you even tell?" Jet snorts.

Ten rolls his eyes. "Obviously she has a completely different shaped hood than the male. She's twice his size. She's clearly a female, probably the queen. Get educated, asshole."

Jet sighs. "I'll take the humans, I guess. Fuck." He barks out the curse as he trots back toward the dark hallway we came from.

Diana turns to me. "Remember, naga see heat, so stick as close to the steam as possible. There's every chance she'll notice us, but if she does, just try to stay ahead of her."

Nodding, I reach out and brush my fingers against the back of Diana's hand. She shivers but straightens her spine, pale lashes fluttering against her cheeks.

The naga lets out a roar as Ten attempts to distract it. Her pained screams echo around the room—she sounds almost heart-broken. Shit. The fallen naga king must have been her mate. This is bad, really fucking bad.

Diana and I sprint to the far side of the grotto toward the locking mechanism. I hear Ten shouting and pleading with the queen, even as Jet's footsteps echo through the chamber. He and Ten nearly collide as Ten sprints ahead of the female naga. Tumbling to the ground, she whips the end of her tail out, cracking it across Jet's back as he screams.

True fear for my brothers urges me on. *Get the door open; we just need to get the door open.* At that moment, a horde of humans piles into the room, roaring in triumph before they slide to a halt. They can't stop the momentum of the crowd, so the unfortunate males at the front go down in a tumble right in front of the naga female.

She screams in anger, whipping her coils out as she dives right into the group of humans, cleaving bodies in two as she throws men left and right. The humans scream and scramble, but there's no escaping her. Some make it back out the door, but I urge Diana on, leaping across the last pool dividing us from the gate lock. When I get to it, Diana screams for Jet and Ten as they flee the queen and run to meet us in front of the gate.

Humans follow them as the naga queen roars and fights off dozens of humans who stab at her with knives, desperately attempting to overpower her.

"Help me with the lever, Noire," Diana gasps as she grips it in both hands and yanks. It doesn't move until I put all the force of my body behind a push from the front of the lever. With a heaving crack, it gives away, and we hear the maze begin to rumble and change.

"Go, go!" screams Diana as we take off for the hidden gate, humans crowding in front of it with Jet and Ten, surrounding my brothers even as they flee the naga.

With horrifying speed, she coils down the hill toward the gate, bellowing her rage at the attack as a newly revealed stone gate begins to lift slowly.

"Fuck, fuck, fuck," Diana hisses out as we pile in a mass of bodies in front of the gate. But it's opening slowly, too slowly.

The queen gets to us first, whipping her tail out as she slashes across the gate with the barbed end. Most of us duck in time, but she manages to eviscerate a group of humans as they fall to the ground screaming. I shove Diana through the widening gap, shouting for my brothers to join us as we roll underneath the bars.

When we get through, Diana stumbles across wet stones and looks frantically at her tattoo, then at the wall. "Got to shut the gate; we've got to shut the gate," she repeats over and over to herself as Jet and Ten stand tense next to me, waiting for the queen to realize what we're doing.

Diana yips when she finds the right stone and depresses it, the gate beginning to creak closed.

The moment the noise starts up, the naga queen whips around, tossing humans away from her as she slithers impossibly fast toward us, heading for the gap that's now wide enough to let her through. The gate begins to slide back down as she slithers onto her side, her head and upper body sliding easily through the opening.

"Run, Diana!" I bellow as I shift and leap on the queen, raking my claws across anything I can reach. She crushes me in strong arms as Diana screams my name. I sense Diana shift before I feel her barrel into the queen and me, knocking us all into the wall. The queen's head hits the wall hard, and she slumps to the ground momentarily.

She shakes her head and starts to move toward us again but not fast enough. The gate continues its downward trajectory, and she doesn't get her coils out of the way in time. The black stone moves slowly as she begins screaming and thrashing, the gate slicing its way inch by inch through her body.

I nudge Diana with my nose away from the queen's thrashing upper body. I have no idea if a naga can survive this, or if we'll still need to fight her.

"She can't regrow an entire body," Ten says behind me, his voice mournful as if he hates to see a creature killed.

On the other side of the chamber, the humans glare at us through holes in the inlaid gate. Most of them lie in pieces on the floor, slippery with blood. But a hissed scream causes them to spin around as Diana sprints to the gate, darting around the naga queen's body as it twitches in the final throes of death. It could only be Cashore and his people.

Seconds later, vampiri stream into the room. In the front, each vampiri carries at least one youngling, Ascelin and Renze flanking the sides as Cashore brings up the rear. Behind him, the manangal hiss and roar, attacking from all sides.

The remaining humans flee around the side of the pools, heading for the far side to get around the oncoming monsters.

Diana scrambles to the stone in the wall, depressing it again as the gate slides back open. I know instinctively that she won't stop until she helps the children, and I find myself drawn to follow her.

"Let's go rescue the vamps." Jet chuckles, always trying to lighten the mood. "We'll never hear the end of it from Diana if we let a youngling get eaten, and they made it this far."

My brothers strip and shift fast as Cashore's group sprints

around the large pool, nearly halfway to us. Diana gets there first, leaping through the air and taking out two manangal with a slice of her claws across their chests. They fall to the ground and flop around as two more separate and dive for her, their leathery wings beating the air as the group keeps running.

Jet and Ten sprint for her with me, Ten breaking off to cover the vampiri carrying the younglings. As soon as he does, Renze splits from the group and spins around, dashing alongside Jet to attack the remaining manangal.

Diana yelps when one of the beasts sinks its fangs into her side, and my vision clouds to red. I barrel into them both, knocking the creature aside before I leap on top of it and rip its head from its shoulders.

Turning to Diana, I find her already up and attacking the remaining manangal, but there are just three left at this point. They seem to decide it's not worth continuing to attack us because they wheel around in the air and speed for the door they came in through.

As a group, Renze, Jet, and Diana turn and follow the fleeing vampiri until we're through the gate once more, depressing the button to shut it once again. Inside the dark stone hall, the vampiri huddle together, hovering protectively around the younglings. Ten sits down like a big dog and nuzzles his way next to Ascelin, sniffing at each youngling, licking a few.

He's trying to calm them.

I wouldn't have expected it, honestly. But then I remember how young he was when Rama threw us in here. I imagine he's seeing himself in these children's faces. It's another reminder that, of my pack members, Ten is the only one with any kindness in his heart. I've got to get him out of here. Ascelin watches him with open shock and surprise on her angular features.

Diana shifts back to human form. "Thank you," she murmurs as she runs a hand up under my shirt. Her blue eyes fill with tears when I reach out and stroke a stray strand of hair away from her sweaty cheek.

"I did not think you would help us," Cashore says, coming around his group to stop in front of Diana and me. "I knew you would not come back when the manangal came for us. I would not have come back either. But I did not think you would help us just now."

Diana turns and stands tall before me. "I could not watch your younglings die, Cashore. I will protect them and see you all to safety if I can. I promise you that."

Despite his earlier assistance in pushing Diana, she seems not to be afraid of the big vampiri king. Cashore takes another step closer to her, too-white eyes narrowing as he looks at her, leaning down so they're face to face.

I snarl, but Cashore smiles, revealing blood-coated black teeth. "You surprise me at every turn, Diana Winthrop. I cannot wait to see how you change Noire for the better."

Diana laughs as I growl and resist the urge to slap the smile off his face.

Cashore smiles at Diana again. "See what I mean? No chest-beating. No grabbing me by my clothes and threatening to kill me. You have made progress already, little omega. He is nearly civilized."

Diana smirks at me but turns and walks to the crowd of vampiri, finding the mother from earlier. "You're still here?" she murmurs to the vampiri woman who responds with a curt nod, a tear sliding down her blood-stained cheek.

Diana reaches out and wipes the tear away, and the vampiri leans into her touch. "I will do everything in my power to get you and your child free of this place. Everything, do you understand?"

The vampiri nods and tucks the child tighter into her chest, leaning forward to press her forehead to Diana's. They hold that pose for a few moments as Cashore watches next to me.

We're frozen, all of us alpha males watching the only omega in this whole place comfort a grieving mother.

Mine. Diana is mine. My queen. A natural ruler. She cares for others in the way an omega should, a way alphas aren't wired to. I know it, watching her caress the child's face in a way that would never occur to me to do.

"That's right," Cashore whispers next to me. "She knows it. Now you know it. So do something about it."

The threads were there earlier, that insistent tug of my body demanding I recognize her. But I didn't allow myself to believe it, to fully accept it, until this moment. The ghost of a smile turns my lips upward. "Diana, what's next?"

Diana turns from the vampiri woman, reaching out to brush the back of her hand across the child's cheek. My thoughts turn to her belly swollen with my own child, watching her birth, feed, and raise my sons and daughters. That's the future I want, the future I will take if I have anything to say about it. She will be mine before this is done.

She looks down at the tattoo running up her hand, following a line as she looks around the hall and points to an open alcove. "There, we follow that for a long time; it takes us around the edges of the maze. I don't know for sure what monsters are down there these days, but we'll just have to be quiet and careful. It's designed for water-based monsters, if a client has a need for that."

"Like what?" barks Jet.

"Water?" Ten grumbles as he turns to Diana. "How would they get water-based monsters in here? I don't understand. I've never seen any water except for the hot springs."

Diana smiles, but it's sad. "The entire maze is a floating island, Ten. That's why nobody ever knew Rama was building it. She built it out at sea across the Vinituvari coast and dragged it toward Siargao. It now sits right at the mouth of the Kan."

Renze gasps. "Are you saying this entire fucking place is what, underwater?"

Diana nods as Ten barks out a laugh. "Have you just discovered you're claustrophobic, Renze?"

Renze snaps his teeth at Ten, but anxiety threads its way through our family bond. Jet actually is claustrophobic, not that I'd ever mention that aloud to anyone.

Renze snarls, "Couldn't be claustrophobic living in this shithole, but I didn't realize water was an option in here. Diana, how much of the maze have we not seen in our time here?"

She looks upward as she thinks, zipping her bodysuit back up. I want to whine when her soft breasts disappear behind the fabric.

I slap myself mentally. We need to get the fuck out of here.

"You've seen about half the maze, give or take?"

Jet and the vampiri collectively gasp.

Cashore's gift scratches at the edges of my mind, and when Diana blanches, I know he's doing the same to her. "Do we even want to know what lies in the other half?"

"Stay out of my omega's head," I snap out in warning as he chuckles and Diana's face relaxes once more. She gives me a grateful smile before pacing toward me.

Diana smirks at the vampiri king. "Probably not. So let's get the fuck out of here."

Threading my fingers through hers, I tug her into my side as we head into the darkest recesses of the maze.

We walk, our group quiet as Diana and I bring up the rear, saying nothing. But the whole time I focus on her, on what I can read from her. Fear, anger, determination, and darkness thread themselves through her emotions. I think back to Cashore's comment about reading her being hard because of likely psychological trauma.

Whatever I need to burn down to fix the world for her, I'll do it.

CHAPTER 16
NOIRE

Our group is quiet, naturally falling into a circle around the vampiri carrying the younglings. It's odd to behave like a pack with the monsters who were my greatest competitors in this place. Cashore and I have been spitting insults at one another for seven years. Yet, now my brothers and bondmate protect his younglings.

He was right about one thing: Diana is changing me in ways I am unprepared for.

Yet I am not trying to stop it. If anything, the need to claim and mark her, to fully bond with her, is driving me wild. My father was a terrible alpha–heartless, callous, and cruel. I don't have to be that. I don't *want* to be that. I want to be something better for the omega who walks quietly in front of me.

"Where to, fearless leader?" Jet jokes as he and Ten hover protectively around Diana.

She's changing all of us.

Diana looks at the part of her tattoo that travels down her forearm, then points along the hallway. "We follow this for a long time, and then we'll come to a big cliff. We need to climb it, and there's an exit at the top."

"What could we run across monster-wise in this part of the maze?" I ask, tilting her chin up so I can look at her.

I need to claim you, I think, pushing my need through our bond, wondering how much she can read since we aren't formally tethered.

Diana's lips part, back arching so she sinks into my chest, one hand coming to my arm. We can't speak in one another's minds, but she senses my need. She looks up at me, concern slinking its way along our blossoming connection. "The cold-climate monsters live on this side of the maze. It's almost completely cut off from your side, with the exception of this hallway and an area at the bottom of the abyss outside the vampiri quarters. I don't know everything Rama could have put in this side, but I've profiled kuraokami dragons, wendigo, and there are some species of cold-weather naga, ironically."

"You must be shitting me," Jet barks out, shaking his head as he crosses his arms. "Dragons? Wendigo? Where is she finding these monsters?"

Diana frowns but steps out of my arms. "I assume she ventures into the Tempang for the monsters I've heard of but never seen… Some of the monsters she's caught and put in the maze are myths I heard of as a child. But most myths have some truth to them."

Tenebris nods. "Kuraokami do actually live in the far north. I've never heard of a wendigo outside of folklore though. Maybe it's from a time when the continents were split differently than they are now, so we have stories about them, but we've never run across them."

Cashore hisses at our line of questioning. "Let us continue on. We can't possibly know what she will put in the maze with us."

"Right," barks Jet, frowning at Renze. "We can assume it'll suck, and that's about it."

"And not even in a fun way," Renze quips back, winking at my brother.

Jet rolls his eyes but looks away, his eyes falling on Diana's tattoo as she references it once more. Looking up the hallway, she points. "We head in this direction for a while. It may start to get cold, so we'll stick close together, okay?"

Renze looks over at Jet again, so I growl with my sneer directed at him. I won't call out his attention toward my brother, but it has not gone unnoticed by me. Renze's black brows travel upward, but then he looks back at Diana.

Our group begins moving, Diana and the younglings safe in the center. Cashore and I bring up the rear, Jet and Ascelin on one side, Ten and Renze at the front.

Cameras embedded into the ceiling swivel to follow us, reminding me that Rama watches our every move. There may be some places in the maze she cannot see, but I'd bet they're few and far between. For half an hour, we walk without saying a word until we round a corner and light fills the stone tunnel ahead.

One entire wall of the hallway is an enormous plate-glass window, and outside that window, the waters of the bay teem with life. Fish swim; a whale passes lazily by. Life goes on, despite everything that's happened here in the fucking maze. It's…normal. It's the first time I've seen the waters of my home-land in any form since Rama threw us in the maze.

"Water," Jet breathes. "It's the fucking bay, isn't it?" He turns from the front, eyes landing on Diana as she nods.

Jet and Ten are enamored, going immediately up to the glass to peer out. Diana paces quietly to me as Ten presses his face up against the glass, clearly in awe of what he sees. Anger stabs at my chest, knowing he spent his formative years stuck in the maze with Jet and me, never swimming in the bay, never experiencing all the things he should have.

I growl as I grip Diana's neck, pulling her close to my chest.

She sinks into my heat, a deep purr rumbling between us as I relax and bury my face in her neck, sucking in great breaths of her scent. Home. She smells like home, and peace, and everything I want for myself. She has surprised me at every turn with her resilient strength, bravery, and kindness. Diana is everything I could never be because it's not in my nature.

But it's hers. And I want to possess it and own it and fucking worship it with every inch of myself.

My fingers grip her throat tight as she gasps and throws her head back. Some of our group watch, but most are enthralled with the sea and watching everything outside the window.

"We need to keep moving," Diana rasps as I let up on her throat, brushing my lips across hers.

"Yes," I growl. "You are a distraction, Diana Winthrop."

"I know," she sasses. "I don't like being by these windows. Do you know how easy it would be to—" Her voice cuts off as an explosion rocks the hallway, knocking Diana and me both to the ground, along with the majority of our party.

We leap upright, whipping around to face the windows. But the long window has a black blast mark stretched across it, and a crack that's spouting water right in the middle of the fucking glass. As we watch, the crack lengthens along the middle of the glass, water spouting out from multiple places.

Something is shooting at the fucking window.

"Run!" I bellow, grabbing Diana and sprinting. The vampiri have already taken off, keeping the younglings in the center as the first big crack sends chunks of glass into the center of the hallway. Another crack springs wide and then another, glass flying across the hall like bullets.

Diana sprints ahead of me as I cover her from one side, protecting her with my back to the glass. We make it to the end of the hallway before the entire pane gives way, the sea rushing in, sending water to nip at our ankles as the hall starts to fill.

"How do we get out of here, Diana?" I growl, still running

with her at my side. She looks down at her tattoo, pointing to a corridor up ahead.

"Go right! Go right!"

Up ahead, Cashore whips around with a snarl. "It is a dead-end, Diana. Are you certain?"

"Fucking go right!" I bellow as we sprint along the hallway, water up to my ankles already. The vampiri listen, and sure as shit, when we turn the corner, the hallway ends in a black stone wall crawling with roses.

Cashore snarls, grabbing his head before snapping his teeth at Diana. "If you are lying, so help me…"

"I'm not," Diana barks, striding past him and depressing stones in the wall in a particular sequence. They slip aside, revealing a much smaller hallway that we all crowd into immediately, pushing the younglings first.

As soon as we're all in, Diana presses a stone and the door slides up, although this small room is filling with water as well.

"Diana," Jet huffs. "The water isn't stopping at the fucking door."

"I know, I know," she barks back, eyeing her tattoo. "Give me a fucking minute."

Behind us, the vampiri click and hiss, nervous energy filling the small room as water continues to seep under the door. Next to me, Jet's eyes dart up to mine, and I could scream at what I see there. Concern. Suspicion. Terror. He's worried if this is all some elaborate ruse, and he's going to die in this fucking room, choking on seawater.

"Steady," I growl at him. It was always our code word for "stay calm, stay vigilant, never let your guard down."

The terror eddies away, his face relaxing as he nods at me, gripping his weapons tighter.

Diana depresses another series of stones, and a new doorway opens in the middle of the black stone wall. The moment it does, a blast of cool air hits us, and one of the vampiri groans.

"You must be shitting me," murmurs Renze. "Of fucking course."

"Hush," barks Ascelin, turning to Ten. "You know about monsters; what can we expect if Diana is right?"

Ten peeks his head through the open doorway, but we can't see anything yet, just more stone. "I'll tell ya when I see something to worry about. But most cold-weather monsters are quieter, so keep the chatter to a minimum. It's likely anything we encounter would see body heat, so you're less of a target than our pack."

"Good," she hisses, smiling wickedly at him. Ten winks back as I struggle not to roll my eyes. We've not been around the vampiri for long at all, and I dislike the interest they're showing in my brothers.

"Get moving," I bark as a few of the vampiri peek around the corner.

"More hallways," someone murmurs.

Diana rubs shoulders with the vampiri mother who still holds the child. "Let's get through here and shut this door. Both together should stop the water. Through here is a forest, built for the quieter monsters. We need to pass through it, and then we'll come to the base of a cliff. If we get separated, look for either ruins or a cliff. Both are safe places to stop."

Cashore turns to his people. "You heard Diana; move quietly and with purpose. If we are attacked, find the ruins or the cliff, and do not stop, no matter what you may hear." He turns to Diana with a frown. "An entire underground forest? How did she accomplish this, Diana? Do you know?"

Diana sighs as she looks up at the vampiri. "It could only be magic, although I don't know what kind or how she did it. But Father wouldn't tell me anything about it. Even then, he was scared of what Rama was doing."

"Let's go…" I murmur, pressing my hand against her lower back. I'll ponder the intricacies of the maze later, once we're free. But right now we are still in danger every minute we stand around.

I fucking hate going into a new part of the maze we haven't seen with a large group. We're practically screaming for attention, but I can't change it. Diana glances up at me, gifting me a soft smile as she follows the mother vampiri into the dark hallway. Nobody says a word as we walk, the hallway opening up into a forest.

The underground forest is dark, complete with snow, white-tipped pine trees and near-freezing temperatures. Renze mutters a string of curses under his breath as the vampiri huddle closer together. For half an hour, we pick our way slowly through the ghostly pines, and nobody risks asking Diana a single question.

Jet hovers by my side, Diana in front of us and Ten on the opposite side, when a sound rings out through the quiet–something is crashing through the trees. Something big.

"Run!" I hiss as Cashore spins in the direction of the sound.

The vampiri take off, led by Ascelin and Renze as Ten brings up one side the way I taught him to. Jet takes off when I nod, but a huge beast gallops out of the trees and follows Jet as Diana screams his name.

It's fucking disgusting, whatever it is. Ten feet tall or more, all saggy, crusted long limbs but a distended stomach. Its face is nothing but a skin-covered deer skull topped with razor-sharp antlers. The monster drops to all fours and gallops toward Jet, who dashes to the side but not quickly enough to avoid one of the antlers.

The force of the beast's headbutt throws Jet high up into the air, blood spraying the snow when he crashes to the ground as Cashore, Diana, and I run for him. Then all hell breaks loose. Jet manages to stab the beast in the eye as it whirls on him again, just as I jump on its back and stab it through the skull.

Cashore sprints ahead of us, slowed by the cold but still quick on his feet as more beasts emerge from the forest, attacking the group as we run through the trees. I jump off the beast's back as Diana drags Jet out from under the beast's bleeding head.

Turning toward the group, Diana yells, "Head straight for the ruins!"

Jet leaps upright and starts running, holding his bleeding side as he turns toward me. "Just a scratch, alpha."

Snarling, I push him forward with one hand on his back protectively, he and Diana right in front of me as we chase the monsters chasing the rest of our pack. I couldn't give less of a fuck about the vampiri, but Ten is surrounded by the slower monsters and whatever this shit is that's chasing us.

Diana pants with worry in front of me, and I know she, at least, is thinking of the younglings as well. Ahead of us, dark stone ruins loom in the forest. "Get in!" Diana shouts. "Get in and shut the fucking door!"

I watch as the monsters barrel through the group once, twice, flinging at least two vampiri high in the air and leaving trampled, bloody bodies as they follow the rest of the group. I don't bother to look down as we pass the carnage, still sprinting to catch up with everyone.

Up ahead, Ten watches the group enter the broad front doors of the ruins and looks at the monsters following.

"Close it!" I bellow, praying Diana is right, and this is the best thing to do.

Ten grunts but does as I ask, slamming the door. I hear a lock click from the inside just as the monsters slam into the door, raging and scratching.

Diana veers off before we reach the monsters, sprinting through the woods along the ruined castle until we're on the far side. She slows and examines her tattoo, finding an appropriate stone and pressing it. Immediately, stones slip to the side, and she dashes in, reaching for Jet and pulling him in beside her.

As soon as I pile in beside them, she presses the stone again and the stones slide back into place.

"Jet, how hurt are you?" she barks out, leaning over his side as he groans, lifting his shirt. Even in the darkness, I can see he's deeply bruised, and there's a long slice down his ribs but no puncture, thank fuck.

"I'll survive," he groans, "but it stings like a bitch. What the fuck were those things? I don't recall that from any of my mother's bedtime stories." His voice is wry and angry as he looks at Diana.

"Wendigo," she whispers. "They've been in the maze from the beginning, but never accessible from your side. They're just stuck here. I don't think they've seen any other monsters in seven whole years, although they're not communicative like hybrids. Wendigo are fully feral."

Jet snorts and rolls his eyes. "Feral wendigo. Kuraokami dragons. I'm suddenly thankful we didn't have access to this part of the maze. This shit is wild."

Diana rubs his chest gently and nods. "Rama is a psycho bitch. Let's go up and find everyone else; Ten will be worried about you both."

I nod as she turns and heads up a painfully narrow staircase that puts us out into a big room where the rest of our group huddles. Ten sprints across the room and pulls Jet into his arms. "Thought we lost you, brother."

"Never," Jet whispers. "I'll always be here to bug you, you big asshole."

Ten smiles and claps Jet on the back as Cashore, Renze, and Ascelin come over, looking furious. Cashore is the first to speak as I step protectively in front of Diana. "What did we just witness, Diana? What else lies in this underground forest? We lost two of our own back there."

She surprises me when she rounds on the vampiri king with a snarl. "And yet we protected you so that most of you made it. I never promised we would all escape this place, Cashore. This is dangerous, even for us. You knew that when you chose to follow me."

Cashore stands up taller and snarls, poison dripping off his fangs and melting the snow at his feet. Without saying anything, he turns and strides across the room, checking in with the mothers who still carry younglings.

"Still fucking surprising me," Jet groans as he looks at Diana.

And I smile. Because she truly is the biggest surprise of my life.

CHAPTER 17
DIANA

S afe inside the ruins, I pace the room as the wendigo rage and scratch at the stone door. The vampiri huddle together, keeping the younglings between them as they mourn the loss of their people. I'm irritated at Cashore's anger, but I feel the need to do something. I cross the space to Renze, seeing that Cashore is busy speaking with one of his people.

Renze's white eyes flash when he sees me, and he straightens up off the wall to take a step toward me. "Do you need something, Diana?"

Hurt blooms in my chest for him and his people. So much pain, so much loss in just a day. "I don't know how to comfort your people, Renze. Rama never televised anything but violence, and I don't know the vampiri ways. Can we do anything for you?" Noire's eyes on my back are practically tangible as he watches me.

The vampiri warrior's frown splits into a sad smile, black teeth poking out from behind equally black lips. "Vampiri are tough creatures, Diana. We will mourn when we leave this place. For now, we need to regain some of our power." He glances behind me with a wicked smile, then leans in close. "Do you know how vampiri derive our power?"

I lean in with my own smile. "From being badasses?"

Renze chuckles at that. "That we are. But our power loves sex, Diana. Vampiri are highly lustful creatures. Sex unleashes our gift, so do not be surprised if you see an orgy begin any moment."

I choke back a laugh. "I'm not trying to yuck your yum, Renze, but I'm surprised anyone feels up to it."

The handsome vampiri smiles again and leans in close, keeping an eye on Noire, who I sense crossing the room behind me, unhappy about the vampiri's proximity to my neck.

"Sex is all about connection, Diana. Sex is life. Already I sense my people's need. Why not partake in a little fun of your own while we wait for the monsters to forget us?"

Noire reaches us then, wrapping one big arm around my waist and shoving his way between Renze and me. He says nothing but growls deep in his throat as he pulls my back to his chest.

Renze smirks and takes a step back, leaning up against the wall again, his gaze traveling from us to land on something across the room. I suspect, when I turn, it'll be Jet.

Cashore's gift claws at my mind then. *I am sorry I snapped earlier. Play with your mate, Diana. Join us as we recharge our abilities.* Hearing the king speak directly into my mind is unsettling.

My second thought is the younglings, huddled together quietly in the corner. But when I look over, most of them are asleep, several of the female vampiri standing guard quietly as the rest mill around.

I snarl at Cashore, turning to face him as he walks my way. "Stay out of my mind. I won't tell you again. It's rude."

"Shall I say it out loud then?" the vampiri king barks with a huffy laugh. "You two should go play."

"We need to get out first," I retort, but there's no real belief in what I'm saying. We're stuck inside the ruins for now, until the wendigo give up and leave.

Cashore smiles, a dark and devious thing that twists his black lips into a smirk. "It is just a suggestion, Diana."

Smirking back, I let Noire lead me across the room toward a quiet corner. Through a window that overlooks the abyss, Alborada roses grow, tumbling along the wall onto the ground where they sneak across the floor. I suspect they're the reason Cashore remains on the other side of the room. I lost my fire starter stone to burn them, but his gift will fade if he comes near them and we have no other fire source.

Noire leans against the wall and watches me, dark eyes locked on me.

I point at the roses, nipping at my fingertip before holding the wound over one of the flowers as I smile up at Noire. "Did you know they're carnivorous? They clean the maze of anything the maulin miss…"

A rich red drop of my blood drips down onto the flower, which springs open immediately, greedily sucking the blood down into the center of the flower. I chuckle as the entire wall of flowers starts to shimmer and move. Noire frowns as he watches the roses rustle and shiver.

"These Alborada are the genetic memory of the maze, Noire. They take in all the blood, all the death, and they hold the memories of what happens in here in a sort of collective consciousness."

"They're thinking? Like a person?" Noire sounds highly skeptical as Jet comes over and watches the dark rose suck at my blood.

I think about the best way to explain it. "It's not that they're thinking so much as holding all that genetic material in a repository of sorts. If you could examine the genes of the roses, you'd

find a mix of all the monsters and marks who have ever died
here. Far more marks, of course, but still."

"That's creepy as shit," Jet deadpans, crossing his arms. "Is
there anything Edson didn't think of?"

My heart breaks anew at the mention of my father.

I turn to Jet with a soft smile. "He didn't think Dore and I
would ever be separated. He was always convinced that,
because we were twins and so close, we'd leave this world
together, the same way we entered it. He had the same tattoo
I do."

Jet's face softens, and even Noire takes a step closer, stroking
my cheek. My big alpha will never be a man of beautiful,
romantic words. I know that. But he pushes sorrow for me
through our bond, bringing the tip of his nose to mine, nuzzling
it gently.

I smile up at him, bringing my hands to his chest.

And then I shove him–hard. Noire stumbles back, snarling,
but as he moves forward, the rose vines wrap around his arms,
dragging him back toward the wall.

I sense his irritation at finding they're strong. Really fucking
strong. Tendrils whip around my alpha's upper body, spikes
poking into his skin as I smile at him. Next to me, Jet holds his
hands up and backs away. "I want nothing to do with this. But
they won't like…eat chunks of him, right?"

I snicker as I wink at Jet, who bites his lip and turns as Noire
bellows after him.

"Dare you to ask for help, alpha," I tease with a wink.

Noire struggles against the vines, but they tighten, dragging
him right up against the wall as they snake around his thighs,
neck, and chest. "What the fuck are you playing at, omega?"

I lean in, kissing the center of his chest. "You've fucked with
me a whole lot tonight, alpha. I'm just reminding you that,
regardless of what you say, no matter how many times you dominate me, I'm still a powerful fucking omega. I will never let it

go, never let it slide. It's like you told me earlier. Every little bit of sass from you is a rolling tally in my mind."

"And?" he barks out, sending alpha dominance rolling over me.

I shudder, my head lolling from side to side as a shiver racks my frame. "Gods, I fucking love it when you do that." Prickles along my skin send heat shooting through my core.

"The vines are attaching themselves, Diana," Noire grumbles.

"That's the idea, Noire," I chirp, dropping to my knees in front of him. "Let's mix a little pain with our pleasure, shall we? I feel our bond, and I want to feel it burn while I tease you."

Noire laughs then, a dark and devious sound that tells me I'm in trouble. "When I get free of this, you better run," he snarls as the roses begin to attach to his skin, their thorns slicing through his clothing.

Ignoring the threat, I pull his thick cock out of his pants, feeling it throb in my hand. The vines tighten across Noire's chest when he moves, eliciting a growl from his throat as he snaps his teeth at me, but can't reach.

"The fuck…" he complains, the noise cutting off into a grunt as I slip the tip of his cock between my lips and bite.

Noire bucks his hips as the roses tighten again. I tsk and lift my head, winking at him. "Be still, Noire. Be still, and I'll let you out faster."

With a swift move, I inhale his cock, sucking it deep into my throat as he gasps out in pleasure. I can sense the sting of my teeth alongside the prickle of the vines has his senses on overdrive.

"I'm going to punish you so hard that you won't be walking after this." It's a threat he fully intends to carry out at some point. Later. After I suck him off. Our bond is heavy with glittering lust as Noire huffs out a whine, trying to thrust to meet me but unable to move.

The rose vines yank tight as he strains against them. I sense he needs to move, to rut, to dominate–but I've taken that option from him. Anger heats our bond as I work him over, humming around his cock.

Awareness prickles at the edges of my mind as I snap my eyes open to find we have onlookers hovering to one side: a few of the vampiri, including Cashore and Renze. Noire groans as I cup his balls in both hands and tug them down, the roses biting into his skin at the same time.

Blood wells to the surface as the vines take from my alpha, all while I work at his feet to drive his pleasure higher and higher. His cock pulses in my mouth as I chuckle, and the vines yank tighter, dragging his arms out to the side as the flowers feed on his blood.

Out. He wants out. He wants to flip me over on all fours and take everything, to claim it all. Noire sends image after heady image through our bond until I'm ready to come from the strength of his desire. I don't know if he's even aware of the growing power of our bond, but I relish every fucking image.

His eyes roll back into his head as I moan around his thick length, deep throating it as I swallow. A hiss leaves Noire's lips when he looks down at me, imagining me planning this. That I chose to do this, knowing there will be repercussions, turns him on more than anything I've done so far. I read all that in our bond as it threads tighter, pulling our souls closer together as Noire's pleasure rises.

With a choked roar, my alpha explodes, filling my throat with release as shockwaves ripple through his system. Around us, other soft groans reach my ears. Our audience approves of the show.

My lips pop off Noire's cock as my eyes find his. I wink as a laugh rings out of my throat, Noire straining against the vines again.

I can feel him examining his feelings for me, looking at me

like I'm a puzzle he can't quite figure out. When he speaks, the blood rushes between my thighs, my body lighting up. "I realize now why all the omegas I've met who bowed their heads to me and didn't talk back never interested me. I need a bondmate to push me, to challenge me. Someone as strong as I am. You," he snarls at me as I rise, "it'll only ever be you, omega."

I grin as I hunt around on the floor and finally find a piece of rock that could start a fire. I strike it against the stone wall, initiating a little spark. The vines react immediately, recoiling away from it. I repeat the action as they untwine themselves from around Noire's muscles until there are only a few left and he's able to yank himself free.

I step right into Noire's arms and run my fingertips up his exposed skin, tickling at the blood that wells from hundreds of tiny wounds. Innocent eyes flick to his, eyelashes fluttering as I pout. There's a thread of deviance behind my innocent look. "Are you ready to get going, alpha? I don't hear the wendigo anymore."

A dark laugh leaves Noire's throat. "You know we need to address this before we go anywhere. Are you ready for me, omega?"

CHAPTER 18
NOIRE

Diana flutters her pretty eyelashes at me, but I hear her heart racing in her chest. Her pink tongue peeks out from between pouty, swollen lips to lick at the cum still coating them. Reaching my hand out, I run it up her back, tugging her hair gently as I bite my way up her neck.

Diana sinks into me with a needy moan. She's so willing, so pliant in my arms. But part of me wonders if at any moment she'll pull more shit to try to test me. Not knowing for sure has me rock hard for her. This omega is a maze herself, her mind layered with inconsistencies and riddles.

"I want to pick apart every piece of you. I want to understand how you work," I growl into her ear.

Diana chuckles as I rip a length of rose vine partially from the wall behind her and wrap it around her neck. The laugh chokes off when I swing the vine up and over the nearest archway, hauling Diana's body up into the air, feet dangling inches off the cold, black stones.

She sputters and coughs, gripping at the vines as they begin to attach themselves to her, suckling at her porcelain skin.

Behind Diana, the vampiri and my brothers are rapt watching

Diana struggle. Jet looks bored, and Ten looks…intrigued. The faint sounds of fucking ring out of one corner of the ruins, driving my need higher.

Turning my attention back to the omega, I find her face is flushed red and flushing deeper as I stalk around her in a circle. "Want to play a game, Diana? Let's take this far enough that you pass out. Maybe I'll have my way with you like that. What do you think…?"

She doesn't respond, the swift thunder of her heart reaching my ears as she claws at the vines.

I stand there, monster that I am, and watch her until her movements slow, and then I unzip her catsuit and lean in to suck at her nipples, wrapping her legs around my waist.

Diana attempts to hiss in a deep breath as I haul her body up, both hands on her ass to bring her pussy right to my lips. I bury my tongue between her thighs as she rocks her hips against my mouth. Omega slick drips from her, coating my neck, chin, and teeth. Slurping noises ring around us as I suck Diana off.

Behind her, I hear grunts and groans. Cashore was right, the vampiri are fucking. I hear it. And knowing that Diana and my show inspired that encourages me to attack her clit, bringing her right to the edge of orgasm before slowly dropping her to struggle against the vines again.

She gasps for breath, straining to reach the ground with long, elegant legs as I glance behind her. I watch in surprise as Ten gets in Ascelin's face, tossing her sword aside and backing her up against a wall. The vampiri warrioress doesn't fight it but wraps her arms around Ten's neck as he takes her mouth.

I'm equally unsurprised when Renze turns to my brother and reaches out to cup Jet's cock, squeezing as he shoves Jet up against a wall. What does surprise me is Jet shoving Renze away, and then giving in when the vampiri yanks his head back to lick his way up my brother's neck. But then Jet pushes the vampiri from him and stalks to the opposite side of the ruins, pacing as he watches the vampiri warrior turn to observe him.

Interesting.

I turn back to Diana, her face nearly purple at this point, and spin us to face the party before picking her up again, granting her reprieve. "Watch our people fuck, Diana. Watch what your little show started. Watch while I bury myself inside you and take my pleasure from your body."

Blue eyes flick from me to the room, Diana gasping as she sucks in deep breaths, pupils blowing wide. Cries ring out behind us as the vampiri rage and Ten starts fucking Ascelin, grunting loudly as the vampiri warrioress hisses encouragement. The room is heavy with pheromones as the collective need increases.

Parting Diana's thighs, I slide into her with a quick thrust as she throws her head back and screams. I grip her chin, biting along her collarbone. "Watch them, omega." It's a reminder and a command, and her pussy clenches around me as she watches the show. I drop her lower so the vine cuts her breath again, but her heat locks onto me so damn tight, I barely stop myself from coming.

When she's at the edge of what she can take, I support her again. Her eyes never leave the orgy going on behind me, not even when Ten bellows his release. Diana clenches hard again as I punch into her, over and over. Reaching between us, I pinch her clit with light, teasing touches as she arches her back.

The move pushes her creamy breasts right into my face. So I bite. Over and over, Diana shattering around me as an orgasm barrels down my spine, sending shockwaves of need through me as I scream into her skin, into the blood and spit coating her as I fill her with ropes of my seed.

For the second time tonight, I imagine her body swollen with my pups, and I want it. I want that future where she is mine, and I am hers, and we build something together. My chest heaves with the aftershocks of pleasure as her head comes up, blue eyes locking onto mine. I feel her, feel that thread that binds us together. It shifts and moves in my chest, centering in a stronger way on the omega in my arms. I want to claim her, but not here. For bondmates, the claiming can lead to abilities, and while we could use the extra help, developing the abilities sometimes leads to temporary weakness. We can't risk it, so we wait.

With one hand, I keep her supported, and with the other, I detach the vines from her neck, reveling in the way she hisses as the rose petals release from her skin. She's covered in tiny wounds from the prickly flowers attention.

Hovering over her skin, I lick my way along her wounds, coating her in saliva. Because she's mine, this show of attention will heal her faster. Her forehead falls against my cheek as she rubs hers along mine, a sign of affection between mates.

"Want to watch the show, alpha?" Despite me halfway choking her to death, she's still in a position to tease me.

"Everything about you intrigues me..." It's an admission, something I wouldn't normally tell the woman I'm bedding. But this woman? She isn't like the many others who came before her.

Diana is...everything.

CHAPTER 19
DIANA

N oire and I watch in rapt fascination as the vampiri orgy rages on. Ten finishes fucking Ascelin and then carries her into a dark corner and starts anew. I watch Renze cross the ruins toward Jet, speaking low under his voice. I'm surprised when Jet yanks the vampiri to him with a hand around his throat and devours his mouth, slipping his tongue between Renze's black lips and sucking. They disappear back into the shadows, gripping one another tight.

It's impossibly hot, watching this connection happen. Through it all, Cashore stands in the middle of the room with his eyes closed, his head cocked to the side as if he's listening to the entire thing and is fucking thrilled about it.

Noire is all warm, sated heat behind me, holding me as we lean against the stone archway and listen to the madness.

Renze and Jet eventually join us, and I'm dying to ask what happened. If they took it further, or not. Based on the heated looks Renze is shooting Jet's way, I think not. But I know Jet's been the star of the Atrium for seven years, so his relationship with sex is probably complicated at this point. For the first time in years, he can choose who he wants to fuck.

And tonight is not Renze's night, it seems.

Jet looks over at me and frowns, shaking his head ever so slightly as if to say "don't ask me right now."

I smile softly and nod, wondering if the deepening bond between Noire and me will work with him like their family bond.

Can you hear me? I think, pushing it to Jet, making sure we're looking at one another.

A faint smile tips the corner of his lips up. *Gods, yes, but please don't start questioning me about this asshole trying to get all over me. We can gossip after we get out.*

I smile as Noire leans in and nips at my shoulder, Jet smirking as he watches us. Reaching out, I grab Jet's hand and pull it up to my chest, sending him comfort and affection the way I would Dore if he were still with me.

Tenebris stalks out of the shadows, Ascelin following behind him as she rebraids one entire section of her long hair. She looks…not put together for the first time this entire night. Her white eyes find mine as her lips break into the barest hint of a smile. So the warrior woman has a softer side? The moment I think it, her smile falls as if she's heard my very thoughts. Maybe she has too…

The orgy begins to slow around us, but I notice a small shadow slip over from the corner—one of the younglings. He's tiny, maybe four or five if he were a human child. He looks up at Ascelin with wide white eyes lined with tears.

Next to Ascelin, Ten drops to one knee. "What do you need, little friend?"

The child looks up at Ascelin, who nods once, and then back at Ten. "I woke up and I'm afraid. Are the big monsters still trying to get us?"

Ascelin drops to a knee alongside Ten and reaches out, stroking the backs of her claws along the child's face. Before she can say anything, Ten puts a fingertip underneath the child's chin and tips it up.

"We will protect you, young one. *I* will protect you. Ascelin and Renze and Cashore will protect you. Come here." With a soothing purr, he opens his arms, and the child steps in, lip wavering.

Behind me, Noire is a solid wall of heat and focus as he watches his brother behave so tenderly.

The youngling reaches up, throwing his arms around Ten's neck and burrowing his face just under Ten's ear. Ten hops gently upright and wraps both arms around the child, rocking from side to side as Ascelin watches him, a strained frown on her features.

For a long time, Ten rocks the child, purring deep in his chest as the orgy dies. Nobody says a word as the biggest of my alphas croons and rocks a youngling. When Cashore joins us, his brows tip up as he watches Ten. Next to Ten, I swear Ascelin's cheeks pink up a little.

Cashore turns from the scene and smiles at me. "I have not felt this powerful in many years. Thank you for getting us started, Diana."

Noire's grip on my hip tightens as he snarls. Choking back a laugh, I stroke Noire's forearm as Cashore chuckles.

"I no longer hear the wendigo," Noire purrs. "Let's get the fuck out of here."

Next to us, Cashore nods and hisses out a series of guttural clicks to his people. Several vampiri grab the sleeping younglings, and we head for the door. I open it using the code from my tattoo, and I'm relieved to see the wendigo no longer crowd the hallway leading into the depths of the ruins.

"I hope they're not right on the other fucking side of this wall," Jet whispers, coming to stand next to me.

"Wendigo are foolish and forgetful," Ten offers. "They didn't get in, so they'll move on. But we've got to be careful not to attract their attention. Keep quiet."

Our group falls silent as we make our way through the last

bits of the tunnel, the air growing stale and cool. As we make our way silently through the pines, the cliff looming ahead of us, the vampiri slow. We're going half the speed we were, and while our group is surprisingly quiet, I sense Noire's mounting frustration as we get closer to the cliff.

They're too slow, he barks into my mind as I turn and stroke his forearm.

There are no cameras in this part of the maze. *Rama can only prepare for us to exit somewhere on the maze island,* I reassure him. This new ability to speak in each other's minds is insanely useful.

A hooting call rings somewhere off to our left, and Cashore whips toward the noise, baring black teeth in a snarl that drips venom. His movements are slower than they should be, slower than they'd normally be, and I know without a doubt that whatever is coming will reach our group faster than we're prepared for.

Dashing ahead through the vampiri, I run through a clearing and sprint through the forest, begging Noire to bring up the rear as fast as he can. Reaching into my pocket, I draw out the firestone I found in the ruins, pushing my tired muscles hard as I exit the forest edge and see a line of huge stone horses. The horses mark the very base of the cliff leading to the outside world, a decorative nod to my homeland.

I love you, Father, I send into the universe as I dash toward the statues. Alborada roses, oblivious to the cold, grow in thickets along the base of every statue, crawling their way up to the top. Striking my firestone against one of the statues, I smile when a spark catches one of the roses, the fire immediately traveling along the vines as the roses crackle and hiss.

My group exits the forest edge, Noire sprinting with three younglings in his arms. I'd throw myself at his feet in gratitude if a dozen wendigo weren't galloping through the trees, antlers lowered as they chase my pack.

Screaming in anger, I rush to light the remainder of the roses, a line of roaring fire separating me from my people. Too slow. The vampiri are moving too slow because of the cold. Pressing the button on my suit to undo it, I shift and jump the fire toward the group, just as Noire bellows for me to turn my ass around and run the other way. *I can't, alpha. I can't leave anyone. Please understand,* I beg as I rush past him toward Cashore, bringing up the far rear. I watch the vampiri king turn to face the wendigo, who have now reached the very edge of the forest, coming into full view. They're just as horrifying as the first time I saw them, all saggy skin and long, cracked limbs ending in sharp claws, decaying teeth, and razor-sharp antlers that are their greatest weapon. The last vampiri passes me, running for safety as I sprint for Cashore.

The vampiri king screams in anger, drawing the attention of all the wendigo as they pick up the pace, falling to all fours and running across the clearing toward him. I bark out a warning as I swoop in and grab Cashore up in my teeth, sliding to a stop and scrambling in the other direction. The vampiri king claws his way up my neck and onto my back as we run for the stone bridge.

Noire breezes past me, bellowing his rage as the wendigo crowd behind me. We run as fast as we can, leaping the fire again to cross the bridge. My only hope, my only prayer, is that the wendigo are afraid of the flames. I don't wait to see if the monsters stop, but when Noire brings up the rear, running just behind me in protective formation, my heart is full to bursting.

You are in so much trouble, little girl, he growls into my mind. *Stop risking yourself against impossible odds.*

Spank me later, I snarl back as we fly to the base of the cliff, grabbing my suit along the way.

"Where to, Diana?" Jet barks out as his eyes scan the cliff. If you didn't know what you were looking for, you'd never see the slight pathway built into the side of the black rock face. I fly past him and run up the first few steps as Jet curses creatively.

"This godsdamned place," he huffs, running up the steps as Ten, Renze, and Ascelin urge the rest of the vampiri on. Cashore leaps off my back with a quick pat on my shoulder as Noire shifts and grabs my snout, bringing his fangs right alongside mine.

"You are a wonder, omega."

A screech is the only answer as the first wendigo gets brave enough to leap over the fire and starts barreling up the stone pathway toward us. At this point, a dozen statues are aflame, the roses crackling and screaming as fire licks its way up them. The noise causes the wendigo to halt, and the next one that leaps over the fire backtracks, fire catching its coat and traveling up the beast's shoulder. It runs off into the forest, screaming, little licks of flame catching the trees.

"Go!" Noire barks the command as he grabs my suit and urges me up the path to follow our pack.

I follow the slow group until we're high enough off the ground not to worry about the wendigo leaping up to catch us. Several of them still pace near the fire, but the forest is starting to burn, and most of them have disappeared, trying to escape the flames. Pausing long enough to shift and put my suit on, I smile at Noire as we pace up the steep cliff.

"What next, Diana?" Ten falls behind to question me.

I smile at him. "A steep fucking climb and then freedom, Ten." I turn to Noire and find him smiling. A real smile, the hint of one, anyhow. A joyous smile too, not the wicked, devious thing I've seen many times tonight. "I can't wait for you to see the world again, Noire," I whisper as he reaches out, wrapping fingers around my throat and pulling me close.

A deep alpha purr rolls out of his throat as he brings his nose to my neck and sucks in a deep breath. "I can't wait to see it with you, mate," he whispers. "I want to rediscover every inch of

Siargao with you at my side. I want to fuck you all over my city, Diana."

Chuckling, I wrap my hands in his hair and drag his face up so I can devour his lips. Noire presses me into the rock face and leans down, hoisting me up into his arms as he takes his pleasure from my mouth.

"You two gonna fuck right here, or shall we get the hell out this place?" Ten's salty proclamation draws a growl from Noire, but I rub his chest.

"Ten is right, alpha; let's get the fuck out of here."

Ten smiles. "We're almost free, Noire. I can almost taste fresh air. Can't you?"

CHAPTER 20
NOIRE

My younger brother smiles, and it's the first time he's looked like himself since we got thrown into the maze. That smile reminds me of how he was a child when we were thrown in here, and how he spent all his formative years in this darkness. I don't know what lasting effect that will have on Ten, but we can unpack that later.

"Love you, brother," Ten whispers as he takes a step closer, bowing his head to me respectfully. I'm not even ashamed to find myself overwhelmed with emotion at the thought of getting the fuck out, of seeing my city, and freeing my brothers. Reaching out, I pull Ten into my arms and crush him close.

"I will see your wrongs righted, Ten. I swear that to you."

"I know you will," Ten whispers, clapping me on the back. "I can already smell fresh air, although maybe that's just the hope talking."

"Let's go," Diana urges. "At the top of the cliff, there's a hidden exit from the maze. Rama doesn't know about it, but it's safe to assume she knows we'll come out somewhere on the island."

I nod as Diana pulls herself up the black stone path fast,

making good progress as Jet and I follow her closely. The vampiri are making their way slowly, but without monsters on our tails, I feel less ragey about hurrying them. Tonight's events have produced an unexpected partnership with the vampiri. I'm feeling far less inclined to kill them than I was earlier this evening.

The scent of fresh air is so heady that I don't even register it until Jet groans and picks up the pace.

"My gods," he sighs. "Crisp dawn air. Can you smell that, Noire?"

"We're almost there, brother. Keep going," I growl. I'll hug him at the top.

Jet nods and keeps pulling himself moving up, up, up until Diana disappears over a ledge, looking back over as we pull our way up next to her. Behind her, the stone is intricately carved with the black Alborada roses we've seen everywhere in the maze. Here, they grow again in plentiful bunches, surrounding the entire ledge and trailing out over the edge.

Cashore growls at the sheer abundance of roses as he turns to Diana. "Tell me please that the surface of this godsforsaken maze island isn't covered with these fucking things?"

Diana laughs, and I want to capture that sound and imprint it on my soul. What other happy noises might she make safe and away from this place?

"Just regular tropical forest." She winks at the vampiri as he sighs happily. She steps toward the stone and runs elegant fingers along the roses. When she looks back down at her tattoo, the part that wraps around her wrist, I find myself in awe of her.

Cashore's gift scratches at the edges of my mind, but this time I don't stop it.

Together, you two have a chance of taking Rama down, he whispers into my thoughts. *But you must claim her, Noire. Make Diana whole once more; her soul aches for yours.*

I smile at him as he turns from me to watch her. Around us,

our group is anxious. Renze, Ascelin, Jet, and Ten still hover around the edges, ever watchful, ever guarding. I sense my brothers are strung out; they're in desperate need of several days of sleep.

Diana depresses four stones in a specific order, and they begin to fall away, revealing yet another black stone hallway. If I never see black stone again after tonight, it won't be long enough.

This is different, though. Moonlight seeps through the roof, cool dawn air coming through the holes in the ceiling. I haven't smelled real air from outside in seven years. Sucking in a breath, I find myself blinking in disbelief.

We're nearly out. In my line of work, hope is a luxury I never placed much faith in. There was always planning and being the biggest and baddest. It's what my father prepared me to do, and it's what I've always done. But now? Hope fills my chest. Hope for the future I might have with my omega if we escape Rama and take her down.

"I always thought I'd destroy this place once we got out," I murmur to Diana, stroking a stray pale hair back from her cheek. "But now, I want nothing more than to track down every person who ever paid to send someone in here, who ever watched with pleasure as we were forced into servitude. I want to throw every single one of them in here and watch them get destroyed by the monsters they forced here. What do you think, mate?"

Diana's smile turns wicked and cruel as she smiles back up at me, sinking into my arms. "I've had fantasies every day since I watched Rama kill Dore about how I'd destroy her. And it starts right here in the maze. There is nowhere that she and the wealthy can hide that we can't find them."

A laugh rolls up out of my chest then as I lean in to brush my lips across hers, sliding my tongue along her own as she leans into my attention. "You truly are the omega I didn't know I needed."

"Good," she murmurs back. "Because I came in here with every intention of claiming you, Noire. You're stuck with me for good."

"You can fuck later," Jet snarls from the hallway. "Let's get going. I haven't had a good martini in seven years, and I fucking want one."

Diana giggles. "Seven years without freedom and that's the first thing you want?"

Jet waggles his brows. "First among many things I want when we get out of here. Like a bath and a week of sleep."

Diana's smile falls at Jet's admission, but I thread my fingers through hers and pull her up the hallway toward him. "Let's go, then."

For ten minutes we walk, the scents of the outside world assaulting my nostrils for the first time. I smell salt, water, and grass. I can hear the faint wash of waves; we're close to the shore. Turning to Diana, I nod toward the sounds. "I smell the bay..."

She nods, weaving her fingers tighter through mine. "The island grew fast, so when we get out, you will see cliffs and the sea, and across the bay, you will see Siargao, Noire." Her gaze darkens. "And if you look up over the city, you will see Paraiso, her floating fortress. She entertains the wealthy there."

"I'm still amazed she was able to build all of this without anyone ever knowing..." grumbles Jet.

"We underestimated her," I bark back, my voice sour. "It will never happen again. We will take over this maze and island until we get the retribution we want, and then we'll burn it down."

Diana squeezes my fingers as we reach the end to find another black door, this one all sleek metal, although it's rusted with the passing of time and the salt air.

"You don't know where this comes out?" Jet questions, grabbing Diana's wrist to look at the underneath of it. She stays still for his perusal as I growl at my brother for touching my omega without asking.

Jet's dark eyes find mine as he reaches into his backpack, groaning when he's reminded the naga crushed all his uppers. "My mind is a top spinning around; I need some focus," he snarls as I growl at him again.

"Jet, you're done. You need to get free of that shit. I need you fully here with me, brother."

Jet snarls but glances at Diana, who reaches out and rubs at his chest gently, purring softly to him. His dark eyes flare, lip curling up as he looks at her, but her soft noise seems to soothe him even as I bristle.

"Let's get the fuck out of here," Diana offers, turning to me. She grabs the door handle and swings it open, stepping through into the light. Grinning at my younger brother, I step through after her, reaching out to put one hand on her hip as I follow her into the cool air.

The scents of a jungle assault me immediately, the early dawn light so bright that I nearly fall to the ground at how light it is. Around me, the vampiri bask in the sudden warmth, their faces turned up to the sky as if they can physically will the incoming sun to sink into their cold skin. Diana smiles at me, even as we blink against the light.

"We're deep in the jungle," she whispers. "We still need to get off the island and into town. I don't have a plan for that part, to be honest."

"That's alright, omega," I reassure her. "We'll figure something out." I've never reassured anyone in my fucking life, but I have a deeply pressing need to do so for my female.

Quietly, our group heads for the sound of waves, and my alpha intuition guides us toward the city easily. We're close enough to the mainland that I can faintly hear the sounds of the Riverside District coming to life. Still, my senses are running circles in my mind. Rama hasn't found us yet, but I'm assuming she could at any minute.

We trek through the dense jungle for a few more minutes, passing a series of horse statues identical to the ones deep inside the maze. "We had these back home," Diana whispers to me. "They remind me of my childhood. They're a nod to my favorite mare, Dove. Dore named her the closest possible word he could find to his own name."

I stroke her hair as we pass through a thick stand of trees and into an open courtyard of sorts. It looks like the ruins from inside the maze, but my senses scream at me the moment our group steps inside the open hall.

Something clicks, and a bright light shines on us, blinding our group as Diana yips and sinks back into my arms. Next to me, Jet barks out a curse as I freeze in place, trying to see ahead of us.

The light cuts off just as suddenly as it started, and when it does, a woman stands in front of me across the courtyard.

Rama.

She's paused right inside the ruins, not forty feet from me, hands clasped in front of her waist as if we're meeting for business.

"Hello, alpha," she purrs, smiling from ear to ear as if she couldn't be more pleased to see me. Not a thing separates us, although noise assaults my ears as soldiers drop out of the sky on impossibly long cords, weapons trained on our group.

My body freezes and tightens as I warn Jet and Ten to stay vigilant and get ready to run if we have to.

Rama cocks her head to the side, calling out behind her, "He's here, Arabella. You can come out now."

A human woman steps out of the recessed shadows of the ruins, watching me with barely concealed glee. That's when I notice there's a sheen to the air in front of us.

It's a fucking force field, Diana whispers into my mind,

snarling as she steps closer to me. *Genetically coded to let through only who Rama wants.*

Jet, Ten, and the two vampiri warriors stand in front of the others, who still carry the younglings protectively.

Rama's gaze levels on Diana, her eyes narrowing. "You surprised me, Diana. Your adventure through the maze was costly, but we had an agreement, and I will honor it. Come here, child."

Angst stabs our bond as Diana steps away from me. I'm too busy processing the words that just came out of Rama's mouth to stop her. Diana passes through the odd sheen and stands next to Rama, her fists balled as she looks at the older omega.

Genetically coded to let through only who she wants.

"I'll take my information now," Diana barks, raising her head without looking back at me. Through my bond with her, I search for answers, but it's dark and cold.

She lured us here on purpose. Jet and I realize it at the same time as he roars, "How could you? You promised to get Ten out. You made a fucking promise!"

I refuse to fucking believe it.

Kill her, mate, I whisper into our dark bond. If Diana can hear me, she gives no evidence of it as she squares up to Rama. Anger rises in my chest as I leap forward to follow Diana, only to be blown back by the odd sheen coating the space between our group and Rama's.

Rama laughs as I stand and roar, "What did you do to Diana? What have you done to my mate?" I fling myself at the barrier again and again, blasted back every time, but raging as I try to get to my mate and can't.

Rama laughs and reaches out to tuck a strand of Diana's hair back behind her ear, but I don't miss the flinch when her fingers brush across Diana's face.

Psychological trauma. It's true then, what Cashore said about Diana. Diana balls her fists tight and lifts her head higher, ignoring my onslaught. "My brother. Where is he? You said you'd tell me the truth about him if I got Noire here. Tell me, right the fuck now."

"Your brother is safe, for now," Rama purrs. "I will give you his coordinates once our business here concludes."

Hot rage fills my system, my fists balling as I resist the need to roar at the sky for this fresh betrayal.

Rama laughs as she crosses the courtyard halfway, the human woman in tow behind her, both women smirking at me. Rama speaks first, "What a knife to the gut, Noire. You discover your bondmate, only to find she lured you out of the maze at my behest..." Rama smiles at me again as the other woman steps forward–the human.

"Why?" My demand for answers is an alpha bark that bowls the human over so hard she falls back into Rama, who rolls her eyes and waits for the other female to right herself.

The human, Arabella, rounds on me with a frustrated, angry gaze as the soldiers behind her lift their weapons higher. "You killed my husband, Andre. I hope you fucking suffered tonight. I hope you found your mate and actually thought she was saving you, you monster."

Snorting, I hook my fingers into the front of my pants. "If you say so. I don't know an Andre."

"How can you not remember? You ripped his head from his shoulders and sent it to me!" the woman screams, incensed as Rama watches, dispassionate.

I smile at the angry human. "What a devoted wife you must be, waiting seven whole years to avenge your husband's death..."

The woman screams again angrily, ripping at her own hair as she turns to Rama with a distraught expression. Rama taps the woman on the shoulder as tears begin to stream down her face. "You paid for his misery, Arabella; have you seen enough?"

"It will never be enough," the human spits, glaring daggers at me. "I scrimped and saved every day for seven years to afford this night. I want him to hurt as I did."

Rama smiles again. "Shall we remove his head? Better yet, we can put him in the Atrium and you can fuck him," she offers as the woman's lips curl up into a snarl.

Diana stiffens behind Rama but still doesn't look up at me, not even when the human female continues with a leer at my brothers behind me. "What if we put the alphas together into the Atrium and make them fuck each other?"

Rama laughs at the suggestion, eyes bouncing upward in surprise. "Your mind is darker than I've given you credit for, Arabella. Perhaps you could come work here. We're always trying to think up more theatrics, although Diana has always been the best at that."

Arabella smiles at me as Jet crouches down. Through our bond, he tugs at me. *We need to be ready to run, alpha.* The vampiri are frozen, even though Ten, Cashore, Ascelin, and Renze stand protectively in front of our pack. I'm not ready to let this go, not ready to believe this was all a ruse simply to satisfy a wealthy human's whims.

"What now?" I bark, taking another step as Rama smiles at me.

"When Arabella approached me about targeting you, I knew we needed a creative way to make you suffer. Something more than just killing another brother. What better way than to dangle an omega in her prime and make you think you were actually escaping?"

Cashore speaks up, snarling as he looks from Rama to Diana. "Diana. You knew we'd end up here? You knew, and you let me bring the younglings. I will tear you to fucking shreds."

Diana straightens her spine and lifts her chin as Rama smiles at the vampiri. "Ah, you see, vampiri, I have something Diana wants: information about her twin brother. And my sweet little profiler was willing to do anything once I told her. I directed her to concoct whatever story she had to, to get Noire to follow her out. Her story was good, I'll give her that. You should not have come with her."

"You've got me here, now what?" I bark, unable to stand still any longer as I pace, rage clouding my vision as I watch Diana stand dispassionately next to the other females, refusing to meet my gaze or respond through our tether. Behind me, my brothers and the vampiri are moving, congregating to one side of the ruins as they prepare to flee.

"I think I'll watch you pace another minute before we toss you all back into the maze." Rama smirks back. "Tonight has been fun, seeing that you believed you would escape. But the reality is you're going back in. All of you."

Cashore bellows out an angry roar as Rama's dark eyes flick over toward him, lips splitting into a devious smirk.

"I underestimated you," I admit. "But I will never lie down and take this. If you put us back in, we will get out again, and again, and again."

Rama smiles. "Oh, I'm counting on it, Noire. Counting on us playing this little game until you lose for good. I've hated you since long before my father offered me to you as a prized brood-mare. Deshali was overrun with monsters from the Tempang, and he begged for your help, alpha to alpha. He offered you money and connections, and you turned him down. We were nearly decimated until I put my mind to work creating inventions to kill and imprison monsters. And that gave me an idea, Noire. The idea for the maze. A place where the monsters do *my* bidding. A place where I never again have to rely on alphas to protect me.

"Here's the thing, Noire," Rama continues, pointing toward Diana. "I have a gift, an unusual gift, not that you ever bothered to learn anything about me."

Diana's blue eyes lift then, and she looks at me but says nothing as Jet tugs on our bond.

Something else is coming out of the fucking jungle, Noire. We need to go. This is a godsdamned trap. I still can't bring myself to run, though, not with Rama so close and my lying mate right next to her.

Undeterred, Rama continues, "I can see mate bonds, Noire. I've known Diana belonged with you since the day I killed her father and took her and her brother under my wing. The thing is, I liberated her *from* alphas. She doesn't need you, and it was fucking glorious watching her make the decision to choose her brother over you. Because that's exactly what she did," she spits the words out, her voice full of venom.

"Is she telling the truth?" I turn my gaze from Rama to Diana, who lifts her head and walks across the courtyard, a guard following her with his gun trained on her.

Diana's blue eyes are filled with tears as she raises both arms up imploringly. "She has my brother, Noire. I'm sorry... I, I have no choice. Please understand? Dore is the only thing I have left in this world. She took everything from me." Diana's blue eyes plead for my understanding as I step back, feeling a knife bury itself in my soul and twist as our bond frays.

Behind me, I can hear faint footsteps. Fuck. I sense the approach of something big as the vampiri huddle together, Ascelin and Renze turning to face the forest. Jet is right. Something is coming. My muscles tense as I realize we have very little time left to flee. I'm not going to get any more fucking answers, and I'm not killing Rama today.

Snarling, I turn toward the forest as Rama barks. "What are you looking at?"

I whip back around as a laugh rings out behind Rama.

Diana.

My mate's head is thrown back as she laughs deviously, her eyes trained on Rama, narrowing to an angry slant.

"I have a gift too, bitch," Diana barks at the other omega. "A wildly inventive father who created mechanical horses that look a lot like statues. They're activated by fire, and they're coded for one fucking purpose–to protect me."

Rama narrows her eyes and sputters, but the swift beat of hooves rings through the jungle as our group mills around, facing the oncoming noise, unsure whether or not to run.

"They'll never get through the field, you useless witch," Rama spits as I pace in front of the force field, looking over my shoulder but unwilling to leave my mate, despite her betrayal. Arabella backs away from Rama and runs toward the soldiers as Diana faces off with the older omega, a gun still trained on her back.

I can't get to her. Fear for her life scratches at my mind as my brothers and the vampiri huddle around the younglings behind me.

"That's where you're wrong," Diana hisses, fists balled as her chest heaves. "You see, despite whatever you held over my father's head, he knew my life was in danger. And he wanted to protect Dore and me in the only way he could. The horses are attracted to electricity, the same electricity you use to power this force field, for example, and your city. And the horses fly, you know. So that weapons system I'm assuming you were smart enough to build—well, that will be a great target for them." Diana points upward to the floating, glittering monstrosity that hovers in the clouds up above the maze.

Rama roars in anger just as the first horse emerges from the forest with a horrible grinding screech. Jet, Ten, and I dive to one side, the vampiri sprinting for the edges of the ruins. The horse still looks like a statue, all gray mottled stone with burn marks crawling along its skin. Except now, it moves as if it's alive, heading straight for the sheen that separates me from Diana.

I snarl when the first horse runs straight into the force field, a loud explosion rocking the forest. The field shimmers once but holds. But when the next one hits, Diana laughs and depresses the button on her bodysuit, shifting into her wolf at the same time. Rama's eyes widen in terror as she sprints and screams for the guards who open fire on Diana as I rage and roar outside the force field.

Bullets pepper Diana's hide but don't bring her down as she bounds across the short space, following Rama and barreling through the soldiers, even as more descend through the sky on long cords, shooting at the horses. Immediately, two of the horses split from the herd and lift off the ground, galloping up toward the soldiers, attacking everything they can reach. Bits of the descending soldiers' bodies rain down on us as the horses scream and attack anyone within reach.

I pace in front of the force field, steering clear of the bellowing horses as I roar for Diana, Jet and Ten hovering just behind me. More horses emerge from the jungle, throwing themselves at the force field and starting to pile around the sides of it, looking for Diana to protect her and attracted by the electricity powering the field.

My brothers shift, sensing the field waver tenuously as Diana bulldozes through the soldiers, tossing body parts in the air as she tries to get to Rama. Rama is already hopping into a ship of some sort that's cloaked in the jungle behind the ruins. The human, Arabella, screams to be let in, but Rama pays her no mind.

The field wavers again as I turn to Ten and Jet. "The moment it's down, we go through," I bark urgently as Cashore and Ascelin join us.

"We are with you," Ascelin says simply. "We are with Diana."

The horses roar and scream as I watch Diana push through the last of the soldiers. They continue to shoot at her as her wolf lands on top of the ship Rama is flying, swiping at the top with black claws just as the horses break through the barrier.

With a whoosh, my pack swoops in, overwhelming the soldiers as more continue to drop down from the sky. Rama screams in anger within the small ship as Diana rips into it with angry swipes of her wolf's claws.

Diana, I'm coming, I bark into our bond as I read her furious intent. She's so focused on getting to Rama that she doesn't turn as I leap through the air and help her drag the ship down, the noise of cracking reaching my ears. Hundreds of soldiers drop out of the sky, peppering the ruins with bullets as my brothers and the vampiri fight.

Anger turns my vision red as Rama's ship falls to the ground and splits. I'm shocked to see that she's shifted into a wolf as well. She leaps out of the box, whirling around as Diana lands on top of her, sending the breath from Rama's lungs out in a whoosh. Soldiers round on us as the fight rages behind us, but I can't take my eyes off the fucking woman who terrorized my pack, my people, my mate.

This is my only chance to take her down. I pounce on Rama, knocking Diana out of the way as I send a message to my brothers. *Help me, brothers, if you can. Help me end this.*

The air rings with the sound of the horses as part of the herd merges to form a circle around Diana and me, attacking anything that comes close. Rama roars with rage when my claws slice their way across her wolf's face. I lunge out, gripping Rama's throat in my teeth and biting tight, crushing her airway. The vicious omega grunts as Diana leaps up from where she fell and swipes at the wolf's stomach, opening deep gashes as bits of intestine start to slide out of the wounds.

Suddenly, I'm flying through the air, breath stolen from my lungs as something blasts its way through the horses and hits us. Diana is knocked the opposite way, howling in pain as I struggle to comprehend. A deep whirring noise assaults my ears as I glance up, seeing small, manned ships flying through the air, shooting at everything. Even the horses were blown to the side, although they leap up quickly, several jumping into air to attack the ship as the rest congregate around Diana where she fell.

An enormous clawed scoop grabs up Rama's bleeding, broken wolf, closing and pulling up through the air, darting from side to side to avoid the flying horses.

Another claw darts out of one of the ships and grabs Ten and one of the horses, gripping them both as I roar. The ships turn and flee, leaving behind dozens of soldiers. The vampiri descend on those left behind and rip them to shreds as we crowd together and watch the ships disappear up into the dawn, heading for the floating city.

Diana shifts and flies to one of the horses, ripping a panel open on its side and punching in a series of codes, clutching her chest as if she's in pain. "Reprogram. Got to reprogram. Got to get Ten," she mumbles frantically as I rush to her side.

"That bitch took Ten," Ascelin grits out. "She fucking grabbed him with one of those claws."

"Oh fuck," snarls Jet, running his hands desperately through his hair as Renze comes over, licking blood off his lips.

"What happened?" he barks out, gripping Jet's chin and turning my brother to face him.

"She took Ten," Jet sobs.

I'm out of my mind with grief as I rock Diana, surprised when Renze pulls Jet into his arms and squeezes him close. "We will get your brother back, *atiri*. I promise you this."

"On it!" Diana roars as she snaps the panel shut, the horse taking off like a shot, spreading metallic wings and galloping up through the air. At least half of the mechanical beasts take off after the first, soaring through the sky and attacking the retreating ships. They manage to take down a few, and then we see them climbing up the side of the floating city.

Explosions rock out above us as the horses begin attacking the fortress. I can scarcely believe it when the city begins to move, until it's picking up speed and moving off into the distance at a rapid clip.

"They'll take out…the…weapons systems and, hopefully,

bring the city down," Diana groans before falling to the ground, covered in blood. In the fury of the fight, none of us realized how many times she was actually hit. The soldiers shot Diana dozens of times, and we can see the damage now she's back in human form. At least a few bullets are too close to her heart.

Roaring, I fall to the ground with her in my arms, holding her close to me as a rattling purr vibrates through me. I can't do anything about this–she's dying in my fucking arms, covered in blood. I didn't get to her in time. I couldn't fucking help her.

"Why, Diana?" I question her as she turns her cheek into my chest, smiling at the purr.

When she looks up at me, blue eyes are filled with tears, but she reaches up and places a palm over my heart, blood beginning to seep out of the corner of her mouth. "When you c–came to visit my father all those years ago and gave me a rose, I knew you were mine then."

"You were a child, omega," I whisper, stroking light hair out of her face as she coughs. Jet and the vampiri mill around, and already, I feel the need to protect her from them.

"Horses…will…try…to get Ten." Diana's voice cuts off as her eyes roll back in her head.

Cashore looks from her back to me, kneeling down to place his palm over Diana's forehead.

She looks up at him, gripping his wrist in one bloodied hand. "You're free, vampiri. I promised you I'd do what I could. Help Noire take her down, get Ten back, and then burn this place to the ground."

Cashore smiles down as Diana looks at me again, eyes rolling into the back of her head once more.

Crushing her to my chest, I hold back a sob as I plead to the gods. I'll give anything, anything, to keep my bondmate here with me.

"I can save her, but it will come at a cost, alpha," Cashore purrs at me, sitting back on his heels as Ascelin hisses and comes over.

"My king, you cannot think of leaving us. Not now?"

Jet roars in Ascelin's face, "If there's a single fucking chance to save her and get Ten—"

Ascelin doesn't respond to Jet but drops to a knee next to Cashore, who puts two fingers under her chin.

"You are my successor until the Chosen is ready, Ascelin. You know what to do. There is nothing outside this place for me with my queen gone. I have always intended to get you all out and then follow Zel."

He turns to me, cradling a limp Diana in my arms. "I can gift her my life force, but it will change her in ways we can't foresee."

I growl. "She'd be a vampiri?"

Cashore smiles but shakes his head. "No, it's not a metamorphosis, it's simply a gifting of my soul, a transferring, if you will. She may take on some of my characteristics. It is rarely done among my people."

"It is a great honor," snaps Ascelin as Cashore hushes her, Renze dropping down next to his king.

In that moment, I find myself grateful to the vampiri for the first time. We worked together as much as we had to to get out, but he could easily be leaving this place right now.

"Please," I whisper as blood from Diana's wounds coats my hands.

"She may retain pieces of my personality or gifts," Cashore warns.

"Then when I fuck her, I'll think about you," I bark as Cashore throws his head back, laughing.

He pushes forward, taking Diana out of my arms to lay her on the stone floor. When he climbs on top of her, straddling her body, I resist the urge to yank him off my mate.

Cashore carefully removes his leather vest and long-sleeved

shirt, placing Diana's hand over his heart before he turns to his people. "You heard Diana. Work with Noire to take Rama down so she cannot do this to anyone ever again. Return Tenebris to his family. And then thrive, my people. Thrive..."

Ascelin chokes back a sob as the vampiri gather around them, Cashore chanting a string of words in an ancient vampiri language. I studied it as a child, but I find I remember next to nothing.

Jet comes to stand next to me, shoulder bumping mine in solidarity. I wrap one arm around his shoulder, comforting him in the only way I know how. I don't have the words for losing Ten and Diana both at once. Around us, the remaining horses stand quietly, stony sentinels guarding my mate's last moments.

As we watch, light travels down Cashore's arms and lands on Diana's chest, seeping into her skin, where it disappears from view.

Come the fuck back to me, I urge her. *Come, mate.*

CHAPTER 21
DIANA

I wanted more in my last moments, more connection to Noire, more love. But Rama took that from me too. I accepted I might not make it out of the maze alive, but I hoped I was wrong. I knew there was every chance Noire would kill me for my betrayal, even though I always had a deeper plan.

My senses slip away as my core and chest heat until my mind squirms to get away from the flames.

But I can't move, and maybe this is already the afterlife coming, but if it is—I've gone straight to the seven hells. Flames lick up my body, eating me alive as I scream and writhe at the burning. I don't think my body's moving, so it's all in my mind.

I push my thoughts to Noire, to the faint read I have on him as I slip away into death. Except that read is getting stronger and stronger until something punches through my core like a knife, my body doubling over on itself.

I'm vaguely aware of a vibration rumbling from Noire's big, hot chest into mine, but my entire body is screaming, stabbing over and over as whispers start in the back of my mind.

Please, gods, let her be fine. I'll do anything. Please.

Is Noire speaking? Or am I just hearing what I want to in my final moments?

My bondmate, don't touch her. She is mine, mine, mine.

Fire eats up my insides as a scream erupts out of my throat, the whispers turning into a rushing roar of blood, the sound thumping in my ears so loud I wish I could move my arms to cover them. The scream turns inward, and then pictures play across my mind: *Cashore being crowned king. An attack, so much pain and loss. And then I wake up in the maze, looking through Cashore's mind, seeing the sulfur pools in my room for the first time. I roar with rage, but the sound travels off into the abyss and disappears.*

My pulse gallops under my skin as feeling returns to the tips of my fingers until I can move them.

Diana. Come to me. It's Noire's thought, struggling to break through the heavy drumbeat inside my head.

I'm trying, alpha, I cry back, struggling to reach my hand up to touch him, to feel him. I never imagined dying would be like this, grappling and scrambling to hold on to the living world.

Try harder. I'm here, omega. I'm waiting for you. Deep in my mind, Noire's insistent purr grows louder and louder until the vibration of it tickles along my chest and neck. I feel him; I truly feel him.

Fluttering my eyes open, I find myself looking into Noire's darker gaze. His forehead is pressed to mine, the tip of his nose rubbing at mine in gentle, languid strokes. His lips crack into a smile as he brushes them over my own. The hint of a kiss is reverent, worshipful. Tender.

"You're back," he growls. "Never leave again. You are mine, Diana."

"Yes." My affirmation comes with a smile as I struggle to reach my hand up and drag my fingers along Noire's stubble. Except, at the end of my fingers, where there were red painted nails, there are now sharp, black claws.

Vampiri, my mind echoes.

"He is speaking in your mind, is he not?" Ascelin drops down next to Noire, looking at me. When I turn to face her, she hisses in a deep breath, searching my face for…something. A string of words in her language flows out of her lips, but I understand them.

"*Hefesh aft inayit,* Ascelin," I murmur, reassuring her wounded heart. *I am still here.*

Did I speak those words?

A tear slides down her face as realization rockets around in my brain. Cashore is present in my mind, but when I glance behind Ascelin, his body lies on the ground, unnaturally still. He's gone.

My gaze flies up to Noire as he strokes my bloodied hair away from my face. "What happened? Cashore?"

Next to Noire, Ascelin breaks down into heaving sobs as Renze drops to his knees and reaches out for my hand, taking it in his own. "Cashore gave his life force to keep you from dying, but that means you're infused with a vampiri king's spirit, Diana. Some things may be different for you, going forward. Like this…" He holds my hands up, flicking his fingers along the new black claws. "There will be more. We can't know yet what changes his infusion will spark."

Sorrow hits me as I look at Cashore's still form, Ascelin turning to lay her forehead on his chest as sobs ring throughout the room.

"We need to get going," barks Jet from somewhere in the recesses of the dark ruins. "Rama could be back any moment with a fucking army."

Shaking my head, I sit upright, watching extruded bullets fall off my skin as Noire wraps an arm around my back, helping me rise.

He leans in, kissing the top of my shoulder, his warmth infusing me as he pours his need and desire for me into a bond that now burns brightly in my chest. "She will most definitely be back, and we need to be ready for that. Diana, do you have any idea what she might do? The fucking city flew away."

"I don't know," I whisper honestly. "She took Ten and one of the horses. So if she's still alive, she will need to regroup. The remaining horses can stand guard, and I can reprogram them to protect Siargao. I don't think she'll further risk Paraiso by coming close, but we need a better long-term plan."

Ascelin turns to me. "Chosen One, we need to retire Cashore's body. You and I must do it together."

"Chosen One?" I'm confused. I don't understand why she's calling me that.

"We have much to discuss, Diana," Ascelin whispers, her lips parting into a soft smile. "Come." The warrioress holds out a hand for me, and Noire lets me leave his grip long enough to take her hand and follow her to Cashore's prone figure.

Nodding, I turn as the few vampiri who remain crowd around their fallen king, kneeling beside him. Somehow, I know what to do. We lay our hands on him, and Ascelin and I speak the words vampiri have used for millennia to send their spirits to their ancestors. Cashore's face is still and beautiful in death, white eyes closed with the hint of a smile on his inky lips.

As we speak, his physical body begins to shimmer and flicker, and then it crumples in on itself until there's nothing left but glittering dark dust. I speak the words over and over as each vampiri cuts a slit in their palm, dripping the blood onto the ashes. We each gather up that mix and draw a line from our foreheads down to our chins.

I can almost hear Cashore mourning alongside us, deep in my mind. I've got no idea how this infusion of his spirit is going to work, but it's something to figure out later. For now, it's oddly comforting, like a cool cloak wrapped around my mind.

When the vampiri are done, I whisper a new refrain, and the ashes lift off the floor into the room, floating away through the stone ruins, disappearing into the dawn light. Ascelin turns to Renze and the remaining vampiri, and they're quiet together in mourning. Even the younglings.

I stand and turn away from them, looking for my mate. Noire's mouth crashes onto mine the moment we touch. Moaning softly, I sink into his heat and return the kiss, grunting when he fists my hair and pulls my head back to scent his way up my neck.

"You smell...different," he purrs. "Deeper. Stronger. Your blood is singing for me, Diana."

Patting his chest, I smile. "It will always sing for you, alpha."

Noire chuckles. "Did you just pat me like a Labrador?"

I turn my eyes up to his, laughing when his widen at what he sees there. "I'm still me, Noire."

"Your eyes are rimmed in black now," he whispers back, his voice soft. "I need you, mate."

"Good idea," I snark with a wink as we turn into the room. I am exhausted and grieving but needy all at the same time.

Noire pulls me close, gripping the back of my neck as his lips tickle the shell of my ear. "Don't think I'm not keeping count of every time you talk back to me, omega. There will be punishment for it."

I roll my eyes, pointing to my head. "Never know what kind of shit I might be capable of with Cashore's help, alpha. You sure you want to start this fight?"

Someone snorts quietly in the back of the room as Noire's smile broadens, sharp fangs poking out from his lips. "Absolutely certain, omega. If you dish it out, I will take and take and take it. And then I will punish you for days."

I lean in with a conspiratorial wink. "I can't wait."

CHAPTER 22
NOIRE

We hike quickly across the island until we come to a small building. "This is the only office on the island," Diana explains. "It's there if something happens to the city above. The entire maze can be run from here."

"So, we could let other monsters out?" Ascelin questions. "I have half a mind to let loose anything with wings. Minus any remaining manangal."

Diana sighs, rubbing the warrioress' forearm. "It's tempting, Asc, but we cannot control the maze's monsters. Our only hope is to eventually return them to their homelands or destroy the maze. First, we need to do something about the disks. We can deactivate them from here."

The disks, I'd fucking forgotten about the disks.

"How much can she really do with them, Diana?" Renze questions, holding out his forearm. The disk is dark like it usually is overnight.

Diana frowns, rubbing at the disk. "I have no way of knowing what she added to the disk technology, but when my father designed it, it was really just a timer. It's likely Rama made it seem like she could control you, but she was just using the maze for that."

"I want it the fuck out," I snarl. "What's the best way?"

"They need to be surgically removed," Diana admits. "If you rip it out, you'll damage your nervous system."

I growl at the dark disk buried deep inside my skin. "I know someone who can take it out, but can we deactivate them here?"

Diana nods, leading us through the small outbuilding until we come to a dusty office with an entire wall covered in knobs and buttons. Our group watches in quiet silence as Diana powers on the wall of buttons and presses her palm against a reader. We watch as a panel of lights flashes then dims, and Diana turns to me with a smile, holding up her hand. "Deactivated! My fingerprints are an override for the maze. If Rama hadn't had her goons follow me twenty-four-seven, I could have swum over here years ago and turned this fucking place off."

I think about the years of emotional trauma Rama caused my omega, and I know with renewed certainty that I will rip this place to the ground.

Snarling, I look at my exhausted pack of two. "Can Rama follow us with these deactivated? I have a place we can go. But I do not want to lead her there for whatever comes next."

Diana shakes her head. "I can never be positive with Rama, but I'm as certain as I can be…"

"I'll take it," I murmur, kissing her forehead. "Let's go. When we take Rama down, we will come back and deal with this place."

Diana nods and smiles at me.

The vampiri refuse to leave us now that Cashore's spirit is infused into Diana's. The dozen or so who remain are piled onto a rubber speedboat, crossing the warm waves of the bay toward the mainland. Siargao glitters ahead of us, and I can practically feel it welcoming me home. I have a few immediate priorities–claim Diana, get some rest, retrieve Ten, take back my town. Not in that order.

The fact that we're free still hasn't sunk in. Not for any of us. The vampiri sit quietly behind Jet in the boat, but Jet's jaw is slack as he lets the air fill his lungs, the wind whipping his dark hair around. He's never looked so peaceful, not since Rama put us in the maze. And despite the fact that we're missing another brother.

When we land on the opposite shore of the bay and I touch Siargao dirt for the first time, something in my dark heart blooms and bursts with joy. This was my home, my town, my kingdom. When I look up, the gray and black spires of the city loom tall above us. The city's skyscrapers gleam and flicker with light, just as they always did. There's a huge jet pad attached to one of the buildings now–it wasn't there before. The first of many new things I'm sure I'll notice.

"That must be how the rich fucks get up to Paraiso, right?" Jet questions. Diana nods and squeezes my arm as I growl. That is a problem for another day.

The Riverside District is as run-down and decrepit as ever, but to be honest, it was always my favorite part of my home province. Riverside is gritty and resilient and glorious.

There's only one person I trust now that I'm back, and we need to get to his home if there's a chance he's still alive. Our group follows me in silence as we head up the riverbank and into the depths of the city. I step into the street and flag down one of the small buses that used to haul workers back and forth from Riverside to the Towers, the area the wealthy live in.

When the driver stops, his eyes go wide with recognition when he sees me. He bows when I give him the address, eyes widening once more when the vampiri follow me up into the cab and take their seats.

The cab takes off toward our destination, but our group says nothing as I turn to the driver. "Tell me what has changed in the seven years I've been gone." I'm curious to hear this from a fresh perspective.

He blanches but straightens his back and glances over his shoulder at me. "Mistress Rama controls everything, alpha. Ayala pack is scattered, as far as I know. Nearly everyone in the city works for her in one way or another."

"Including you?" I purr, letting my dominance roll over him as he jumps in his seat.

"When I have to," he admits, unable to lie to me.

"What's it like with Rama in charge of the province?" It's something I've wondered about. I ruled Siargao with an iron fist, but I was fair to the common people, good even. I took a share of every transaction in the city, so it made sense to ensure the city's businesses thrived. I highly doubt Rama rules that way, but I'd like additional perspective. Diana has eluded to some of what's gone on, but I am eager for more news.

The driver sighs. "She plays with people simply for the sake of her own entertainment. She's needlessly cruel and terribly unpredictable. She fucks with people for fun. She's a psychopath."

His words make me think of everything Diana has endured since she was a child. Rage at her treatment blisters my soul as I vow, pressing my lips to her forehead, that Rama will never fuck with her again.

The driver stops in front of a long row of low-slung houses. I owned every one of these houses before I left. I wonder who owns them now? I'm praying the alpha I knew before somehow escaped the slaughter. He was out of town visiting family when I was thrown into the maze, although I don't know if he would have even tried to come back here.

The vampiri follow Jet and Diana out of the aircab as I pause by the driver. "I have nothing to give you in thanks, but I will not forget your help this evening. Spread the word that I'm back, please. And find me if you ever need anything. I owe you a favor."

The cab driver's eyes widen, but he nods, a splash of relief darting across his face. "Thank you, alpha," he murmurs as I stand and hop down out of the bus.

Gripping Diana's hand, I walk up the middle of the street, watching as people peek out and close their windows when they see us coming. Ah, I still strike fear in peoples' hearts then. I imagine seeing me walking up the street with a vampiri pack in tow, all of us covered in blood, will do that. It's a good fucking feeling. An older alpha comes out of the last house on the left, staggering when he looks up the street and sees me. He yells over his shoulder into the house for someone, then jogs up the street.

When he's close enough, he falls to a knee in front of me, head bowed. "Alpha, you escaped."

Laughing, I reach out to give him my hand and lift him back upright. "It is good to see you, Thomas. I thought you might have stayed abroad. I had help getting out. This is my mate, Diana."

The alpha who raised me when my father couldn't smiles broadly at my mate and reaches out to shake her hand. "It is so incredibly wonderful to see you." Thomas' eyes dart over Diana's shoulder, a growl rumbling out of his chest at the vampiri contingent behind us.

Jet comes forward, wrapping Thomas up in a hug. "They're with us, Thomas. They helped us out of the maze."

Thomas turns to me as a woman flies out of the house and barrels up the street toward us. I smile, opening my arms as she flings herself up into them, squeezing my neck so tightly I can barely breathe.

"Maya, Maya! I can't breathe, woman."

Rheumy sobs ring in my ears as she refuses to let up, crying into my neck with her arms crushing me. I glance at Diana to find her biting back a smile.

So you're a big softie? she asks in our bond.

There's not a single soft thing about me, omega, I bark back into her mind. *But Maya and Thomas are family.*

Maya finally stops crying long enough for me to put her down and introduce her to everyone. She cries again when she sees Jet, throwing herself into his arms too. "Where's Tenebris?" Her voice wavers as she asks the question.

"Tenebris was taken by Rama during our escape," Jet says the words, and they're a dagger to my chest. I went into the maze with three brothers and came out with one. I'll never let this stand. Rama is playing a game with me, a game that's going to eat her up.

Maya sobs quietly as she looks at me. She was a mother to the four of us when our own died and our father lost his way to insanity without his bondmate. He came out of it eventually, but Maya and Thomas raised us in the meantime. They're practically my grandparents.

"Let's get inside and get you settled," Thomas encourages, waving at the vampiri. He waits for me to nod my agreement, and then we follow him up the steps I played on as a young pup, into the house so many of my happy memories were made in.

You grew up here? Diana asks the question in my head as we walk down the hall, past the stairs, and into the kitchen at the back of the house.

For a time, mate. I'll tell her the whole story later, but for now, I have questions that need answering, and I sense everyone is ready for food and rest.

The vampiri need sleep, Diana whispers into my mind again. The feel of her connection is a lick of smoke curling along the edges of my consciousness, warm and comfortable. I want to press her into the wall and tease her until that smoke becomes a raging bonfire big enough to burn me to ash. It wasn't that long ago I was on the edge of a rut because of her, and now that we're out, my predatory need to take her is starting to eat at me again. Maya flits around the kitchen, gathering food to heat. Jet howls with excitement when she pulls his favorite roast out of the fridge. He helps her, but I read how broken he feels underneath the busy exterior. He's coming down from the uppers and destroyed about Tenebris.

We'll get him back, I promise, I whisper into our family bond as Jet freezes, then relaxes.

Linking my fingertips with Diana's, I tug her across the kitchen, where I fall into a chair with her in my lap. "What do your vampiri need, mate?"

When Diana doesn't react to the fact that I called them hers, I smile. Cashore's spirit is already changing the dynamic of our group, tying us together in ways we couldn't possibly foresee. The vampiri are Diana's, and she is mine, so they are all mine now.

She hops up off my lap like a naughty girl and walks across the kitchen, going straight to the vampiri with the child. "Do you prefer to bathe or rest?" Diana's fingers stroke across the baby's forehead as the mother's eyes flutter from exhaustion.

"Rest, my queen," the woman whispers.

At the word "queen," Renze sucks in a breath before hiding it behind a cough.

There's going to be an interesting dynamic here. Cashore's spirit lives inside Diana, and clearly, at least some of the vampiri are taking that to mean Diana's in charge. I'll sort that out later, figure out how we can use it to our advantage to destroy Rama. I glance over at Ascelin, but her eyes remain trained on Diana, her expression unreadable. Whatever Diana being their Chosen One means, I can see Ascelin will be a big part of that.

Thomas sets bread and butter on the table as he watches Diana warily. "What do they need, alpha?"

"Is the house next door ready?" The house next to Thomas

and Maya's was always a safe-house of sorts when I was a child, always ready should one of our brethren need a place to stay at a moment's notice.

"It is." Maya grabs the key, handing it to Jet. "Jet, honey. I'll finish this and have it ready for you. Why don't you take them next door? Everything is in the same place."

Diana's eyes find mine, unsure.

You don't want to part from them? How curious. I cock my head to the side and watch her nibble at her lip. *I promise they will be safe there.*

I'll go with them, just to make sure they feel settled, she whispers finally into our bond.

Stay here, I bark back. When she raises her brow in challenging irritation, I add a *please* to my command. I've never said please to anyone, except for maybe Maya and Thomas when I was a child.

Diana nods, rubbing the vampiri mother's shoulder before pressing their foreheads together. She kisses the child, who yawns and blinks up at her with huge all-white eyes.

Maya crosses the room and smiles at the mother. "The house is not stocked for young ones; can I get you anything for your child?"

The vampiri smiles, but she's clearly exhausted and grieving from everything that happened tonight. "No, thank you. She feeds from me, and I just ate. Rest is the best thing for us."

Maya nods as Jet passes her, gesturing to the vampiri. I don't miss the way Renze's eyes follow my brother again–hungry and wanting. I thought it was the heat of the maze orgy, or maybe how few options we had for connection. But there's obviously something deeper there. I'll unpack that later with Jet. I'm still not sure how I feel about the vampiri thrusting themselves on my pack because of Diana, but if Jet could find a real connection, I would be happy for it.

Now that I have that bond and know what it is, I would never begrudge him the feeling, even if it's with a vampiri warrior.

Thomas watches the vampiri go before clucking the way he always does when he's thinking and unhappy.

"Speak, Thomas. What are you thinking?" My alpha command rolls over him as dark eyes flick back to me.

"The world has changed in seven years, alpha," Thomas begins as Diana comes back to my side, wrapping her arms around my neck. Reaching up, I stroke my fingers down her forearm as her warmth seeps into my back.

"Talk to me about what has happened while we were in the maze. Who is left from Ayala pack?"

Thomas blanches. "When Rama took you, she destroyed most of the pack. I've heard some escaped, and I've looked over the years, but I've never been able to find anyone. You know we were abroad, and we came back before the news spread of your capture. But we couldn't bear to leave, so we remained here—quietly."

"No one is left?"

Thomas nods. "An alpha from Dest passed through here once and stayed next door. He had heard whispers of some Ayala pack settling there. But it is difficult to leave the city, so I haven't traveled there to see if that's true…"

"Dest? That's on the far side of Lombornei," I murmur as Diana starts up a soothing purr behind me. She senses my distress. I can't believe my pack is gone. Actually, I refuse to believe it. Why would Rama decimate an entire pack when she could use them somehow? I add it to the long list of things to explore quickly. Every move Rama makes has a purpose, it seems.

When Diana speaks next, the news sends my blood hot through my veins. "I was never allowed to roam far from the riverside district, but I've heard rumors that *this* maze is one of several. That Paraiso is another maze of sorts, even though Rama entertains the wealthy there."

Thomas' eyes narrow as he looks at Diana. "You know this how?"

I dislike the bark in his tone. "Diana is my bondmate, Thomas. Treat her with the same respect you treat me. She worked for Rama but spent years planning how to get us out. It is only because of her that we are here today."

Maya blanches but sets steaming food on the table, nudging it toward Diana and me. "Eat, please. You must be exhausted."

Am I? Behind me, my mate feels vibrant with energy, with need. We should be exhausted; we've had a hellish fucking twelve hours.

Diana unwraps herself from my neck and sits next to me, piling a plate high with food before placing it in front of me. "Eat, alpha." It's an omega command that washes over me the same way mine does her, a rolling tidal wave of omega dominance, the way only a bondmate can do. Our connection compels me, and I take the food, spearing a piece of roast before offering it to her first.

She bites it daintily off the fork before making a second plate for herself. Thomas and Maya watch us the whole time, guarded but interested.

They've never seen me like this with an omega, and even among our people, bondmates are rare. Most packs marry for money and stature, and that works. But bondmates are nearly unstoppable together; the joint power that connection unleashes is a force of nature. Diana and I will become stronger and stronger together. And when I claim her with my bite, either or both of us could develop powers.

Shifting in my chair to ease the building pressure between my thighs, I begin eating.

Thomas leans back and sighs. "Rama doesn't come into Siargao as much as you'd think. She spends the majority of her time up on the sky island Diana referenced." Maya rolls her eyes, placing more food on the table and pushing it across to Diana as Thomas continues.

"In her absence, Rama created something called the Council, and the Council took over the prior Siargao government, taking directives from her. They're a bunch of fucking assholes. You know them all, but they stay up in the Towers."

"Who?" I bark out.

Thomas lists off the names of every smaller pack that wanted what I had when I ruled Siargao. Packs that take and take and take and give nothing back.

"And how is the city doing under this rule?" I question.

Thomas looks around with a frown. "It isn't thriving the way it did when you were here, alpha. The common man is crushed under the Council's heel. Nobody can ever excel because, the moment you make something of yourself, the Council and Rama swoop in to take it. The best of the best everything goes up to the sky island, Paraiso."

I can practically feel Diana rolling her eyes next to me, irritation skating along our bond before she tamps it down.

My need for her builds as her anger grows. I want her to unleash it on me. I'm done talking for tonight.

Turning back to Thomas, I smile, showing him the disk in my arm. "This needs to be surgically removed. Jet has one as well. Can you do it?"

Thomas pulls his glasses to the tip of his nose and examines the unlit disk, poking at the edges as he frowns. "It looks very intricately placed, alpha. I can do it, but it'll take me a few hours for each of you. Do you want to do that now?"

Shaking my head, I glance at my mate. "Diana deactivated them, but even so, I want it out soon. Let's get it done tomorrow, unless Jet returns and wants you to do his. For now, I need space and a room. Where do you prefer we go?" I ask because I'm going to be fucking Diana for hours, and my pseudo parents may not want to hear it.

"Stay here," Maya offers immediately. "Thomas and I will go across the street."

Turning to Diana, I smirk. "We've had a long night, omega. I think it's time for bed."

CHAPTER 23
DIANA

T*ime for bed.* Noire's words are full of the dark promise of the pleasure in front of me this evening. I should be exhausted; we both should. But instead, I can't wait to be alone with him, outside the maze for the first time. I've fantasized about this since I was much younger, too young to fantasize about the alpha in front of me. He was mine the moment he handed me a rose all those years ago. And I've spent every moment of every day plotting and scheming to get him out of the Temple Maze.

Maya stands and smiles at us both. "Please feel free to finish your meal, and leave the dishes. I'll clean up in the morning. Do you need anything before Thomas and I go?"

"Did you keep any of my things?" Noire's deep baritone travels straight to my clit. I thought I was doing a good job of being polite, but knowing everyone is leaving to give us space sends a feral need through my system. I want to throw Noire across this table and take him.

Rein it in for sixty seconds, mate, Noire chides through our mental link. *I'm going to lose my mind.*

I struggle not to let out a whine as Thomas nods at Noire.

"Your chest is at the foot of the bed in the first guest room. We've never opened it."

Noire chuckles aloud. "Good, I would hate to scandalize you both."

Thomas snorts. "Had a mating chest myself once, you know…" His voice trails off as he looks at me, but I sense he's happy and relieved. "Do you need anything else, alpha?"

Noire doesn't turn to look at me but shifts in his seat, leaning forward. "I need a piercing kit, Thomas."

Maya muffles a giggle behind the back of her hand as my head whips to Noire. "A piercing kit?" *What the fuck are you talking about,* I scream into our bond. I know better than to question him aloud; he's my alpha. But a piercing kit? That's a big hell no from me.

Noire doesn't bother to respond as Thomas turns from the kitchen and disappears into the depths of the dark house. Across from us, Maya sucks at her teeth and holds in a smirk, refusing to meet my eyes as I glare daggers at the side of Noire's fucking face.

I start tapping my nails against the kitchen table, but I don't miss how Maya's eyes fall to the unusual black tips before Thomas comes back into the room, carrying a small wooden box. "Everything's here, alpha. I don't know if there are any fittings though."

"Thank you, Thomas." Noire's voice is a thanks and dismissal all at once as he turns in his seat toward me. I barely notice Thomas and Maya leave quietly out the front door. Instead, everything in me focuses on Noire, on the way his pupils overtake his iris as he leans forward in his chair, setting the box on the table.

I'm going to bed, I hear in my mind. It's Jet. *I'll catch up with you both tomorrow?*

Bed is the perfect idea, Noire purrs back into our family bond.

Ugh, don't start with a play by play. I don't want to hear it.
I snort, but a moment later his voice rings softly through my mind again. *I can't reach Ten through the bond. I can't feel him at all.*

Noire growls but speaks down the bond to both of us at once. *Tonight we will rest and regroup. Tomorrow we get the fucking disks out and make a plan to retrieve our brother. I will not stop until we get him back. You have my promise, Jet.*

Thank you, brother, Jet whispers back to us. *Night.*

Distress and longing snake their way along my bond with my alpha. I reach up to run my fingertips along his forehead, smoothing out the wrinkles from his scowl. "We have a few more tricks up our sleeves, alpha. I'll do everything I can until we get him back."

"I need to claim you," Noire whispers. "Bond you to me for good. Tomorrow we will plan for everything else." He reaches out, stroking my cheek as I lean into the touch, purring like a godsdamned cat in heat. My mate chuckles as I slide off my chair and into his arms, straddling him as my hips rock up against his hard length.

"I'm mad about the piercing kit, but I want you," I grumble into his lips as he throws back his head and laughs, a deep laugh I haven't heard from him yet. I love it, and I want more of it, this bright and unbridled joy.

The moment Noire's neck is presented to me, I lean in and bite my way up it, his laugh morphing into a groan as he brings his claws to the front of my suit and shreds it with two swipes. The top half of the black fabric falls away as Noire hoists me higher in his arms, bringing one nipple to his warm mouth and biting hard enough to bring blood welling to the surface of my skin.

Hissing and moaning, I punch my hips against him, a moan rising out of my throat when he tugs my nipple between his teeth, standing with me wrapped around him. Noire holds me with one hand, and grabs the kit with the other, heading for the front of the house. He takes the stairs easily, still nipping and sucking at my chest. At the top landing, he heads right, down a long hallway, up another few stairs into a room with a steep angled ceiling and tons of windows.

I can't take the time to enjoy the simple beauty of the room because all I want is my mate, undressed completely in front of me. A thread of sorrow is still buried in our tether, a reminder of how much we lost tonight. But I want us to claim one another, to grow in power and tear Rama to shreds, once and for all.

Noire tosses me into the bed roughly, smiling as I bounce and yell through our bond.

"Every little bit of sass will earn you a punishment, mate," he purrs, letting the vibration travel through the room. His promise lights me up as I arch my back on the bed, shimmying out of the remainder of my destroyed suit.

"Promise?" I whisper as he chuckles. When I'm fully naked, Noire drags me to the edge of the bed, pressing my legs open as his eyes devour me. Already, slick wets the sheets, dripping out of me as he licks his lips and breathes, heavy and deep.

My mate leans over me, holding my thighs wide as he licks a path straight up my core, my scream echoing off the rafters.

"Godsdamn, Diana. You're so ready to be claimed."

"I am, mate. Please." I'm begging at this point, but I've wanted him for years, and the scent he's giving off makes me want to eat him alive. We're as safe as we can be, for now, while Rama licks her wounds. The horses will stand guard. And I *need* to take my alpha.

Noire nibbles at my clit, sucking it into his mouth as one hand strokes my entrance. And then he stands and stalks out of the room through a different door as I whine and protest. The sound of water cutting on hits my ears as I hop to a stand and growl, following him into what must be the bathroom.

My mate pulls his shirt over his bulky frame and crooks two fingers at me. "Come, Diana."

"I'm trying to!" I shout back as he laughs again, that same deep belly laugh I'll never get enough of.

"And come you will, dozens of times before I'm done with you. But we both smell like the fucking maze and the roses and the vampiri, and I want to smell nothing but you and me. I don't want the distraction or the reminder."

"You did promise me a bath at the beginning of this adventure," I huff out, crossing the room into his arms as he purrs.

"You have a need, omega, and I'm going to fill that need. You won't leave this room wholly unsatisfied. I promise."

"Do you always keep your promises, alpha?" I snark back as Noire's smile falls, fingertips gripping my chin hard as he turns my face up to look right into his eyes.

"I don't make promises lightly, Diana. Which is why I can promise you now that we will take Rama down together. We will find Tenebris and bring him home. And you will not leave this bathroom without screaming my name."

So many promises. So much to do lies ahead of us.

The warmth of Noire's mouth over mine surprises me. His kiss is far from gentle, a demanding push that forces my mouth open as he sucks on my tongue and nips at my sensitive, still-bruised lips. Blood wells along the cuts and bruises at the corners of my mouth as Noire groans and licks the blood away.

He lifts me bodily, setting me in an ancient claw-foot tub, hissing when he steps in after me. The water is scorching hot, but Noire is gentle as he soaps a sponge and commands me to turn. I sink my back into his chest as he rubs the sponge along my shoulders, cleaning the dried blood from his and the maulin bites. He rubs soft circles along my arms, my chest, using his fingers to part my legs, and washes there too. He's careful around the still-healing bullet holes, the hot water burning my sensitive skin.

And then he pushes me forward to scrub my back and the base of my neck. His breath tickles along my skin as I pant and whine. He's so close, so warm, so hard behind my body. Reaching between my thighs, I grip his cock and nestle it between my folds so I can tease myself as he washes me.

Noire's first grunt of pleasure encourages me as I rock my hips along his length, reveling in the way his piercings tickle my swollen folds.

My mate pours water over my hair and turns his attention to that next, fingers rubbing at my scalp until I'm gasping at every touch. Truthfully, I'm half a second from coming right here in the tub, all over his thick cock. And he's barely teasing me. When he punches his hips against me, rocking himself between my thighs as he reaches with one hand and pinches my clit, I do come.

The wave of pleasure hits me as my back bows off Noire's chest, his fingers still tugging at my clit as his dick rubs between my legs. I can't tell if I'm screaming or just gasping for air as my body lights up from the inside, hot tingles traveling down my spine as I struggle to make sense of it.

When my orgasm fades, I fall back onto Noire's chest with a huffy pant. "That was...so good, mate," I gasp out as he reaches down, taking my hand and placing it on his cock, rocking his length through our joined hands as he groans.

"We're just getting started, my queen." Noire's whisper against my neck lights me up as he fucks himself through my fingertips, grunting as he gets close, and then stopping to shift us both up out of the tub.

I whine with need as Noire wraps me around himself, dripping water as we fall into the bed. Without further preamble, he parts my thighs and slides in, burying himself to the hilt with a deep growl.

"Mine," he snarls, snapping elongated fangs into the air as his jaw clenches. Noire falls forward, pulling my left knee with him for a deeper stretch as I moan underneath his big body. I'm caught under him, taking his thick cock, his knot already swelling between us.

"I'm going to pierce you tonight," Noire growls, nipping at my chin before turning his attention to my nipples. "First here and here, and then down below."

"Fuck no," I bark out as Noire pulls out of me. "No, Noire..." I cry, desperate to feel his incredible knot lock us together.

"You get to pierce me too, mate," he growls, reaching for the box on the bedside table. He rummages around in it before turning to me with a glittering needle, a curved half-moon-shaped gold trinket attached to the end of it.

"Why?" I bark. "Is this a thing alphas do? My father never gave me that particular talk."

"Mhm." Noire chuckles, pulling out and flopping onto his back on the bed. "Get on my face, Diana. Ride me, and I promise I'll make it good for you."

"I think the good is gonna stop the second you stick me with a needle, but we'll see," I grumble as I straddle Noire's neck.

He slaps my ass with a deep growl, eyes sparking as I yip and move my hips forward, settling them on his stubble. Noire brings one hand to my ass, playing with it with his fingers there as his tongue slides along one side of my clit, fire traveling to my core as his other hand plays with my nipple.

My mate brings me to the edge over and over and over again until he's covered in slick and I'm ready to scream and demand things. And then I feel the needle, the sharp prick at my nipple, and searing, burning pain as he slides it through the sensitive skin, tugging until the bearing is firmly lodged. At the same time, he sucks my tender clit into his mouth rhythmically, sending me into an intense wash of orgasm just as the bite of the piercing dulls to roaring pain.

I rock my pussy against Noire's face as I ride out the orgasm, heat and pain and pleasure confusing my system as I scream. Does it feel good? Does it hurt? Noire is all of those things. But as the orgasm fades, he groans, and even that threatens to make me come again.

"Good girl, Diana," he purrs, tapping at my tender nipple with two fingers. "Take a look at the first of many ways I'll claim you tonight."

Panting for air, I look down at the golden, glittering half-moon piercing that enters one side of my nipple and leaves the other. I'm wholly unprepared for Noire's teeth to close on my nipple, sucking it into his mouth before tugging gently with his teeth.

"Owwww…" I scream as pleasure and pain rocket through my system, warring with one another at the forefront of my brain.

Noire nips at my other nipple then, and before I can protest, he slides a needle through that one too. I pant at the heat and sting as he reaches into the box, twisting a second half-moon piercing onto the end of the needle. He sucks my clit into his mouth again before pulling the piercing through and tossing the needle onto a bedside table.

The moment that's done, he flips us so he's on top again, rubbing his cock through my folds as he groans. "I need you at least once before I pierce this." His fingertips come to the nub between my thighs as I spread my legs wider. My nipples hurt like a bitch, but he feels so good. I'm confused, horny, and needy.

"You're going to run out of things to pierce, Noire," I growl as my mate smirks at me.

"Oh, I think you'll find me highly creative about the various types of pain I can inflict on you, mate."

I grumble again as Noire leans forward and bites his way up my tummy and chest until his beautiful lips find mine. His tongue demands expert entry into my mouth, taking and possessing until I don't know where he stops and I begin. The first pressure of Noire burying himself between my thighs has my body producing enough slick to drown someone.

I grunt into the kiss when he bottoms out inside me, his knot partially swollen.

"I need to claim you, mate," he murmurs. "We'll get to the piercing later, I think."

"Good," I bark as I push up onto my elbows and throw my head back. It's a plea and an invitation, and I'm ready to beg when Noire simply chuckles and presses greedy, teasing nips to my neck.

"Gods, Diana. You smell so fucking good." Noire's voice loses some of its command and takes on a raw edge as he thrusts rhythmically between my thighs. His lips, his touch, his incredible thick cock–they're all sending warring sensations through my brain.

Noire collars my neck and flips us in one smooth move, parting his thighs for leverage as he grips a hip and starts punching up into me. This angle hits differently, stroking along a different part of my walls, and an orgasm builds fast as I clench around my mate.

He groans as if the connection isn't enough, not nearly enough. Wrapping both arms around me, he hops to a stand with me still impaled on him, trying my best to get friction and get off.

Stalking across the room, Noire thrusts me up against the plate glass windows that overlook the city, tugging my arms above my head in one of his big hands. Black eyes travel down my chest, his lips curving into a wicked smile as he looks at my new piercings.

"You're bleeding, Diana. And the sight of that pretty red blood does things to me."

"Wanna lick it off and make me feel better?" I pout for my best effect as he laughs, capturing my mouth again.

The first hard punch of his hips shakes the window, rattling the glass with its intensity. Noire grunts as he does it again. All I can do is be captured in his arms, taking what he's got, Noire's particular brand of violent dominance. Through our bond, I send him my desire, my need, the connection I've felt for years waiting for him. I think about all the nights I went to my bed with my toys and hands between my thighs, thinking only of him.

Need builds between us as sensation and emotion overtake Noire. He's all gnashing teeth and clenched jaw as he works my body like an expert, bringing me to the very edge. He'll fall with me, locking us together.

"Noir–" I gasp out, his name cutting off as an orgasm hits me with the force of a hurricane, my head hitting the glass as he leans in. My mate's mouth descends on that sensitive flesh where my neck and shoulder meet, fangs sinking deep into the muscle as he roars into the claiming bite. Hot seed bathes my womb as Noire's knot balloons and locks us into place.

His voice is ragged against my shoulder as he clenches harder into the bite, pain rocking through my system along with his incredible pleasure. The orgasms are a continual tidal wave of fire as he rocks into me, coming and biting, cementing us to one another for the rest of our lives.

When Noire releases the bite with a gasp, my hands fly up to the wound. It hurts like a bitch, but touching it also sends pleasure straight to my clit, causing me to rock hard against him.

"Easy, mate," Noire growls. "You're knotted, and you could tear if you're not careful."

"I can feel you," I whisper, searching his face, flushed from pleasure.

Noire pulls my hands down from over my head, placing them over his heart. "I feel you too, mate. Deep in here. Where you belong."

I'm half-tempted to make a joke about him going soft on me

with those sweet words, but I'm a little scared he'll decide to get into more piercings if I do that.

Noire laughs as if he read every thought. "I haven't forgotten about the piercing, Diana. It's happening because I want it."

"And if I don't?"

"You will," he counters. "You get off on my dominance, mate. The day I stop pushing you is the day a crack rocks our foundation. I will always strive to be at my best for you."

"I think I'm gonna cry," I tease, wiping a pretend tear away as Noire throws his head back to laugh. But something about seeing that muscular neck sends heat through my core, and I lean in to bite him hard.

Noire grunts as my teeth sink in, his hands going to my hair. "Claim me too," he whispers, letting his head fall to the side, eyes fluttering closed.

I release the bite and look at his neck, running my fingertips along it, looking for the perfect spot. "Maybe I'll just leave you hanging. It's kind of cute to watch you waiting for me like this." Another tease. I'm probably going to get punished for poking the bear.

But Noire simply smiles. "Don't think I'm not counting every time you sass me, Diana. I've got plenty of piercings in that box…"

Leaning over, I find the perfect spot along his collarbone and sink my fangs into his hard muscle, pouring my want and need into our bond. Noire bellows, pushed into release by my bite, rocking me hard against the windows as connection burns bright between us.

Feeling his pleasure sends me over the edge with him as I bite harder, reveling in the blood that wells to the surface of his skin, dribbling into my mouth. He's all dark temptation, pure sin wrapped up in a big, dominant package. Deep in my mind, I recognize a more fervent need for his blood, and I assume it's because of the vampiri spirit. I want to suck Noire's deep richness into my mouth and revel in his taste.

We come together until that sharp need fades, his knot deflating as I retract my fangs from his muscle. He's bruising already, but I bring his fingertips up to skate along the edges of the mark. He groans at the way it feels to touch it. Our claiming bites will be an erogenous zone for us going forward.

When I lean in and nip at the bite, Noire shudders and grunts, dropping me to the floor long enough to spin me so I'm facing the windows. "Hands up high, mate," he snaps as both of his come to my waist, lifting me back up until I'm crushed against the cold glass. "I'm gonna finish this night the way I started it, Diana," he groans. "Buried in your ass, fucking you within an inch of your life."

The first press of his cock against my back hole has me clenching, but Noire nips at my shoulder. "Open. Relax."

His cock sliding into my ass prompts a pained grunt from me. He goes far slower than the first time he took me here, but I've taken a lot of abuse this evening. When he shifts out and back in, that pain dulls to throbbing pleasure. A mewl leaves my mouth as I press my hips back into him.

Noire chuckles as he slides back in. "There's nothing like your ass, Diana. Hot, perfect, so fucking tight around my cock. Look out at the city while I fuck you, mate."

I struggle not to let my eyes roll back into my head, looking out the window at the glittering, dark high rises of Siargao.

Out and in, Noire slides, his growl turning into a deep groan of pleasure. "This city was mine, Diana," he grunts, rocking hard into me as I pant in response. "Now, this city will be ours. We'll destroy Rama, and we'll make Siargao something new, something better."

"Yes, alpha," I beg. "More, I need your knot again. I need your bite."

"You're gonna finally get that rut you were angling for,"

Noire growls, crowding me hard against the glass, teeth grazing along my shoulder as his thrusts take on a faster cadence, my hips crushed against the cold surface. "I will burn this world for you, omega," he whispers into my ear. "I will destroy everyone who ever hurt you, whoever forced you into something you didn't want. And then I will rebuild my kingdom with a throne for you to rule from."

Another orgasm hits me at his words, the city disappearing behind my eyelids as I throw my head up against Noire's. He bites my neck and shoulder over and over, all claiming bites, all bruising and bleeding as he comes with me.

When that finally fades, Noire bathes me again as my head lolls. I'm done. Absolutely done. He tucks me under his chin in the bed and strokes my back until I fall asleep.

I wake in the morning to find Noire between my thighs, sucking and licking with a devious hint to his gaze. He brings his head up just long enough to wink at me. "Hand me the piercing kit, Diana."

Not bothering to disobey, I lean over and hand it carefully to my mate as he sits up, slick coating his face. Noire wipes it off his mouth and rubs it along his chest and neck, over the black bruises of my claiming bite.

Fierce pride rockets through my system when I look at him. This incredibly powerful alpha male, locked to me for all time.

"All mine," I growl as Noire's dark eyes find mine and light up.

"Always," he agrees. "Now spread those legs for me, mate."

CHAPTER 24
JET

I thought I'd sleep for days after we escaped from the maze, but between coming off the uppers and my terror for Tenebris, sleep eludes me. Noire is in the house next door, fucking Diana six ways from Sunday, having a great time, I'm sure. I can't begrudge him this happiness. Liuvang knows he deserves it, and I'm sure he's thankful he'll never need to have a marriage of convenience.

Lying in a bed in one of the guest rooms, I growl. It's early morning, and I'm done attempting to sleep. I need to move. My body is sweaty, my palms clenching and unclenching themselves as pain hits my core.

I've been on uppers for seven years, and we lost my bag with the uncrushed bottles somewhere in the pine forest. The next week or so is going to be a fucking hellscape of pain and night sweats.

Snarling, I hop into the shower to wash the sweat off, then dress and go outside for some fresh air. Faintly, I hear Diana screaming Noire's name from next door. Gods, he must really be working her over.

The main street is already busy and bustling with people

commuting or doing whatever they do now that Rama rules everyone. That needs to change. This city didn't run scared when we were in charge of it. It didn't look frayed and desecrated around the edges the way it does now. Ayala pack ruled with a heavy hand, and we took plenty. But we kept people safe, and we kept order. We committed every crime imaginable, but the city thrived because of us.

I sense Renze come onto the porch, despite how quietly he moves. He stops next to me, looking both ways up the street before leaning against the brownstone's half-wall. "Couldn't sleep?"

I grunt my assent, not turning to look at him. We did things in the maze, deeply sensual things that awakened something in my soul. I had a lot of sex in the Atrium, Rama's clients using me for their shows, for their own pleasure. But I took the uppers so I wouldn't have to feel.

And then Renze and I kissed, and something clicked and changed in my chest. Even now, it's twisting its way through me, making me want more.

"I feel it too, *atiri*," he growls, taking my hand and spinning me to face him.

I yank my hand back immediately, growling at him. "There's nothing, Renze. What happened in the maze should stay in the maze, all right? I don't know what an *atiri* is but don't call me that. I don't want anybody getting ideas about us."

Hurt and anger flash across his face before he frowns. For half a second, I feel guilty, but I squash it down. "We have a lot of work to do to take Rama down. We need to find Tenebris and the truth about Diana's brother. Let's focus on that."

"If you say so," he growls before leaning into my ear, a shudder racking my body when his breath tickles my skin. "I'll give you the space for now, but we aren't done with this conversation, alpha."

I growl again when movement catches my eye. Across the way from us, a woman exits a brownstone, dressed in a simple wrap dress that highlights her thick curves. Renze pivots to watch her at the same time I do, his lips still too fucking close to my neck. She pauses at the bottom of the steps, green eyes flicking from me to Renze and back again. She cocks her head to the side, assessing, before catching herself staring and turning to move up the street. I watch her go, even when I feel Renze's eyes on me, asking a question with his gaze.

When she rounds the street corner, she passes a man who stands just in the shadows. They nod at one another as she walks by, but he doesn't watch the beauty go as we did. Instead, he looks at me, eyes locked onto mine.

He's an alpha, a pack alpha. That much is clear from the aggressive stance and the eye contact. He steps out of the shadows, and I get my first look at him. Tall, taller than Noire by a bit. Thickly muscled. The next thing I notice is a jagged scar running from one side of his neck to the other. Someone slashed his throat, but he survived.

Renze follows my gaze and growls. Before I can say a word, I'm down the steps and heading toward the alpha with Renze at my side.

The alpha smirks, sliding both hands into his pockets, then turns and heads into the busy street. Renze and I pick up a jog, but when we get to the corner, there's no way to see him among the crowd.

"Who the fuck was that?" Renze barks, running both hands through his dark hair.

"I don't know, but a pack alpha for sure. I have no idea what's changed in the last seven years, but it looks like we have a lot to figure out. Like who the hell even lives in Siargao anymore." I dislike being out of the maze and not recognizing my city. There could be new packs in charge; anything could have happened. Already, people are watching us now that we've returned. This is just the beginning, really.

Renze cocks his head to the side. "We will figure it out, *atiri*. I feel we should tell Diana and Noire, but they are still busy."

Grimacing, I turn. "We'll talk to Thomas about the city later. You can hear Noire from here?"

Renze smiles. "Vampiri kings are able to spread pleasure among us all when they experience it themselves. Diana probably doesn't realize she's doing it, but we've all been buzzing since last night."

"That explains you trying to get all over my ass then," I grumble as Renze's smile falls. He purses his lips but follows me back toward the brownstone as irritation and anger swirl away in my gut. We're not out of the maze a full day and it begins.

Siargao is its own unique brand of maze, just in a different way from the one we came out of.

Renze stares around at the quiet side street before opening the door for me. "Welcome to the maze, level two," he grunts in a sarcastic tone as I sail through the door, bellowing for Noire.

Level two indeed.

Half an hour later, Noire and Diana emerge, my brother looking happier than I've seen him...well, ever. Even before the maze. There's a lightness to his step, and the way he pivots to keep an eye on the omega is shocking. It's like they're magnets, perfectly attuned to find one another in a room.

It terrifies me. There's never been something for Noire to focus on other than Oskur, Ten, and me. And now, Ten is gone. Oskur is gone. There's just me. And Diana.

Noire was less than thrilled to hear about the alpha we saw and grilled me within an inch of my life while Diana bathed somewhere in the depths of their room.

Now I'm standing on the stoop outside Thomas' house, watching my alpha lead his mate out of the kitchen and toward the front stairs. Renze stands across from me, silent in the porch's shadows. He hasn't said much since this morning, but I can tell he's anxious to do something, anything, now that we're out.

Noire opens the door and pulls Diana out, smiling as he tilts his face up for the beautiful Siargao sun to warm it. "Godsdamn, it feels good, brother." When he turns to me, I see a smile I haven't seen since we were children.

Noire is happy. Truly happy. Despite what lies ahead of us.

"I think it feels a hell of a lot better for you two than the rest of us," I grunt. Noire chuckles and pulls Diana into his arms, sliding his tongue into her mouth suggestively. She sinks into his touch, ignoring Renze and me. Over Noire's shoulder, Renze's dark lips part, eyes on my brother and his mate.

"Liuvang-be-damned, keep it together, would you?" I snap at Noire. "We got out. What's next? Rama won't take this lying down, if she survived."

"Oh, she survived," Diana murmurs. "She's too much of an asshole to simply die on us. She was deeply injured, though, and she'll need time to recover. I suspect she won't want to risk Paraiso since the horses already attacked the city. So she'll pick apart the one she got to figure out how to disarm them."

"Why wouldn't she just blow this whole place up?" Renze asks. It's something I've been curious about as well. "With one word, Rama could probably destroy us. Why hasn't she?"

The frown lines around Diana's pale eyes deepen. "She thrives on playing with peoples' lives. Plus, we've got the horses. She didn't see that coming, so I suspect she's trying to learn more about what else my father might have created before she takes another step."

I glance up the street to where one of the horses stands at attention. It gazes up and down the street as if it's alive, and a shudder travels down my spine. "It's creepy as fuck," I murmur as I scowl back at Diana.

She huffs out a laugh. "I never knew what Rama held over my father for her to force him into architecting the maze. But I knew he would never leave Dore and me completely without protection. The horses were his way of looking after us in any way he could, knowing he wouldn't always be around."

"You had a much different childhood than we did, omega," Noire whispers into her lips.

"All alphas don't have to be asshole fathers," she murmurs back, nipping at Noire's lower lip. He closes his eyes, sinking into her caress until finally opening them and turning to look at me, his stance all alpha command again.

I fall into it the way I always do, straightening my shoulders and spine, standing tall next to him just like we used to before the maze. "What do you need, alpha?"

"I want to bury Oskur before we do anything else." Noire's voice is all alpha, but there's a thread of sadness that sinks like a dagger into my chest.

"Do you want us to come help?" Renze asks from the shadows. "Or would you prefer to do this with your pack alone?"

Noire turns to the other warrior. "It would honor me if you came, but if everyone is still resting, I understand." I don't think I've ever heard Noire say anything so…thoughtful.

Renze dips his head. "We will be there, alpha."

"Even the kids?" gasps Diana, whipping around toward Renze. There's an odd moment where she pauses, cocks her head to the side and then relaxes.

Understanding passes over Renze's face. "Are you remembering vampiri customs, Chosen One?"

Diana shrugs. "I'm not accustomed to Cashore's presence in the back of my mind, but hopefully Ascelin can help me."

"I would be happy to," Ascelin says, emerging from the house next door and leaping over that porch and onto ours, settling herself in the shadows next to Renze. He turns to her with a soft smile.

"Get some sleep, Asc?"

"Not hardly," she barks back. "I cannot stop thinking about what Rama might be doing to Ten, how she might try to use him against us. And I am sorry. Sorry that we could not save him." Noire snarls, but it's not directed at the warrioress.

"I echo that sentiment," I bark in response to my brother. "Let's go bury one brother and make a plan to retrieve the other. Others," I clarify, looking at Diana. "She will try to use the information about your brother to hurt us."

Diana frowns. "She has used Dore to hurt me for years, Jet. It can't stand in the way of us getting clear of her once and for all."

We head for the main street as Diana smiles. "How about a walk, alpha? You can see your city once more, and the people can see you and know you're back."

Noire nods and looks at me.

As always, I know what he needs without asking. I walk beside Ascelin, Renze taking up a position across from us as the vampiri begin to file out of the house. In a group, we walk through the riverside streets of Siargao's river district. The scents of the wild jungle surround us–wet leaves, brightly colored birds, raindrops everywhere. So much has changed, and nothing has changed. It's disconcerting.

For half an hour, we walk until we reach Diana's apartment. She stops in front of the door, looking at the bao vendor across the street. I watch her blink slowly, twice, a big smile crossing her face as he leans his head back and laughs. It's clearly a signal of some sort. "Chat later?" she asks the man.

He glances at Noire, and the smile falls a little. "Later, Diana. It seems you didn't share everything about your plan with us."

Diana nods. "I'll find you."

I have questions. Many, many questions. But we'll get to those as soon as we bury Oskur.

There's a resistance of sorts, Diana whispers into the family bond that more easily connects us all now that Noire bonded her. *We should meet with them as quickly as possible.*

I follow Diana and Noire up the stairs to the second floor of a shitty, shabby three-story apartment building. It's seen better days. When we ruled the city, we were controlling assholes, but nobody lacked basic necessities. Nobody lived in run-down homes. Noire put our pack first, but Siargao thrived under his strict rule.

Angst curls in my stomach when Diana opens her door and strides across the room, yanking her television stand out of the way. Noire follows her, keeping an eye on her open patio window and glancing around the apartment. He's keeping an eye out for her.

Diana yanks a panel off the wall behind the stand and pulls out a box.

It's small. It's horribly fucking small. "Oskur's in...that? All of him?"

Diana shakes her head. "I don't know if it's all of him. Gods, that's fucking horrible to say. But there are hundreds of bones here, so it's got to be close...."

Noire and I stare at the box like it's a viper, but he reaches out first, opening the box slowly. The first fucking thing I see is a skull, and I know it's Oskur immediately. He was in a terrible accident as a child, and there was always a knot in his skull afterward. There's clearly a lump in this skull in exactly the same place.

Anger and the need to rage fill my chest until Noire comes across the room and presses his forehead against mine, getting right up in my space. "We will avenge this, brother," he whispers, wrapping his hand around my wrist and pulling my hand up to his shoulder. "I will never let her do this to Ten. We will get him back. And we will honor Oskur's memory. I need your help to do that. Are you with me?"

"Of course," I bark. "You know that."

"I know that," he repeats, using his fucking alpha purr on me. "We need to let you detox off the fucking uppers, and we need to make a plan. But right now, we're going to bury our brother. Come on."

Noire stalks out of the apartment as Diana crosses the room and threads her fingers through mine. Blue eyes are filled with tears, and as the first one falls, I'm compelled to reach out and brush it away. She's Noire's, which means she's ours—our pack's. Diana is Ayala now. I will care for her as if she were mine because she belongs to my alpha.

"I'm so sorry, Jet," she whispers.

"Let's go, omega," I bark, smiling when she lifts her head high and lets me tug her out the door to follow Noire.

When we get outside, the vampiri line the street, and the citizens of Siargao have filled the street too. The neighbor across from Diana's building, the guy with the bao shop, raises his fist high in the air above his head. "We stand with Diana!"

The rest of the people take up the chant, and my heart clenches as the city chants for her, Noire smiling as he watches her hug the neighbor and a few others who come out of the crowd to greet her. Whatever this resistance is, it's clear the city is in support of it, and Diana is somehow a huge part of it all.

Renze falls in behind me as Diana plays the politician, greeting the people and chatting. Noire cuts it short after about five minutes, turning to stride up the street with Oskur's box under one arm and Diana's hand wrapped in the other.

The vampiri follow us, and most of the fucking town does too, until we get to the graveyard at the end of the Riverside District. Up here, the hills start to roll, and skyscrapers pepper them. The wealthy live there. The people who took from us.

I snarl as we turn into the graveyard. Two shovels stand up against a tree. I grab one, and Renze grabs the other. When Noire moves to take it, Renze shakes his head. "Let me, alpha. Let the vampiri show their support of this new, joined pack." There's a moment where Noire says nothing, and I expect him to bite the vampiri's head off, but he nods and takes a step back, reaching for my shovel instead.

"Let me, brother," he whispers. "This is not your burden. I am responsible for Oskur."

I don't hand it to him though. "Step back, Noire. I've got it," I bark. Because I do. I couldn't save Oskur in the maze, and I can't save him now. But I will bury him.

Renze and I dig in silence for a quarter of an hour until there's a hole big enough for the box that holds Oskur's bones.

I'm surprised when I hear the clicking of the maulin foxes from the maze, but Diana murmurs and hisses to them, and they surround our group as we lower the box into the hole. One of the foxes trots forward, dropping a small bone into Diana's open hand before hopping up onto her shoulder and sitting like a damn bird.

We cover the box back up with dirt, and Noire speaks the words all alphas use to encourage our spirits to pass to the next life. "Oskuredad Ayala, may the goddess receive you. May she keep you. May you run free in the Dark Forest, Liuvang-blessed."

I choke back an angry bellow at my brother's death. A sniffle reaches my ears, and when I look over at Diana, tears roll down her cheeks. She stands stiff and tall next to Noire, her fists balled as she looks at the small grave. The fox on her shoulder leans in to rub its cheek along hers, the same way alphas and omegas do.

I told Diana once that nobody had ever surprised me in my life. And it was true–until her.

All I know is that, whatever comes next, I want Noire and Diana by my side for it. I want this new pack in all its glory.

And I will kill Rama and return Tenebris if it's the last thing I ever fucking do.

THE END

Want more alphas? Sign up for my newsletter to receive spicy deleted scenes, bonus epilogues and get the latest news from my world!

Wanna know what's next? Jet and Renze are going to embark on a highly sexualized adventure in book two of the Temple Maze series.

GET IT HERE on Amazon. It will also be available in KU. Flip to the next page for a QR code to find all my books!

BOOKS BY ANNA FURY

DARK FANTASY SHIFTER OMEGAVERSE

Temple Maze Series

NOIRE | JET | TENEBRIS

DYSTOPIAN OMEGAVERSE

Alpha Compound Series

THE ALPHA AWAKENS | WAKE UP, ALPHA | WIDE AWAKE |
SLEEPWALK | AWAKE AT LAST

Northern Rejects Series

START THE SERIES

Scan the QR code to access all my books, socials, current deals and
more!

@annafuryauthor
liinks.co/annafuryauthor

ABOUT THE AUTHOR

Anna Fury is a North Carolina native, fluent in snark and sarcasm, tiki decor, and an aficionado of phallic plants. Visit her on Instagram for a glimpse into the sexiest wiener wallpaper you've ever seen. #ifyouknowyouknow

She writes any time she has a free minute—walking the dog, in the shower, ON THE TOILET. The voices in her head wait for no one. When she's not furiously hen-pecking at her computer, she loves to hike and bike and get out in nature.

She currently lives in Raleigh, North Carolina, with her Mr. Right, a tiny tornado, and a lovely old dog. Anna LOVES to connect with readers, so visit her on social or email her at author@annafury.com.

Made in the USA
Las Vegas, NV
15 November 2022